Embrace the Moment

Book two of the Shifting Series

ANDREA MICHELLE

Published by:

Andrea Michelle

Embrace the Moment

Cover Design: Artistry in Design

Cover Photographer/License: Coka and Veer

Interior Design: Andrea Michelle

Editor: Monique O'Connor James

*Warning: Recommended for readers 17+ due to sexual content, underage drinking and adult language. This is book two in the series and the story will continue in the next novel.

Synopsis for Escape the Doubt (Book 1 in the Shifting Series)

Is taking a chance with your heart worth the escape, or was it better to have never loved at all? Can forgiveness really set you free?

After the unexpected death of her Dad, and the haunting manner in which he died, Riley Shaw built invisible walls around her heart. Barriers she created to protect her from splintering into broken pieces that couldn't be repaired. She was unable to move forward from her past, letting the guilt of her parent's mistakes dictate her own choices.

Dean Warren was safe. Being with him was innocent and peaceful because she didn't truly love him. His words held her captive in a false sense of security. His eyes were deceptive, and his promises of never pushing her beyond what she was willing to give were broken, leaving Riley in a state of regret and doubt.

Joshua Parker had the power to take what was left of Riley's splintered pieces and ruin her completely, or make her whole again. He was her best friend, her next-door neighbor—everything she wanted and settled on never having. Loving him was as easy as breathing air. The fear of losing him forever was more real to her than the feelings she couldn't escape.

When faced with the very thing she feared the most, and in the arms she thought were safe, Riley finds herself questioning every decision she has made over the past two years. When she finally escapes the doubt in her head, and accepts the truth in her heart, is it too late?

"I'm so close to the edge of the cliff that I know one more breath, one more inch, I could fall." –Riley Shaw

Acknowledgments

TO MY HUSBAND *OMG I wrote a second book and you didn't ask me for a divorce. ;) I love you so very much. Thank you for being my biggest fan, my best friend—my everything. I told you last summer I was going to write a book, and you said, "that's great, baby. Go for it." I don't think either of us knew this would become my obsession. I sincerely appreciate all that you do for me, making this opportunity even possible. You are awesome, and I am one very lucky girl to have such a great man in her life.

TO MY DAUGHTERS (Princess, Sassy and Trouble) *Please, stop growing up. Now! As I write this novel, I'm reminded of how hard it is to be a young female. I hope that I am the mother that you need me to be—that you receive the support you need most as you grow and change. I believe in all three of you. You are precious, smart, beautiful, and full of potential. The world is your oyster. No dream is foolish and out of your reach.

TO MANY AMAZING LADIES *My editor: Monique, I am so happy we were introduced. Your detailed suggestions, changes and critiques are so helpful. You make my writing better, and I look forward to working together in the future. *My Beta Team: I heart you ladies so much. Thank you for not stoning me after you read ETM. You were patient and just amazing while I changed my mind over and over again. Special thanks to: Jess Danowski, Erica Westfall, Heather Young, Jen Andrews, Trista Baldwin, and Jamie Turner-Norton for reading and re-reading the many chapters I sent your way. Your comments, suggestions and rants on my craziness made this all possible. *My street team (The Working Girls): y'all make our street corner an exciting place to be. I love your pimping skills something fierce. You believe in me, and that means more than you know. I am so very thankful to have y'all in my life, and can honestly say that I have found some friendships I adore. You girls have been my rock and I thank you so much. Some of you have been with me from the beginning and others have joined the journey along the way. No matter how long we have known one another, though, your support has been amazing to me. *My Facebook group (The Indies Round Table): I am so glad I started that group because the support we give one another is priceless. ALL OF Y'ALL ARE AMAZING, AND I LOVE EACH OF YOU LIKE CRAZY! You've answered my crazy questions, given encouraging words, opened your arms and without that I'd surely be lost. MaryAnn, Emma, Victoria, Ty, Jen, Chelle and Meg—my love for you is endless. Y'all keep me sane and get me. Without you, this would not be possible.

TO THE READER *Thank you again, from the bottom of my heart for reading my book(s). This story wasn't an easy one to write. In fact, I was a blubbering mess throughout most of it. I had to make some decisions that I knew would either be loved, or hated. I took a risk, hope that you loved it and will continue riding this roller coaster with me. I kindly ask that you leave a review behind on Amazon. I read each and every one of them. Your thoughts mean the world to me.

TO ALL THE LOVELY BLOGGERS *YOU ARE AMAZING! I love you all. None of this would be possible without you. Special thanks to: Jess Danowski with Inside the Pages of a Book/Promotions. Not only did you handle the cover re-reveal for ETD, but you also took on the cover reveal for ETM *and* my review tour. You are just amazing, and I am so glad that we are friends. Christine Michelle with Sinful Thoughts for my release day blitz. YOU LADIES ROCK! To all the bloggers that have posted, shared, reviewed and participated in my events—THANK YOU from the bottom of my heart. It means the world to me.

❤️ About the author

Once upon a time in the boot of Louisiana, a young girl made a mess of things and began writing dark poetry to cope. She often found herself daydreaming and creating stories in a far away land that didn't exist and was always out of her reach. Her mission was to move on, find love and a reason to believe in the beautiful things in life. She didn't expect to be counting her blessings daily for all that she has found since then. Her once dark poetry became colorful and bright—it became music. She found purpose and her make believe stories slowly vanished away. Her poetry also sat in the backseat, as more important things took priority. However, life can catapult you in the blink of an eye. A long forgotten coping mechanism of writing would once again become her escape. This time, though, she realized that this escape where she created stories was not a curse, but a gift. Embracing her voice, she breathes life into her characters and poetically weaves together stories for readers to enjoy. She is no longer the young girl who feared the unknown, but is stronger and has faith that beautiful things will always be in reach. She is married to her best friend, and is a mom to three beautiful daughters who are her favorite cheerleaders. She is excited to have the opportunity to share her love of writing with readers. The stories are fictional, but they are real to her. She has always felt things passionately and this new journey as an author is no different. She is no longer looking back, but looking ahead to this amazing adventure with all of you. She invites you to connect with her if you desire to do so.

Social links:
Blog:
http://authoramichelle.blogspot.com/
Twitter:
www.twitter.com/AuthorAMichelle
Amazon Author page:
http://www.amazon.com/author/andreamichelle
Wattpad:
http://www.wattpad.com/user/AndreaMichelle_8
FB Friend:
https://www.facebook.com/andrea.michelle.79025
FB Author Page:
https://www.facebook.com/booksbyandreamichelle/info

Goodreads:
https://www.goodreads.com/author/show/2665501.Andrea_Michelle
Join my Support Group:
https://www.facebook.com/groups/AndreaMichelle.fan/

Dear Reader,

I truly believe music is the perfect healer for a bad day or the inspiration to a beautiful story. I love to listen to music while I write; actually I find it necessary. This is the playlist that I felt moved me while I climbed inside Josh & Riley's heads. Enjoy :)

PLAYLIST FOR THIS NOVEL:

To listen and follow on Spotify: http://t.co/KYfnF4Kzzn

All Around Me (Acoustic) – Flyleaf
Iodine – Icon For Hire
Say Something – A Great Big World
Inscape – Stateless
Get Around This – SafetySuit
Satellite – Rise Against
23 – Mike Will Made it
All of Me – John Legend
Anywhere but Here – SafetySuit
Like A Waterfall (Flipside Ambient Mix) – Jes
Life Left to Go – SafetySuit
What if – SafetySuit
Glory Box – Portishead
Pieces – Red
Broken – Seether (feat. Amy Lee)
Crave You (Adventure Club Remix) – Flight Facilities
Pushing Me Away – Linkin Park
In the End – Linkin Park
All Those Pretty Lights – Andrew Belle
Flawless – The Neighbourhood
Afraid – The Neighbourhood

Rewind – Rascal Flats
Damaged (Redemption Extended) – Plumb
Snuff – Slipknot
Love & Loss – Mattia Cupelli
Let Me Go – Avril Lavigne
Keep it Together – Puddle of Mudd
Rest in Pieces - Saliva

Table of Contents

Torn apart by a tragedy, pushed together by fate. Nothing is coincidence.

Riley and Josh have been through it all together, first as best friends and now as a couple.

Faced with a decision that will test their relationship, these two learn to fight harder than ever before to keep their hearts intact. Once the decision is made, there is no going back. With the past creeping into their present, and miles between them, they learn nothing is easy. Every moment matters.

Can Riley and Josh survive the first year of college apart? Will their love remain strong enough to embrace every moment that belongs to them? Or will someone from the past interfere, take what he wants and ruin them forever?

"For each star in the sky, I have a reason why I love you. When you look up at night, never forget this truth." ~Josh Parker

Not recommended for anyone under the age of 17 due to underage drinking, sexual content and adult language.

Riley

PROLOGUE

Travel back in time...

THE FUNERAL

I was still in complete shock. Completely numb. Completely shattered. My dad was dead. He had been there a few days ago, arguing with my mom as usual, but alive. I just didn't understand—and Josh—God, Josh. My dad had killed his mom. He'd run her off the road driving drunk, and he'd fucking killed her. How was Josh handling it? Jesus Christ that was such a stupid thought, but it was all I could think about. How was he? Of course he was crushed. I thought for sure that he must hate me. What the hell was wrong with me? I was sitting at my dad's funeral listening to hymns that I hadn't heard since I was a young child, and my thoughts were on how the accident affected Josh and me. I was so selfish.

I glanced over at Josh sitting with his dad and his sister, Joey. He didn't look at me. He hadn't looked in my direction all day. He definitely hadn't looked at me the day before when we'd gathered together to say goodbye to his mom. A funeral, everyone mourning and grieving, then watching as the earth swallowed her casket under the dirt.

I will never forgive my dad.

My eyes were still glued to, Josh. He looked so vulnerable, so broken. I wanted to hug him, to hold his hand. I'd have loved to go back to a few days before and have none of it happen. We'd been so happy before, so close to becoming more than what we had been.

It was hard to believe that just the Wednesday before, Josh and I had been walking home together when he'd complimented me. It was a small something. I didn't do well with compliments, and any time Josh tried to step over the line with me I would get cold feet, but everything that day was just the perfect pieces of sweet, and I'd felt completely comfortable when Josh had told me that I looked really pretty with my hair straight. My mom had bought a new flat iron, and I'd tried something new, removing my wavy tendrils for a day.

"Thanks, Josh," I shrugged sheepishly as a shy blush warmed my cheeks. He'd grinned, tucked a free strand behind my ear, and kissed my forehead just like always. We walked home with his fingers interlaced with mine. I'd smiled a lot that day. I'd been building the courage to tell him that I liked him—a lot.

But now all that had changed.

He couldn't even look at me anymore. He was pulling away, putting distance between us—it hurt.

My heart didn't feel sad like it should have as we said goodbye to my dad. It felt cold, hard and angry—not with Josh. I was angry with my parents—at my dad. They corrupted everyone around them, damaged everything in their path. It apparently wasn't bad enough that my dad had been having an affair, and he and my mother had spent years hating each other because of it. Did they need to ruin a perfectly happy home, a perfectly happy marriage too? They'd shattered a family that had been completely intact. I hated them.

My eyes were still on Josh as my mom quietly cried next to me. Tatum sat stoically still. She hadn't cried yet. Neither had I. I wondered what that meant about us.

A hand squeezed mine from my other side and I almost didn't feel it because I was so distracted by the boy I would never be able to have. I turned my eyes to find a concerned Dean. Internally, I recoiled at his nearness. He had been trying for weeks to get my attention, to convince me to go on a date with him, a real one. He had always been flirty with me. We'd gone to one dance together the year before, but it never went further than that. He had been trying to change that though. Of course he would use my vulnerability to get close to me now.

"Hi, you okay? Sorry that was a stupid question. Of course you're not okay," he said in a hushed tone at my ear as he scooted over next to me uninvited.

I looked at Dean and wondered if I told him the truth about how I felt—that such dark feelings of bitterness lived inside of me—would he still be sitting there willing to comfort me, or would he find me disturbed and suggest anti-depressants?

"I'm okay, Dean. Thanks for worrying about me but you don't have too," I whispered back.

He looked at me with sad chocolate brown eyes. They were beautiful in their own kind of way. I just happened to love hazel ones.

It had been two weeks since we'd buried my dad, two weeks and one day since they'd buried Josh's mom.

It had been two agonizing weeks—fourteen days, some odd hours, and minutes of lonely pain without my best friend's laughter and teasing behavior. I missed Josh. I felt so broken, and wished I had him to hold me, except he was also broken, and his brokenness was the fault of my parents—a bloodline directly connected to me.

I'd asked my mom where she had been the night my dad had been driving drunk, the night he'd killed himself and Josh's mom. She'd frowned, swallowed a lot of air, shivered even—then she'd told me, I wouldn't like the answer and wasn't ready to hear it. I didn't like her response and I hated his choice for whatever had transpired between them.

Later, I agreed to go on a date with Dean. I regretted it already but he had been so sweet and supportive. I wasn't much of a talker, at least not with him, but having him nearby strangely enough comforted me, and I appreciated his attentiveness. He didn't ask me questions, respecting me enough to know I probably didn't want to talk about it. He didn't talk to me about why Josh and I weren't as close lately. He didn't make me talk much at all and I liked that. I needed that.

Josh finally began talking to me again after a few weeks of the silent treatment. Our friendship was, by no means, completely back to normal. He looked at me with what I perceived to be pity or sadness. It might have been in my head. What did I know about how he felt? Everything in my head was screwy. I knew Josh genuinely cared for me. Things were different now between us, though, there was no mistaking that.

We were at our spot by the lake, the very spot we declared ours as kids because it was our favorite place to go together. He was sitting by the tree with one of his legs bent. One of his arms rested atop his knee and the other behind his head. He seemed beautifully broken. His eyes were watching what was happening at the lake. A mother was handing her toddler son pieces of bread and he was throwing them into the lake for the ducks. His little laughter made me smile as I heard it, but my joy was short lived when I saw the blank expression Josh had masked across his face as he watched them.

His hazel eyes had lost their sparkle, and it killed me to see that it was missing.

When he looked back at me, he almost seemed dazed momentarily. I couldn't read the expression I saw there, and that frightened me. It was just one of many things that had changed between us. I couldn't read him anymore. His eyes were glassy, and he shook his head apparently to erase his thoughts it seemed as he cleared his throat.

"You and Dean have been hanging out a lot lately?" He stated it like a question, and it hung there in between us until it settled on my chest with heaviness. I hadn't expected that to come out of his mouth.

"Yeah, um...I guess we kind of have. He's been a good friend," I replied truthfully, even though I wished Josh had been the one I'd been spending time with. Just the thought of Dean in his place made me uncomfortable. Josh and I needed each other now more than ever; at least that is how I felt.

He nodded, looked away, and ran his hand behind his neck like he always did when he was nervous or irritated, and then he turned back to me, his eyes suddenly unsure. "Is that all he is?" he asked in a soft tone with his head tilted to the side. His eyes studied mine, searching for something. They weren't warm and sweet. No, they appeared cold and full of judgment. I hated that set of hazel eyes. I missed the set that were warm and sweet.

I was confused. "All he is?"

He narrowed his eyes and raised a brow. "A friend?"

I shrugged "Oh...um, I think so," I said gauging his reaction closely, which kind of confused me, because he grinned like this news made him happy and his cold eyes instantly became warm again. His dimple that I loved so much made an appearance and it tickled my stomach like the flutter of a butterfly's wing. He shook his head and then stood up in front of me where I was sitting on the tree swing.

He gazed down at me with a strange intensity, and a slight tingle traveled up my spine. Squatting down in front of me, he placed his hands on the tops of my thighs. I didn't really know what was going on, or what he was thinking right then, but I was focused—one hundred percent focused on everything he wanted me to see and hear. Nothing mattered, but the breaths of air we were sharing and the look in his eyes.

"I want you to be happy, Riley," he said seriously. I believed he meant that, but he'd said it like he thought my happiness hedged on being without him.

I wanted to scream at him, *'No, no, no. My happiness lives in your eyes, Josh. My happiness is inside of you. With you.'* But I didn't say those things.

I nodded, because it was the only response my brain seemed capable of with him that close, the look in his eyes and his hands on me. We just silently stared at one another with a thousand unspoken thoughts being exchanged under the warm afternoon sun. I hoped mine told him the truth, since my mouth was betraying my heart.

Within seconds the crushing blow came, and that was the moment my heart was ripped out of my chest and thrown into the lake where it drowned a slow death. The realization that Josh and I could never be anything more than best friends. A tear rolled down his cheek, and then another. With a choked strained voice he said, "I miss her so fucking much, Riley. It isn't fair. She should be at home cooking her famous chili, making my dad a very full and happy man. She should be in the bathroom braiding Joey's hair or painting her nails like they would do on Friday nights sometimes. She should be my cheerleader in the stands, or the nagging voice telling me to pick up my socks for the third time. But she isn't any of those things. She's gone."

His lost eyes with tears streaming down his cheeks were locked with mine. I had no words. I had nothing that I could say to take away his pain and God I wanted to take his pain away. Saying 'sorry' wasn't enough. Saying 'I hate my dad for doing this to you and your family' wasn't going to bring her back. So, I said nothing. Instead, I cradled his head in my lap and trailed my fingers though his hair and down his back as he cried with his face pressed into my stomach. He held me, and I held him, as he missed the woman who had given him life, the woman my dad had stolen away from him. I crumbled on the inside. Our future as more than friends died that day. I would always be there for him and he would always be there for me, but it would never be more than friends. It could never be more than that.

ONCE UPON A TIME
THERE WAS A GIRL WHO MET TWO BOYS
ONE BOY MADE HER FEEL CHERISHED,
BEAUTIFUL AND STRONG
THE OTHER BOY MADE HER FEEL LOST,
CONFUSED AND WEAK
ONE HAD HER HEART
PROMISED TO KEEP IT SAFE FOREVER
THE OTHER WANTED IT
NEEDED IT TO MAKE HIM FEEL BETTER
SHE CHOSE WRONG
BETRAYED HER HEART OUT OF SHAME
HEART IN A BOX
SAFE UNTIL ALL THAT WAS LEFT WAS PAIN
TIME AFTER TIME
FATE LED HER TO WHERE SHE BELONGED
SAFE IN THE ARMS
OF THE BOY WHO MADE HER STRONG
EMBRACING FIRSTS AND TAKING RISKS
WITH LOVE AS THE BIND
FOREVER ON THE HORIZON
EXPERIENCING MOMENTS OF A LIFETIME

For those cherished moments that steal your breath.

CHAPTER 1

Overcoming multiple fears in one day has my head feeling fuzzy. This day has gone from sad and depressing, to shocking, to beautiful and with my hand in his. My heart belongs to him. Joshua Parker, my boyfriend, my best friend and just EVERYTHING. Then like a light switch is flicked, the night takes yet another turn I didn't expected.

Imagining Josh having sex with Preslee is torture. Thinking that they shared something so intimate together and that a baby has been created is beyond brutal. But now I know the truth.

Josh never lied to me. He was never with Preslee, and my tortured heart and brutally beaten spirit has a flicker of hope. After I have the worst day, thinking the worst of Josh and finding out the worst about Dean, I begin to see the light at the end of the tunnel—the light that Josh helped me run toward and not away from. I'm no longer lost and drifting. Josh found me. He knows what I need. He helps me release my doubt, my fear, and to embrace the future—the future that is meant for us.

As we walk away from the Cheesecake Factory where Josh just spoon fed me the most deliciously rich peanut butter cheesecake, I find my mind wandering to the things he said to me earlier tonight as we sat at the cemetery where our parents rest. I'm still stunned at how so much has changed in mere hours.

"Everyday for the rest of my life—if I'm lucky enough to keep you that long—I will not see that accident. I will see a beautiful girl who is lost in a sea of uncertainty and wants so badly to dive in but thinks she can't, but you can and I will hold your hand when you do. I will see my best friend and the girl that I am desperately in love with. I will see you, Riley. Just you."

I can't believe how much time I wasted—lost without him—time spent held in the wrong arms. I'm still shocked to my core that Dean has been deceitful for so long. I don't know what I did to deserve Josh still being here—waiting as I get my shit together and realize it is in his arms that I belong. With everything that has happened this past year, in just a few short hours, Josh has made it seem like a distant memory.

With stolen kisses at the table, longing glances in one another's directions, and a simple touch like his hand in mine—I am completely and utterly lost to him.

"Are you ready to do this?" Josh asks, squeezing my hand and looking up at the ticket booth at the movie theatre. *Right, I owe him a scary movie.* I inwardly cringe even though I smile. It is an almost sincere smile, but I know it doesn't quite reach my eyes. I really, *really, really* hate scary movies. But for him, will do anything. I will tackle every fear, but only with him because he makes me feel safe.

"No, but I have you to hold me. So, I will be okay, right?" I answer with what I honestly feel.

He smiles down at me and appears pleased with my answer. "I will always hold you, pretty girl. No movie required." I think my heart just swelled in my chest with that statement. *Always—yes, please!*

I turn to him and wrap my arms around his neck; standing on my tippy toes where I can meet his stare. A curious and happy grin lights up his face as he peers into my eyes. It's been so long since I've seen contentment in his gaze, and it warms my heart to see it. "Did you mean everything you said earlier tonight?" I ask, placing a contented kiss on his lips.

He wraps one arm around my waist and with the other he tucks a curl behind my ear. "I mean everything I tell you. Which part are you referring to?"

My eyes study every speck of his. I love his eyes. The way the green and the whiskey color dance together—it's such a beautiful dance. "The part about everyday for the rest of your life. Do you really see that for us? Together—for the rest of our lives?" I whisper and bite my lip nervously.

It seems like such a crazy statement, given that, for the past two months, I've been ignoring him, and thinking the worst of his intentions. Now, I'm here—in his arms—*HOME*—and discussing forever. It's the only thing on my mind that makes sense. We share our childhood memories together, had our own secret language, and have never told anyone about our stolen ice cream sandwiches that we took from his mom's deep freezer in the garage. It was her secret stash and we always took them. She would blame the brats, otherwise known as our younger siblings—never once suspecting us. We've shared our teen years together, had our own secret feelings, and I've never been kissed the way he kisses me—brownies will never be the same. That night freshman year, when Josh and I chased each other around the kitchen with brownie mix, and then kissed for the first time, will forever be one of my favorite memories of us. *Why wouldn't we share the rest? Right? Right.*

He smiles sheepishly and nods his head. His eyes flick to my mouth and he licks his own causing my stomach to flutter. "I do. You have always been my best friend, Riley. I've imagined the day I could call you *mine* a thousand different ways. I can't picture my life without you. So yeah, everyday—forever. I see it spent holding your hand, and kissing your lips—which I want to do so badly right now."

Our eyes study each other before we gently let our mouths touch—once—then twice, until we finally deepen it. The sound of a revving engine nearby filters out the sound in my chest of my rapid heartbeat. He tastes like peanut butter and sweetness, and just everything I've become addicted to.

He pulls away smiling—seemingly sated. He runs both his hands through my hair, and then grabs my cheeks as he leans down to place a tender kiss on my forehead. I lay my head on his chest as we embrace—loving the sound of his heartbeat. "We'll be old and gray sitting on rocking chairs with ice cold sweet teas, and little rug-rat grandkids causing havoc in our front yard. They will always be full of laughter," he says pressing his lips to my hair. That makes me produce the goofiest of grins ever.

I lift my head and stare at him just waiting for the rug to dissipate beneath us. This moment, while we are embracing feels too perfect. Something always happens—our happy always gets interrupted. I push the thought into the back of my mind and try to hold onto this feeling. "I'd have my Kindle or a journal to write in, and you would be playing your guitar with a bouncing toddler nearby making up songs just like I used to when we were kids." His lips curl up at the side into the biggest grin—even his eyes are smiling at me.

His knuckles brush my cheek, and I reach up to take his hand and bring it to my mouth where I kiss his palm and then we hug. We freaking hug—it's the simplest of gestures, but it makes me feel warm—and like his arms are my home. He is home to me, and I'm so completely happy to be back home where I belong.

"Well, isn't that cute," I hear a familiar voice say from behind me. I feel Josh tense instantly and when I turn around I find disgruntled chocolate eyes looking at me. That warm and fuzzy feeling dies a quick death being buried underneath years of wrong decisions. Dean takes off his helmet, places it on the handlebars and swaggers as he moves toward us, never breaking eye contact with me. His eyes appear to be bloodshot, which shoots up a red flag for me.

I'm not sure what my face is portraying right now. A little shock, and a little irritation I would presume. "Hey, Dean," I reluctantly say to the guy that is more like a stranger to me than an ex-boyfriend of two years, and a good friend since childhood.

His eyes are speaking to me without words. For a second they soften, but with just a breath they become cold and foreign again. "Riley, I see you found your smile again." He smirks, but it's strained and seems to taunt me not congratulate me. "Good for you. Strange though, how it seems to slip right into place when only Josh is near you, huh?" he says full of sarcasm and bitterness. It slaps me right in the face with the truth.

Josh reaches a hand around my stomach protectively. I interlace my fingers within his and let myself relax against his front. I feel I need to or I might lose my balance. "She's been through shit today, man. You already know that. We don't want trouble, so back off," Josh snarls from behind me, squeezing my hand tightly with his fingertips.

I can feel the tension radiating from both of them. It's uncomfortable. The air suddenly feels thick with threats of something to come—something bad. Dean's eyes are staring at Josh's hand on my stomach. He seems to grow angrier at seeing it there. Then he smiles wickedly, and his eyes dart to Josh's, as though Josh's words have now become a challenge he's accepted and wishes to trump him one. "Funny how you tell me to back off, dude. Dont'cha think trying to get in my girlfriends pants for the past two years is asking for a shitload of trouble?" he snaps.

I gasp, shocked at his audacity to say that. Josh has never tried to get in my pants, whereas Dean has tried and epically failed many times.

"Ex-girlfriend," Josh clarifies.

Dean stares blankly at Josh, no expression on his face, and a chill jolts up my spine. He turns his eyes away from Josh and meets my glare. "I tried to call you. I was worried about you after what happened earlier tonight," he says in a soft tender voice. It's bewildering. He didn't act worried when Josh exposed all of Dean's secrets to me. He was cold.

I can feel Josh's gaze on me. I don't return it. I didn't tell him Dean was calling my phone. I just turned it off and ignored him. I don't want any more trouble, and yet I have been strangled with it anyway. Trouble followed me here. "I know," I whisper.

"Then why didn't you answer? I needed to talk to you. We're friends remember? Friends should be able to talk to one another when they need them," he mutters.

What? "I didn't answer because I was on a date, and that is rude. I didn't answer because I don't know if we *are* friends, and I don't think there is anything left to say," I reply truthfully. We are not friends anymore. I don't know if we ever were anything real.

He steps into my space, and Josh squeezes me closer to him. I feel a mental tug of war going on and I don't like it.

"Of course, we're friends. Don't say stuff like that. We can be more than friends again, Riley. Just let me explain everything. I didn't earlier because you were so angry, and I knew you weren't in any frame of mind to hear it, but I miss you, baby. I miss you so goddamn bad some nights. You're all I think about." *What the hell?*

His breath? Holy shit. Now that he is close enough to me, I can smell his breath. It reeks of beer. He's drunk. *SHIT!*

I'm shaking my head back and forth. I'm speechless. I'm here...with Josh—where I belong. And he wants to say he *misses me* and *thinks about me?* Did he miss me and think about me when his dick was inside Preslee? NO!

"You're delusional, Dean. We are not getting back together—ever."

"C'mon baby? Don't be like that," he says slurring his speech and stepping even closer.

I feel Josh ball his fist beside my waist, and if Dean's eyes hadn't gleamed so sinfully with satisfaction at Josh's reaction, I wouldn't have intervened. I would have stepped aside and let Josh pummel the shit out of him. I don't do that though. I don't want Dean to win. I know he's trying to get a rise out of Josh, or maybe in his drunken mindset he thinks I'll agree with him. I don't know, but before Josh can react I turn around, grab his face and whisper my plea. "Don't. He isn't worth it. Please, let's just go."

Dean laughs and then opens his evil mouth. "Oh, please, Josh. Please don't. You fucking pussy."

Josh growls and meets my eyes. I can see his inner turmoil. He is holding back and his restraint is barely existent. His body begins to vibrate as his temper unquestionably flares. I need to get him out of here. *Now*. Screw the movie. "Riley, I can't let him talk to us like that. I mean...fuck—he just called me a pussy."

I shake my head back and forth. "I don't care what he says, Josh. I think he's drunk. Besides, what he thinks doesn't matter to me anymore. You matter. Just you. Please, let's go. We can see a movie another day. We have forever, remember?" I try to smile, to lift the weight I can feel on his chest. My smile is forced, my insides tremble and my stomach churns. That rug just dissipated beneath us, as I feared it would. Nothing with love comes easy.

He squeezes his eyes shut, and inhales deeply as if to calm down and regain some semblance of control. "Forever," he breathes as he slowly opens his eyes with a quiet resolve in place. I nod. I'm successful in calming him down, but inside I'm scared as hell.

Dean is drunk and obviously riding on his bike. My mind is conflicted between right and wrong. If I leave with Josh, and Dean leaves on his bike, he could hurt someone. I can't be responsible for that. I just can't, not after everything. If we stay, then nothing good will come from this. I decide without informing Josh that I need to get him in his truck away from Dean, and then I need to somehow convince Dean to call someone to come get him. However, to do that would mean coming back and talking to him alone. I figure that is what I have to do.

Josh grabs my hand and we turn to walk away from Dean as I'm thinking this over—coming up with a plan to separate them and still help one without hurting the other. But it's not over—it never is.

"Oh, Riley? Before you go, I'm just curious of something," Dean inquires in a voice that is no longer friendly.

I halt with my back still turned away from Dean. Josh looks down at me with curious eyes. His grip tightens on my hand. I shouldn't have turned around. I shouldn't have. I don't know why I did. "What's that, Dean?" I ask, ignoring my own advice and turning to face him. *I'm such a hypocrite. I just told Josh to let this go and I turn around. Why did I do that?*

Once the words left his dirty mouth, it was too late to change my mind. I should have never turned around—I had a plan. Now, it's too late to stop what was about to happen—I never should have turned around.

"It's been a few hours since you left me standing stunned in your living room wondering what the hell y'all were talking about. Then running down the road in the rain and falling into his arms. Those arms you apparently have always wanted to be in, right?" He laughs bitterly, and then walks right up to me, looking down into my eyes. His nearness and the hatred I see in the brown depths I used to find so adoring spike a fear in me I've never felt before with him. His voice takes on a low menacing tone, and his eyes never drift away from mine. He wants me to hear every word and I am listening.

He doesn't let me speak. He just keeps throwing mean words at me in between stale alcohol-infused breaths. "I'm just curious, though. Two fucking years...you strung me along never giving it up—waiting for him, I assume." He glances behind me and then flicks his eyes back to mine. He leans down and whispers words so harsh and laced with vileness that I shiver. "Is that pretty little cherry of yours still intact, or did you let him pop that in the minutes it took for you to forget I ever existed?"

My heart leaps to my throat because I know nothing I say now will stop this. I should have never turned around. I should have stuck to my plan. Why can I never do what I should?

My mouth falls open, and I have never felt words expose me so deeply. Dean hates me. I don't care what he said earlier about missing me and us being friends. We are so not friends. We are enemies.

He has never spoken to me like that. He means to rip me to shreds just now. He means to cut me open and let me bleed out right here in this parking lot. *Who the hell does he think he is?* He had sex with my best friend and lied about it for two years. He had sex with Preslee and knocked her up while we were dating—probably screwing her the entire time. I'm hella glad I kept my legs closed. I respected my body, and my heart enough to know that Dean wasn't the one to give that cherished piece of myself to.

How dare he?

Josh gently pushes me aside, and his fist collides with Dean's mouth and nose in one sharp punch. Blood spatters onto my shirt. Dean spits all the while laughing. I think he has gone mad. I think he has truly lost his shit. Déjà vu times a million is what this is.

"Oh my God!" I scream, but they just keep throwing punches, and pushing and shoving at each other. Josh grabs Dean by the shirt, and yells in his face. "You're the fucking pussy, you bastard! You made her question everything. You used her, manipulated her and when you didn't get what you wanted out of her, you broke up with her. She was of no use to you anymore, and you want to call me out?"

Dean shakes him off and yells back at him, "She *never* saw me. All she ever saw was you. And you just ate that shit up, Parker. I tried like fuck to be something to her, but I didn't have a chance in hell, because of YOU!" He shouts as he shoves Josh in the chest.

People are watching as though it's entertainment. *What is wrong with people? Why won't they step in and stop this?* No one does though—just me.

If given a scale of the shittiest decisions I've made in my life, I'm pretty sure the scale would be tipped on the shitty side, because I'm not the best at making the right ones. Choosing Dean to be my safe haven for two years was one of those shitty decisions. I've made many mistakes today. This would be another—another tip on the shitty side of the scale. *Why the hell not?*

I jump in the middle of them ducking and putting my hands in front of my face. "Please, stop. Just stop. It's not worth it." I cry.

I push them apart the best I can, but they continue to punch and push over and around me. Josh tries to move me out of the way, but I keep moving back in the middle of them. "Dammit, Riley. Let me handle this. Go wait in the truck!" he shouts as he throws the keys toward me.

Tears are streaming down my face, and I watch as the keys fall to the ground. That was another moment to do the right thing and back away. I never make the right choices.

I don't step away. I stay right where I am—in the middle of them. Dean shouts directly in my face, "No, *you're* not worth it." He yells things at me, but I can't hear it. I'm just stuck in this bubble of darkness and fear as the sting of his hands hit my chest.

I just want them to stop. I just want Dean to leave me alone. I just want to go back to two years ago and tell Josh I love him—that I've always loved him. I just want to go back to the day when I let Dean convince me that he cared for me and not believe it, because he doesn't. He hates me. He uses me. He lies to me. He tricks me. He makes me hate myself. Josh makes me love myself. He makes me feel like everything I feel makes sense, and it's okay. Dean makes me feel guilty. He makes me feel lost and confused. I am lost and confused when he is around.

I don't see him do it, but I feel it. His hands push me on the chest, and I'm shoved back and into the air. I stumble as I try to catch myself, but I lose my footing on the curb falling to the concrete, hitting my head on impact. I land on something sharp, and the pain shoots through me like electricity. It all seems like slow motion—Josh yelling—Dean looking angry then scared with his hands in the air.

"Riley, NO! Oh, fuck! What did you do?" I hear Josh shout as he runs towards me.

I felt the wind leave my lungs, and the pain in my head shoots fire through my veins. I try to sit up, but dark spots clouded my vision, and I immediately feel dizzy.

"I...oh, shit! Riley, I'm sorry. I didn't mean to. I'm so sorry. Is she okay?" Dean asks, trying to come near me. His voice is like an echo.

"Get the fuck away from her. Haven't you done enough? Just LEAVE.US.ALONE!" Josh hollers as he is cradling me in his arms.

I blink my eyes trying to get the spots in my vision to clear. My head hurts. I reach behind it to hold the spot that hurts and feel wetness. When I pull my hand back in front of my face my hand is red, and I hear Josh curse again.

I don't know if it was the red on my hand, or the shock of everything, but I shut my eyes as everything goes black.

"Hey, Riley. I missed seeing your adorable face in History yesterday," Dean said as I was standing at my locker.

"Yeah, sure. Whatever," I spoke with sarcasm. *"I had a dentist appointment yesterday, and my mom just let me skip. We had a shopping day. I bought some new jeans,"* I said looking down at my new MissMe's.

He smiled. "I appreciated those as I watched you walk down the hall to your locker." He looked me over for emphasis.

I peered up at him, feeling the flush reach my cheeks with embarrassment. He watched me walk, which implied he was staring at my ass.

He grabbed a curl, twirling it around his finger. I wondered why he always did that. Why I liked that he did that. Then I remembered why, because Josh used to do that—that was why I liked the way it felt.

I missed Josh. Nothing had been the same since the accident and the funerals. He'd pulled away from me and it hurt—a lot.

I looked past Dean, and saw Josh leaning against the wall with one leg up. His eyes were on us. I tried to read them, but I couldn't. He just looked curious. He hadn't talked to me in a few days. I missed his voice. I missed everything about him.

A group of cheerleaders walked over to him, they tried hard to get his attention. He nodded, his mouth moving as though he was interacting with them, but his eyes remained locked with mine. I couldn't look away. I was trapped in his gaze—trying so hard to read him.

Dean must have noticed I wasn't paying any attention to him, because he grabbed my chin and turned my face to his. I blinked a few times—feeling hypnotized. "Sorry, what?" I said. Why did Dean always make me feel that way? Flustered and confused—I wondered about all of these things.

He laughed lightly. "I said that I'd like to take you out tonight. We can go bowling, or to dinner. Whatever you want. I just really like being around you.

You're funny and cute as hell. What do you say? Will you go out with me?" he asked for the third time in a matter of weeks.

I looked back towards Josh, but he wasn't looking at me any longer. He was laughing at something Collin had said. One of the cheerleaders dropped her textbook on the ground—probably on purpose. It was pep rally day and she was dressed in uniform, which was the shortest of short skirts—nothing was left to the imagination, and by the looks on Josh and Collins faces—they preferred it that way. She bent over to get the book she'd dropped. Collin and Josh admired the view before them appreciatively. Collin covered his mouth and slapped Josh's arm with the other. I read Josh's mouth as he said, "Dayyyuumm"

Did he say, damn? That meant he liked the view, I thought.

Shit! It was the only word that matched the way I felt—like shit!

It made me furious. It made me feel jealous. It made me feel a lot of things.

Just for a second Josh's eyes flicked to mine. He knew I'd noticed. He frowned at first, like he was contemplating something, but then he smirked as he looked back at Collin continuing their conversation—ignoring me.

I looked back at Dean as he looked between Josh and me. "You still have that crush, huh?" he asked.

"What? I don't have a crush on Josh." I lied, clearly in denial.

He smiled, moving into my space—continuing to twirl my curl and making me feel nervous. "No? Then what's stopping you from going on that date with me tonight?" he asked with a flirtatious tone.

I swallowed down the feeling in my stomach that it would be a mistake, but for whatever reason I shrugged and said, "I guess nothing. Tonight it is."

He smiled, "pick you up at 7." He kissed my cheek, and when he walked away, I noticed Josh punch his locker and storm away.

"Miss, can you tell me what happened?" A guy in blue asks me as I blinked my eyes rapidly, trying to gain my focus. I can't seem to get the stars to go away.

"Look, Bill. This is going to have to wait? I need to get her to the hospital." A lady with pretty blue eyes says, applying pressure to the back of my head and wrapping something around my forehead. It hurts. She kneels down in front of me and asks me a question of her own. "Can you tell me your name?"

"He pushed her. That's what happened." I can hear Josh yelling as she asks me that, "her name? Why the hell are you asking her that? Of course she knows her name." He berates the lady questioning me.

I can't concentrate enough to understand what either of them is saying—my head feels like pressure is building inside of it. "I...I...I'm Rrriley," I say, my speech sounding slurred.

The lady looks up at another guy who appears blurry to me. She nods to him and they pick me up and put me on a stretcher.

"It was an accident. Damn it. Baby, it was an accident." Dean's voice sounds muffled and distant. *Dean? Why is Dean on my date with Josh? I'm so confused.*

"Don't call her baby. She is NOT your baby. She's mine," Josh shouts to Dean.

"I ffffell ddddown," I whisper as loudly as I can to the guy in blue as they are wheeling me away. He nods, but backs away, not pressing me further.

I feel Josh grab my hands as he tries to follow beside me. "No, you didn't fall Riley. Don't cover for him baby. He pushed you." Josh says, trying to convince me to tell a story I'm not sure is the truth. His eyes are moving rapidly to each of mine. I'm trying to focus on them but the dark spots in my vision are making it hard. He looks so nervous.

Josh looks at the lady wheeling me, "Please. She is confused or something. He pushed her down," he says sounding so distraught. It makes me panic on the inside. *Did Dean push me down?*

I turn my head to find Dean. My head feels fuzzy and I'm not sure if what I see is real, or if I'm hallucinating. He is sitting next to a cop car in handcuffs, looking right at me.

I didn't feel well. "I didn't mean to hurt you, Riley. I'm so sorry. It was an accident." His voice is muffled behind the ringing in my ears and the distance between us.

The people helping me are pushing Josh back—away from me. When I turn to where his eyes were just a moment ago. I can't find them there. For the life of me I can't seem to understand, or remember why my head is hurting, or why everyone is fighting like this, or why Dean is in handcuffs.

I just remember delicious cheesecake, and peanut butter kisses on Josh's lips. I remember promises of forever and a scary movie I owed him. I don't remember watching it, though.

"Don't talk to her." Josh shouts over to Dean. He pushes his way back to me and holds my hand. He kisses my forehead and wetness blankets my face from his tears. Dean is shouting he didn't mean it and to please forgive him. Josh is grumbling back to him while holding my hand. It's too much.

I shake my head and try to blink away the spots. "Stttoooppp it. Stop, please. I...I...I don't know. I ddddon't remember. I'm sssorry, Josh." My head hurts. I feel dizzy. I just—can't think. I grab my head and squeeze my eyes shut and it's like my head is swirling, my stomach suddenly turns and I get sick off the side of the stretcher. My body wretches and dry heaves overtake me.

Josh is worried about me. I can see it in his eyes when I look back at him, confused as to why I'm suddenly suffering a massive headache and a stomach bug.

"Step back. We need to get her checked out. I'm pretty sure she has a concussion." The lady with pretty eyes explains to Josh, as the friendly man across from her separates us. I look up at the lady just as they are lifting me into an ambulance, his hand slips away from mine, and I feel bereft without it.

"I'm scared. I don't know what's going on." I admit to her. Josh is begging to come with me, but they tell him no. "Josh? JOSH!" I whisper then shout for him but a glass separates us.

Somewhere within that time I must have fallen asleep, because I don't remember the lady with blue eyes, or the blurry guy. I don't see Josh or Dean or the guy in blue again. I don't see anything other than a tunnel of black, and strange stars that aren't in the sky.

 *Josh*

CHAPTER 2

Had someone told me years ago that this girl would become crucial for me to breathe—I wouldn't have believed them. But here we are—her lying in a hospital bed, and her cold hand feeling fragile between my own. The beeping from the monitor hooked up to her is annoying, but reassures me that her heart is strong and she is okay—just sleeping. Nonetheless, the fear I feel is strong. She has become the air I breathe, the reason my own heart has a pulse, the cause for my senses to go into overdrive—just everything. She is everything to me and she is hurt—and I hurt.

"Why isn't she waking up?" I ask her mom again for the third time since I've arrived. I rub tiny circles underneath Riley's palm as I watch her chest rise and fall with each breath she takes.

According to the paramedics, she lost consciousness in the ambulance briefly—a result of shock or the concussion.

Thankfully, a brain scan has reassured us all that she is okay. She does have a concussion, as suspected, and two small staples have been placed in the back of her head to close a small gash. She has officially freaked me out, with her slurred speech, not remembering what happened, and the fact that she has fallen asleep, and hasn't opened her eyes since I arrived here hours ago. She won't wake up.

"She is okay, Josh. The doctor said it's normal for her to sleep like this. Don't worry," she says placing a sympathetic hand on my shoulder. "You should go get some sleep. When you get back in the morning, I can assure you she will be awake and happy to see you, as always. Okay?"

I don't want to leave her. I don't want to go home without her. I am tired, though, and I have nowhere to sleep here. Her mom is staying, and it would be rather inappropriate of me to try and stay in her place. I'm just her boyfriend, not her husband. *Fuck, where did that come from?*

I place a kiss to Riley's forehead like I always do. I lean in to whisper in her ear, "Baby, I'm so sorry this happened to you, and I'm sorry I let my temper get the better of me. I'm sorry you got hurt and that I didn't protect you, but more than that baby... I'm sorry I might not be here when you wake up. I love you so much. So much that it hurts." I let my mouth linger there even though I have stopped speaking. The beeping on her monitor begins to accelerate. It catches my attention, so I lift my head and glance at it. I look back down at her as I feel her squeeze my hand, but she doesn't open her eyes.

That's something though. She heard me. I believe she heard me.

With that, I stand and give her mom a hug. "Please, call me if she wakes up. I don't care what time it is. I want to be here with her. Please," I plead.

She smiles and pinches my cheek. "You're a good boy, Joshua."

I laugh. "Shhh...someone may hear you. Girls don't like good boys, Mrs. Shaw. You might ruin my reputation."

She glances at Riley and then to me. "Nah, you're wrong. It's the good ones they give their hearts to."

I suck in a breath of air. I'm momentarily stuck on her words. *Give their hearts to*. Riley trusts me with her heart. She has never trusted anyone with her heart. She trusts me, and I acted like a jackass with a temper. Now, she is here with staples in her head, a confused memory of tonight's events, and a headache from hell I would presume. God, I'm stupid. I should have listened to her. We should have just walked away from Dean and never looked back. Tonight was supposed to be a beautiful beginning for us, and it ended up being the beautiful hell that we always seem to get thrown into.

Every time I attempted to shut my eyes, my mind replayed watching Riley fall and hit her head. I tossed and turned for what seemed like hours, and then I plugged my ears with my iPod listening to anything and everything to get my mind to shut up—it never did.

I am in the kitchen when Joey and Tatum come wandering in, wrapped up in a single blanket. They both jump two feet in the air when I say, "Hey." I guess they don't see me sitting at the table. I laugh, which made them laugh, and for a minute it feels good to let go—until I remember why I was feeling sad—and the reason why I can't just climb into Riley's bedroom window and hold her.

"What are you doing up so late?" Joey asks me pulling down two mugs and two tea bags.

"I can't sleep." I say, thrumming my fingers on the table.

"Awww...you've got it bad for my sister, huh?" Tatum says, giving me that look that says I'm sweet, and she loves me. It makes me smile. I nod.

"It just sucks. The past few months have been hell. You know? And then it was like we were getting a second chance. We finally seemed to cross that invisible line and then this happened." I'm not meaning to sound whiney or wallow in my own pity part, but it does truly suck. It's like every time Riley and I take one step forward—something happens, or someone happens, and we are sent hurdling backward again.

Joey walks back to the table holding the two mugs of tea for her and Tatum.

"So, why are y'all still up?" I ask.

Joey yawns and points to Tatum. "It's her fault. She was talking in her sleep and—,"

"She tried to smother me with a pillow. It was attempted murder. Some best friend your sister is to me." Tatum says, sipping her tea. "Truthfully, I was probably telling her to quit snoring. I'm sure that is what I said in my sleep," she adds.

"I do not snore."

"So do."

They go back and forth like two year olds for a few seconds before Tatum puts her hand over her mouth. "OMG! I forgot to feed, Tink," she says.

"Where's your key? I'll go," I offer a little too eager.

She grins and walks to Joey's bedroom returning with her keys. She kisses my cheek and says, "I hope one day I find a guy as sweet as you, Josh."

There is that word again. *Sweet.*

So, I'm a nice, sweet good guy. My reputation will be burned to ash before graduation.

As I walk next door, I wonder if Riley will always be attracted to the sweet, good guy persona, or if she is secretly attracted to the asshole that put her in the hospital. She spent two years with Dean. She had to have been attracted to something about him. I just don't know what it was. Dean is definitely NOT the nice, sweet, good guy. We are definitely nothing alike.

Once inside Riley's house, I am enveloped in the scent that is—*her home.* It's cinnamon and vanilla, always reminding me of baked goodies, like a honey bun or something.

I go about my task of feeding Tink and refilling her water bowl. Next up, I open Riley's bedroom door so Tink can find her comfy sleeping spot next to Riley, but then I remember she isn't there.

Riley.

Shit. My heart is splintering.

I don't know why I get hit with a moment of nostalgia with my hand halted on to the doorknob. Maybe it's the feeling like I'm invading her privacy. Maybe it's the memories of the last time we were in here, when Riley could barely look at me because she thought I lied to her and that I was the father of Preslee's baby. It most definitely is the gut wrenching way her eyes looked when they met mine earlier today—the sadness and disappointment, the way they desired me, and then with a deep inhale and quick blink—they hated me for everything that had happened.

"Well, Tink? Ready to go to sleep?" *I've officially lost my cool. I'm talking to a cat.* She purrs and rubs against my leg. As soon as I open the door, she takes off to Riley's bed, finding her pillow, kneading and curling up until she's set.

I stare at Riley's door as I remember the way her body looked wrapped in nothing but a towel and how much my hands itched to feel what was underneath it and the way her eyes pleaded with me to be careful with her because she was broken—all that has changed now. Riley knows the truth. She knows I love her and only her, and she loves me.

I've always thought bedrooms tell a story about a person. For example, my bedroom says I'm a football player. My guitar and music collection express my love for the art. Random pieces of paper with scribbled lyrics are scattered around my own room. Just like I see in her room—just one example of how Riley and I are two kindred souls entwined.

I take a minute to study the story Riley's room tells me. I've been in her room countless times, and have paid attention to the way it changes from year to year. Like the lime green walls with Tinker Bell stuffed animals and decor, switching to N'Sync posters and nail polish to what it is now—one black wall covered in colored chalk poems, and a bulletin board with random snapshot photos with Post-It notes of more jotted down poems. I smile at the photos and frown at the poems. Her writing is dark and a bit depressing. I stand there looking around at it, thinking that must be what lives inside Riley. Sadness—it breaks my heart.

I spot a photo in a frame on top of her chest of drawers. It piques my curiosity, and I look hard at it, feeling the sudden urge to cry for this little girl, and for the familiar face in the background I long to see each day. It's a picture at Riley's fifth birthday party. She is dressed in her Tinker Bell costume that she used to *always* wear. Her mom must have taken the photo because she is the only one not in it. Riley's dad is leaning over her sitting at the table blowing out the candles. She looks so happy. Her hand is in my hand, and I'm looking at it with a boyish grin. My mom has her finger pointed at us and is smiling up at my dad. She thought we were the cutest thing together. My parents are standing just to the side, and dad's hand is placed on her stomach, where Joey was beginning to grow. It was placed as though he was actually holding her tiny hand before he really could. It's a picture perfect moment.

They don't come often, and that one had hidden flaws. Just moments after that picture was taken, I gave Riley the toy car that has been sitting secretly in her jewelry box for years. My mom gave her the Barbie, which led to a memory she had kept to herself. Everything spiraled into chaos.

The darkness seeped through that happy moment when Riley unknowingly told a secret she'd promised to keep, not realizing exposing her dad's affair would result in lasting consequences for her family—for her. No child should be placed in that position, to have seen at such a young age the lies behind someone's eyes, to realize the one they love the most in the world has a facade, to walk in on her own father having sex with her babysitter and being asked not to tell—no wonder she didn't trust easy.

Nonetheless, the picture captured one of the first connections between Riley and me—for that—I smile. I touch my mom's face, swiping with my other hand a tear that I didn't even realize had fallen down my cheek. Shit, I miss her so goddamn much.

I find a shirt of Riley's lying on her bed and bring it to my nose, inhaling the scent that is just...her. It's not perfume or any fake smell that girls douse their skin with to make them smell pleasant.

No, this smell is a treat to my nose—like lotion or bath wash mixed with everything that is, her own sweetness. It wraps around me like a blanket, warming me with images of her hands tangled in my hair, as I taste just a bit of the sweetness off of her neck. Maybe it's creepy, but I take the shirt with me when I leave. Maybe it will give me pleasant dreams.

CHAPTER 3

I'm cold, scared and confused. I can hear them talking around me, but they can't hear me. No matter how hard I try to open my eyes, they are just too heavy. No matter how hard I try to make my lips move, they just stay clamped shut. What happened?

"Why isn't she waking up?" I hear Josh ask my mom again as he rubs tiny circles on my palm—it's soothing.

"She is okay, Josh. The doctor said it's normal for her to sleep like this. Don't worry. You should go get some sleep. When you get back in the morning, I can assure you she will be awake and happy to see you, as always. Okay?" My mom's sympathetic voice assures him.

I can feel him whisper in my ear, but I can't respond. "Baby, I'm so sorry this happened to you, and I'm sorry I let my temper get the better of me. I'm sorry you got hurt, and I didn't protect you, but more than that baby...I'm sorry I might not be here when you wake up. I love you so much. So much that it hurts." I want to respond, to ask him what he is talking about, but my mouth won't move. My eyes won't open, and it scares me. I try so hard and feel as though I squeeze his hand, but I'm not sure I really do.

Then I'm bereft and cold.

"Please, call me if she wakes up. I don't care what time it is. I want to be here with her. Please," he pleads.

"You're a good boy, Joshua," she explains.

He is.

"Shhh...someone may hear you. Girls don't like good boys, Mrs. Shaw. You might ruin my reputation." If I could laugh, I would. His reputation of a bad boy with a cold heart is just a facade. I know the truth.

"Nah, you're wrong. It's the good ones they give their hearts to."
She is so right. *You have my heart, Josh. I could never give it to anyone else but you.*

I want to wake up. I'm done sleeping. I want to wake up now. Please, wake up now.

I'm just too sleepy.

"He's a good guy...that Josh. I always knew I needed to watch out for him." A deep voice says, but this voice is different. This voice isn't like the others. This is a voice I haven't heard since—he died.

Oh!

"Daddy?" I screech, frantically trying to open my eyes, but I can't. I'm in the dark with him. *Oh God, I'm dead aren't I?*

"Am I dead?" I ask.

He is laughing now. "No, Tinker Bell, you aren't dead. Just sleeping."

"How can I talk to you then when no one else can hear me?" I ask.

"You wanted me here, I guess." And like a light switch is flipped on, he is illuminated before my eyes. We are walking side by side along the banks of the lake. It's the part of the day where the pink and oranges in the sky mingle beautifully.

"How did we get here?" I ask him.

He turns to look at me, "It's your favorite place. It's a happy spot," he answers. "This is your dream, princess."

I look around at it, and I see Josh pushing me on the swing as my hair blows in the wind. We are smiling and laughing—content.

"He loves you." My dad states the obvious.

"And I love him," I say, turning my eyes away from happiness and to the source of the darkness that has enveloped me for so long.

"I've made so many mistakes, Daddy. Why would you come to me now? Why did you leave in the first place? I'm scared." I admit and feel the tears fall down my cheek.

He reaches his hand up to touch me, and I freeze. It falls away. "I'm sorry, princess. You can't stay in the past anymore. What happened between your mom and me...what I did—it's not your fault. I want you to promise to let it go, to let yourself be happy. You deserve to be happy. Okay? Moments come and go, and so many slip by without us truly living them. Promise me that you will embrace the moments as they come...live in them and make mistakes. It's okay to make them."

And then it's dark again. *No!*

I don't know how long I sleep, or what else I dream about, but I know it is happy. It is dreams of time spent with Josh at our spot embracing sweet moments.

"You will always be my Tinker bell. Always my princess." My dad says next to me. I slowly lift my eyelids as he lifts his hand again to touch mine.

This time, I'm not scared to let him touch me—I'm curious. I lift my hand and place it flatly against his palm in the air. It's not cold, and it doesn't go through me. He smiles as he interlaces his fingers with mine. I suddenly feel stronger—suddenly warm and safe.

"Let him love you, okay, princess?" He whispers to me, slowly vanishing into thin air.

He's gone.

 *Josh*

CHAPTER 4

I was wrong about the pleasant night's sleep. It was anything but sweet. I've never given much thought to the meaning behind someone's dreams or nightmares. That is, until this morning when I realized what mine had been about.

I had finally fallen asleep well into the middle of the night. It's only natural that I would dream about Riley, when my last thoughts were of her, but my dream was a result of my fear of losing her and had left me feeling restless.

Riley called me crying. She said she was so sorry for everything bad that ever happened to me because of her. She promised to fix it for everyone. She told me she could never let the same mistakes happen to someone else, and because of that she was leaving me.

I begged her to explain what she meant, but she didn't. I could hear the rain falling, and the thunder from the storm brewing on top of us—she was outside. I could tell by her breathing that she was running.

"Riley, tell me where you are, baby. I'm coming to meet you," I pleaded.

"I'm by the lake. You're too late, Josh. I have to make this choice. I can't let someone else die because of me," she said between sobs.

"No one died because of you, baby. Your dad killed my mom. Not you. We've been through this. Stop talking like that." I groveled with her as I took off running towards the lake.

You're wrong, Josh. I needed to get you away. I had too. Because of me you are alone."

"I'm not alone, Riley. I have you."

"Had me Josh. You had me, and now you don't anymore. I'm so sorry. I let this happen to you again." She choked on her tears.

"What are you talking about, baby? I do have you."

"No, you don't," she whispered into the phone, just as I caught up to her at the lake, except it wasn't the lake anymore. We were back at the theater, no rain in the sky, just a still motion picture of the events from last night.

I'm standing there, watching it. It's weird.

I'm watching the 'me' from last night yell at Riley to back away, but she doesn't listen. And then Dean pushes her to the ground. She falls, and I run to catch her, but I don't get there in time. My eyes are as wide as saucers when I see her hit the concrete with a thud.

"Riley? Oh—fuck! What did you do?" I yell at Dean as I cradle her in my hands. She doesn't open her eyes and blink rapidly like she did last night. She doesn't talk to me like she did last night. She doesn't move, or act confused like she did last night. She doesn't do anything at all. She's not waking up.

She's not waking up. I yelled it. "She's not waking up!"

"HELP! Someone help her!" I shouted to anyone around me, but the sky had gone black, and nothing existed but me—and her—and this moment as I embraced her fragile body.

I kissed her forehead, her cheeks and her lips. I blew my own breath of life into her, but it isn't enough. I would give my own heart to her if it would make her's beat with life again. My tears would drown her if she were still able to drown.

"Please, wake up. Please. WAKE UP! WAKE UP!" I screamed it. She doesn't

I do.

I wake with a jolt, drenched in sweat. It was just a dream. Riley is okay. She had hit her head, but she-is-okay. I repeat it multiple times until my trembling ceases and my heart rate slows.

Clearly, I am afraid of losing Riley. Dreams don't ever make sense so I can't rationalize any of the things that happened in it, just that I had been fearful. I know that I was. I have been scared for Riley many times.

When her dad died, and she drank his booze until she puked and felt like shit, and when she told me she was just like him for numbing her pain with alcohol, I had been scared for her then, she wasn't like him.

At the cemetery this past year, I had been worried about her, seeing the lifelessness in her eyes. At Brandt's party, when she'd drowned her emotions at the expense of her liver—again—I had been scared for her—and thought that maybe she did tend to numb her pain with booze.

At her house, that night when she thought I'd rejected her—her tears had ripped me into two halves. I had hurt for her then, too.

At school when she'd passed out, and on the street when she'd almost run into the car—all more moments I had been scared for her.

None of those moments came close to the fear I'd felt last night—the sound of her skull hitting the concrete—the blood that was on her hand, and the way she didn't make sense when she spoke.

That was fear.

"I'm going to the hospital." I told my dad as I walked past him heading out the door. I didn't expect to see my worst enemy sitting on the hood of my truck, though.

I was beyond shocked, and a hell of a lot pissed off to see him sitting there.

The nerve.

I guessed they'd let him out, but how dare he show up here to what—finish this fight?

I have no more fight left in me. Between getting Riley to admit that she loves me and losing her for months—thanks to a misunderstanding and rumor, then getting her back only to end up here—and then, that fucking nightmare—I was mentally drained.

I was angry at the world, and the shit hand cards it kept dealing to the table. *I FOLD so now can we move on, pretty fucking please,* I mentally begged of fate.

I feel the blood begin to race in my veins just thinking about it. I reign in my temper, take a deep breath and climb down the steps. "What do you want?" I ask crossing my arms over my chest and leaning against the porch.

He hops off my truck. "To talk. I just want to talk...that's all." He begins to pace and grab his hair looking up at the sky. I need him to leave so I can get to Riley, but I am curious as to what the hell else he has to say about what happened last night. He takes a deep breath and looks at me.

He doesn't appear to want to fight. In fact, I see defeat in his eyes, and then he starts, "Do you remember when we were kids? You, me and Riley?" He doesn't even give me time to reply before he continues, "I do. I remember every moment of every second we were all friends growing up. I can't pinpoint when it was that you and I became enemies, or when it happened that Riley began to look at me with the same eyes you do, but I remember it—the good times—before it all turned to shit."

I sigh heavily. "I remember when we were friends, Dean, and I remember the exact time I began hating you," I admit.

"When?" he asks. "Because I have no fucking clue what the hell happened man? We were friends—all three of us, at one time."

"*Were*. We were friends, Dean, and then you became an asshole." I push off the porch and step forward.

"Asshole? How? What did I do?"

I pause—trying to form the thoughts in order to make them clear to him. "Seriously? Dean, how do you not know this? You knew she meant everything to me. You knew I had feelings for her, and you still went after her. That's a dick move man."

I continue...

"Did you know that the night you kissed her for the first time was the same damn night that she and I kissed for the first time?" His eyebrows draw apart, and his eyes widen. I can tell he didn't know that. *Well, now he does.*

Before he can reply, I add a little more information for him. "Yeah, it was the best damn kiss I'd ever had in my life, and I thought—*finally*—Riley and I could cross this invisible line she'd drawn. She had so many damn walls built up around her. Every time I tried to break them down, she would panic but that night, it was different. And hell, if you didn't come along to confuse the shit out of her."

He stares at me for a beat and sighs. "Josh, I could say the same to you dude. Y'all may have had this special connection, or barrier I couldn't break through too, but I cared for her just the same. You knew that too. You knew I liked her."

It was my turn to sigh because I did know, but he didn't deserve her. "She was special to me. She was everything to me, and I know I sound like I'm pussy whipped, but it's true. She belonged with me and the second an opportunity came, you swooped right in."

He throws his hands up in the air, "so, that's what it's about? She gave me a chance and not you? She let her walls down for *me*?"

I stare at him not sure if he is right or not. Have I hated him all these years because she let him in first? No, I was sure as shit that I'd hated him because he was a douchebag and didn't deserve to be the one to break down her walls. "I don't know, to be honest, but I know you didn't deserve her," I said

"And you did?" he shouts.

"Damn straight," I deadpan.

Dean shakes his head, "When her father died, you put distance between the two of you. You weren't treating her like you once had. You pushed her away, Josh. *You did.* She told me it hurt to be near you because she could feel your pain, and she knew you saw her differently. I was there for her—because believe it or not—I do fucking care."

I run a hand over my face and grit my teeth, "I know that. And you're right, Dean. You were there—ready to take advantage. I was hurting, too. I didn't push her away. I needed time to sort *myself* out. I lost my mom, too. You know? We both lost a parent that day."

I begin to pace and hate myself for the way I acted then. I needed her, she needed me and instead of pulling together—he was right— we'd pulled apart. I pulled away. I don't know why I did. I just did, and she found comfort in him. He was there for her when I wasn't. I couldn't blame him for that. I should thank him because she wasn't alone, but then he fucked her over. So, fuck giving him thanks. Fuck him and the way he cares for her. His 'care' meant shit. She needed someone. She needed me, and I wasn't there.

We stare at each other, neither knowing what to say next, not exactly. Except I do. I have a question I needed answered. "If you cared for her then why did you do it? Why did you lie all these years, and make her think she would be your first when you know she wasn't even your second?"

He swallows and then grimaces. "I never thought she would find out. I just wanted to be with her, and I thought if she would give me that last little piece of herself, then she would truly be mine. She wouldn't forgive me if she knew who I really was."

"That's a bunch of bullshit and you know it. She wouldn't have sex with you, and you got it on the side, and you made her feel guilty for that. That's low dude, and you know it."

"I never claimed to be the best for her, and you're right, I'm not deserving, but...truth? I knew deep down the reason she wouldn't sleep with me was because of you. It was always you. Even when we were kids, it was you. I would tell her a joke, and she would look at me confused. I would tell you the same damn joke, and you would laugh because it was funny. It never failed, as we walked to school together the next morning, you would always share with her the very same joke I'd already told her—ya know... the one she thought wasn't funny. She would laugh and look at you like you hung the damn moon. It was the same damn joke, just coming out of your mouth, not mine."

He sighs. "When we were together... I wasn't in denial about what I saw, Josh. She was always looking at you, telling me shit you said like I gave a flying fuck—staring out her window when we sat on her bed, as though she were dreaming about what was on the other side of it. It ate me up inside. I wanted her to want me, dammit, but she was always wondering about you. I cared. That's not a lie. I still care. It's not an excuse, but I just wanted to feel wanted, and sex did that. In my mind, it was Riley I was with."

I ball my fist ready to kick his ass again. The only thought I have hearing his words is, *She is mine.* He needs to understand that, and never, *ever,* picture her that way again. "She.Is.Mine." I tell him through gritted teeth.

He growls softly as he sits on the step, his eyes cast down to the ground. "I know. She always was," he whispers. Then he looks back up to me, "Wasn't she?" He stares at me for a beat longer without my reply, and then his eyes downcast again.

Was she? I wonder.

I wonder if he is sincere in everything he is saying. He gazes up at me, "Is she okay? I never meant to hurt her. I don't know why I pushed her. My head was all fucked up last night. I didn't mean to hurt her, Josh." He grabs a handful of his hair and looks toward her house.

I hop up on the hood of my truck, "She is. She has a concussion and seems confused about stuff. She has been asleep for a while, but the doctor says that is normal, and she will be fine."

He nods, "That's good. Not that you care or anything, but I spent the night in jail until I was sober. I guess I should be somewhat thankful for that. They fined me a shitload instead of revoking my license, though. So I guess I got lucky. Oh, and her mom called the cops. I had to promise to stay away from her, or she would get a restraining order against me."

I didn't know that, but I play it off and nod, "I see. Well, it could've been worse. You could've gotten on your bike and hurt someone—killed yourself. How could you be so reckless, especially around Riley? Dude, I should kick your ass just for that alone. That is how my mom died. The very reason her dad is dead."

He doesn't meet my eyes. He knows, and when he says, "I did hurt someone. I hurt the best damn thing to ever exist to me. I never meant to, though," I begin to feel angry again. She is the best damn thing to ever exist to ME.

"Dean, whether you meant to hurt her or not, is irrelevant. The point is you did. You put your hands on her out of anger. Her mom is just protecting her." *Something I'd failed to do,* I thought.

He stares at me with a blank expression, and his eyes look desolate, "I know. I guess I am like my dad, after all."

I want to correct him, to tell him he is nothing like his asshole of a dad, but I don't because I'm not exactly sure if he is or if he isn't like him, people change. It's been years since I knew the Dean that was once considered a friend.

"I should go. I won't be around for a few days. I need to clear my head. I spoke with her mom this morning, apologized and explained my side. I asked if I could come say goodbye to Riley and she agreed, but only if Riley agreed to see me."

"No, you can't do that," I say defensively. "You just said her mom didn't want you around, Riley."

His narrowed eyes dart to mine as he stands, squaring his shoulders. "Look, I get it. She's yours... whatever. Like I said, she always was. I just want to talk to her and apologize. Say goodbye. Okay? Besides, her mom is the one to make that call, Josh—not you—and she says it's fine."

It wasn't fine.

Another thought hit me. "What about Preslee?"

With a raised brow, he asks, "What about her? What was that yesterday at Riley's house? What the hell were y'all talking about anyway?"

He didn't know? "I told you to go talk to her. Did you not?"

He shakes his head back and forth. "No, I didn't want to be around her. After a few bottles, my thoughts were on Riley."

I ignored his thoughts being on Riley—I say, "Dude, she is pregnant, and she claims it's yours."

His eyes go wide, and I see the panic set in and then the realization of it. "What? No!" He shouts and then drops his voice lower, "No, she can't be. She said she was on the pill."

Aha! "Well, then she told a lie, brother. She said one time... No condom and hello baby."

He looks up to the sky grunting, "Fuck! I, well...ain't that some shit. I've gotta go." He pauses, "Look, Josh, last night was a wakeup call for me, and I get it now. She belongs with you. I can't say that I don't wish it were me—because I do. I wish she thought I hung the moon for her, but I will respect her enough to let her be happy. I should have done that a long time ago." He says, as he turns to walk back down the street towards his house.

I have no reply. I have nothing more to say. I just hope he is being honest and will leave her alone.

After stopping to get Riley's mom some breakfast and coffee to go, I head to the hospital, and my heart beats erratically as I hope to see Riley's beautiful eyes this morning.

I get off the elevator, finding Dean standing with Riley's mom outside her room. They are talking in hushed tones. She is giving him an earful, and he is hanging on her every word holding flowers and a teddy bear, obviously for Riley.

I feel sick. I thought about it the whole way over here. Dean is a dick, and I hate him no less, standing here after his apologies and explanation than I did yesterday. He may care for her, *fuck*, he may even love her, but it doesn't change the fact that he doesn't deserve her. She belongs with me. She always has.

They both turn to meet my eyes, and I hide my insecurity and nod my head.

"Good Morning, Mrs. Shaw. I brought you breakfast and coffee." I offer with a smile, full of the confidence I don't really feel on the inside.

She smiles wide, Dean frowns. *Suck it, motherfucker!* "You go on inside. I'll be in there in a few minutes." She turns to grab Dean by the elbow and pull him out of the walkway.

I nod my head and make my way inside, disappointment crashing in my veins when I find her asleep. I brush the hair out of her face, and find dried tears on her cheeks like she has been crying.

I lean down and kiss her forehead. I study her to memory. She is so beautiful. I reach my hand down and interlace our fingers as I look to the door to find her mom coming in without Dean.

 *Josh*

CHAPTER 5

I'm beginning to think Dean has multiple personalities. The nice Dean and the cruel Dean. I also think I must be crazy because I feel like I had a visit from death.

My eyes flutter open as I realize my hand is still interlaced with my dad's hand, except it isn't his hand any longer—it's Josh's.

"Riley? Baby? Oh, God. It's so good to see those beautiful eyes. She's awake," he says over his shoulder to my mom. She joins him in gushing, hugging and welcoming me back to wherever I just came from.

"Josh? Mom?" *Oh, my head hurts.* I feel groggy and confused. I blink my eyes a lot. The light hurts my eyes. "What happened? Where's my dad?" I ask.

Josh looks at me perplexed, and then he looks at my mom with evident worry in his expression.

"Your dad?" he inquires with a raised brow.

I nod, "He was just here. Right there." I point to the spot next to my bed that is empty. "He held my hand, helped me wake up."

I pull my hand from Josh's and touch my fingers with the other hand. "I think he held my hand. Maybe, I dreamed it." I rub my temples and try to relieve some of the throbbing.

They are both looking at me like I've lost my mind. I'm wondering if I have.

The doctor takes this moment to enter the room, "Well, good morning, sunshine," he says in a friendly voice while smiling at me. "Can you tell me your name?"

That is a weird question. *Shouldn't he know my name if he is my doctor?* I lift my brows and answer, "Riley."

Another question rolls off his tongue. "Can you tell me who the president is?"

Really?

"Obama," I answer without hesitation.

"Can you tell me what year it is?"

This is strange.

"2013."

He smiles like I just won some contest. "Perfect. Now, how do you feel?" He asks pulling out a pen from his pocket. He starts flashing this annoying little light in my eyes. He checks the machine next to me and makes a humming sound.

"Like shit," I answer truthfully. My mom gasps, scolds me and apologizes to the good doctor for my choice of words. Josh just laughs.

The doctor checks my pulse and grins, "That's to be expected. You look good, though." His eyes cut to my moms and his face falters, "and how are you, Claudia?" The way his voice softens, and the way he says her name like a purr makes me wonder if he knows her. *That's odd.*

She smiles fondly, "Nothing to worry about, Dr. Peters." Their eyes linger on one another just a little too long for my comfort, so I clear my throat. Dr. Peters blinks his eyes a few times and turns to look down at me. *What the hell was that?*

"Can you sit up?" he asks as he writes a few things down in a chart by my bed. I nod, sitting up with Josh's assistance.

"This looks good, too," he says as he coaxes me back down.

"What looks good, too?" I ask confused.

"You have two small staples in your head back there—nothing to worry about.

I look confused back and forth between the faces in the room. *What happened? Why am I even in the hospital?*

"Staples? Why do I have staples?" I begin to freak out.

Josh looks at the doctor concerned, and my mom walks over to stand in the spot my dad was just in. *My Dad? What the hell is wrong with me? Am I going crazy?*

I guess the doctor senses their concern as he proceeds to explain, "Like I told y'all last night, it is common for patients with concussions to not remember the incident, or to suffer slight amnesia. This will pass as she heals."

Incident? What incident? I look around at all of them with wide eyes, "A concussion?"

Josh brushes his knuckles along my cheek, "Something happened. You, um, you hit your head," he whispers.

"What happened? I can't remember. I remember we ate cheesecake. We were going to the movie, I think. I can't remember anything after that."

I grab my head again and try to blink the fuzziness out of my eyes. "Dean? Was Dean there?" I ask. Josh puts his head down.

Or maybe, I dreamed about Dean, but why would I do that?

"I was." I hear his voice say from the doorway. *Or maybe not.*

My mom stands up and makes her way to the door, Josh curses under his breath. "Now isn't a good time, Dean. She just woke up," she tells him pushing on his chest.

"I won't stay long. I just want to apologize. Please. I promise not to touch her. I promise, Mrs. Shaw. I just need to talk to her." Dean pleads with my mom to let him in the room, and the whole altercation is bewildering.

I can't look at Dean, though. I'm too busy looking at Josh's eyes. They look lost, worried, sad and maybe even apologetic. I don't understand the expression on his face, and it's holding me captive.

"Josh?" I whisper, reaching up to smooth his brow line. His eyes squeeze shut, then slowly open and move up to meet mine. They look glassy like he is trying not to cry.

"What happened?" I ask again in a low voice that only he can hear.

He looks to the door where Dean is stood. They exchange something with one look that I don't understand. The door is propped open, and I can't hear what my mom is telling Dean in a hushed whisper.

Josh looks back at me, he grabs my hand, kisses my palm softly and then he sighs. "I'm going to let Dean explain it to you, if your mom agrees to let him talk to you. But now that you're awake, baby, there is something you should know…"

"Oookay? So tell me," I whisper again feeling a pit in my stomach grow uneasy.

"I love you. Okay? I love you so much and—and I think that maybe Dean does, too," he says.

My eyes dart to the door and then back to his, "What? What the hell are you talking about? Why would you say that to me?" I feel my pulse begin to race. I begin to feel angry not confused. *Why would he say that? Josh loves me, right? RIGHT?*

The doctor who is still standing in the room observing all of this finally intervenes. "Look, she just woke up, and she needs to get her bearings. I'm going to have to ask you all to step outside, so I can evaluate my patient further. Okay?" He starts shooing them out the door. And as much as I don't want to be alone—I want to be alone.

After some bickering and protesting, the room falls silent, other than my monitor beeping, the drip in the IV and the racing thoughts in my mind—it's not quiet enough. The doctor walks back over to me and checks the machine again, "That is better," he smiles.

He seems warm and sweet—eyes like a grandfather. I bet he is a nice man. "I'm taking your cues, okay? You seem to be just fine, Riley. The confusion is absolutely normal so don't fret over that. Also, you need to eat something. I'm going to let you go home after that, and you might feel drowsy for a while, again that is to be expected."

I nod. "Can you send Dean in? I need to speak to him. He's just outside. He's the one that was trying to come in earlier. Will you tell my mom it's okay? I need to—well I don't know what I need, but I think I need to speak to him."

The doctor's mouth forms a straight line, and I can tell he is reluctant to allow this, and I'm not sure exactly why that is. "I will ask your mom, but ultimately it's her decision on if Dean is allowed in this room with you. Okay?"

I stare at him trying to read into that statement, but I'm stumped, "Okay."

When the door opens to my room, I try really hard to stay calm. I don't feel calm. I don't like not knowing what happened to me, and why I'm here with staples in my head and a visit from my dead father. I don't like that Josh said he loves me and in the same sentence, says Dean does too. I don't like that Dean has any part of any of this at all.

Dean reluctantly walks forward to me and takes a seat in the chair that I gesture to. "Hi," he says whispering.

"Hi," I reply with a whisper in return. I don't know why we are whispering.

He lifts his hand and reaches it to my hair but stops himself when he sees me tense. He places his hand back into his lap. Dean has a habit of grabbing a curl and twining it between his fingers.

His brown eyes look lifeless. "I'm sorry, Riley. I never meant to hurt you. Not just last night, but—ever. I never meant to hurt you." His voice cracks and fear prickles within me. He hurt me?

"What happened to me? I don't remember," I ask.

He looks at the door and then to me. "You don't remember?"

I shake my head back and forth. He stares at me for the longest time as if contemplating his reply carefully.

"I pushed you." He puffs the words out like air as he looks away from me.

"You what?"

His eyes move back to mine, and he pauses, gauging my reaction. I don't have one just yet, I feel a little numb.

He swallows hard and clears his throat. "Josh and I were fighting, and I pushed you, Riley. You got in the middle, and I was so angry, I don't know what I was thinking. You hit your head, and a piece of glass just happened to be on the concrete where you fell. It's my fault. I hurt you. I'm sorry. I'm so sorry." He puts his head down on the bed, and his shoulders shake. I'm not sure, but I think he is crying.

I remember the two of them fighting. I remember what he said. How mean he was to me. I remember it now as though a cloud has been lifted, and my vision is cleared. So why do I find myself lifting my hand and rubbing his hair? Why am I consoling someone I hate? That hates me.

We stay this way for a moment before he lifts his head and pulls away. "I really made a mess of things. Didn't I? I talked to Preslee this morning. I'm gonna have a baby, apparently. God, I'm such an asshole."

I nod my head, "This is true," I say smiling. He *is* an asshole.

He shakes his head and grins. "I'm sorry for the things I said last night and for being so irresponsible. That was stupid."

"It was. Were you drunk, Dean?"

He nods slowly.

I feel sick that my suspicions are correct. "I...um, I don't want to sound vain, but I need to know. Were you drinking because of me?"

He studies my eyes—I guess trying to figure out why I would care or ask that. I don't want to be the reason for someone to make a decision as reckless as that. My mom was the reason my dad drove drunk. I just don't want to be the reason.

He lifts one shoulder and sighs. "I don't know to be honest. I think yes, a little, but not completely. After you ran off, I knew I had deceived you in the worst way, and I pussied out by not giving you an explanation. I made it seem like you meant shit to me, and that isn't true at all. When I saw Josh cradling you in his arms in the rain, I think my heart broke. You never looked at me. You never gave me a second thought. It killed me, and I just replayed years of longing for you, and you longing for him in my mind until I just needed it all to shut up. I drank a few beers, not a lot. I tried to call you, and then I called your house. Your sister told me you were at the movies with Josh. She was a little snotty about it, and I realized that even your family wants you with him. When I saw you with him—like everything was fucking perfect, I think for a brief second, I hated you."

He looks away and doesn't say anything else. "I know you hate me, Dean. It's okay because some days I hate me too—some days I hate you, as well. The thing is—with Josh, I don't hate me as much."

His eyes dart back to mine and his whole demeanor deflates. "The thing is...for me, Riley. I don't hate you at all. I never could. It would be easier if I could or did hate you, though. I should hate you. I said a lot of things I shouldn't have, but it wasn't out of hate, it was out of hurt. I know I fucked it all up, but I do care about you. I might even love you." He swallows, "I must...to have gone through all this shit to just try and be with you..." He says rubbing his hand behind his neck.

Love me? "Clarify. What do you mean *all this shit?*" I ask. Didn't he put me through a bunch of shit?

His eyes lock with mine, and I see a lot clouded within them. A silent storm brews behind them as though he has been hiding behind them for two years. "Ever since we were kids, I've wanted to be near you. Not just wanted, though. I needed to be near you. You smelled like strawberries, and your laugh was contagious—a laugh that was like a rope pulling me to you. I just really wanted to get to know you. You never did make that easy on me, you know? I had to work pretty damn hard to even be your friend, in the first place. As we grew older, my feelings for you changed, they shifted somehow without me realizing it. I began to notice things—things that I liked, *a lot* actually. You no longer smelled like strawberries, but I still loved the way you smelled when you were near me."

His eyes have been looking past me, through me, like he is somewhere else altogether. "I was a fool for trying, though." He looks back to me like he is actually here with me again. "I couldn't help it, though. I had to try."

I swallow the lump in my throat. He's never talked to me like this or told me these things.

"Try what?" I breathe.

His expression doesn't change—it's flat and unreadable. "To get you to see me, too."

I inhale a deep breath and slowly release it. "I saw you. I was with you for two years, Dean."

He shakes his head. "No, you weren't. Not really. You may have been my girlfriend, Riley, but you were never mine. I never had your heart. You saw him. It was always him for you. I knew that. That is why I say I was a fool for trying. I knew it was a matter of time. It wasn't an, '*if*' you left me for him, it was a '*when*'. It was going to happen. I knew it from the start."

He stares at my eyes studying them, and he lets his hand grab the curl like he always did, like he can't help but do so now. He begins twirling it around his finger mesmerized by the movement. He drops it and looks into my eyes again.

"I thought if we had sex, if you and I took that next step...that somehow you would connect with me. It wasn't about the sex really, though. I wasn't just a horny bastard," he laughs. "Well, I was...but it was more than that, too. I thought that maybe I could seal us together. Give you and me something that only we had shared together. You and Josh already shared the rest, the stuff I couldn't have with you."

My mouth falls open. "But Dean, you and I wouldn't have been the only one to share that together. You were *sharing* with a lot of girls. I think I understand what you're saying, but I'm glad we didn't go there."

"Me too," he says flatly.

"Huh? But you just said— ,"

"I know what I said. It would have been a mistake. You don't belong with me. Like I said, I think I've always known that."

I stare at him unable to form any words to reply. I don't really know what to say.

"It's okay, Riley. You don't have to say anything. The more I thought about it, the more I see the things I tried not to see...like how you would look at me confused sometimes. You would go somewhere in your head that I couldn't reach. I think you even asked yourself sometimes why you were with me, huh?"

I go to open my mouth. "Don't answer that. I don't want to know." I shut my mouth, and he frowns. "Look, I'm gonna leave town for a little bit, go clear my head."

I nod, "But what about school? You can't drop out."

"I'm not dropping out...just taking a few days. I'll be back for the last week. I won't be far...just not around here. Anyway...I'm sorry. I really am. Guess I need to get my shit together since I'm gonna be a dad and all that," he says without enthusiasm.

"I don't really know what to say to that, Dean." I really don't. He cheated on me and got someone pregnant. Saying 'Congratulations' just doesn't seem appropriate. I don't know how to feel about any of it right now. I was upset, and then I became angry, and now I feel numb, but the nicer side of me feels sorry for Dean.

So, I tell him what I think I can say that makes sense to me. "I'm sorry too, Dean. You're right. My heart was always with, Josh. I shouldn't have used you like that. I think I never really realized I was. Either way, we both fucked up, right?" I rub my temple, which is beginning to hurt again. I feel a little dizzy, but it passes.

"Are you okay?" he asks concerned. He appears worried, and as if he is fighting the urge to touch me again.

"I am. Just dizzy, but I'm good. I'm tired, though." I admit, feeling sleepy again.

"Okay, I'll go." He stands, hesitating for a moment before he leans down and kisses my cheek.

My heart flutters a little, and I think that without trying to, without meaning to, and even if just as a friend, he had a piece of my heart—a piece that I wasn't even aware until just now that I had given to him.

He opens his mouth and shuts it, obviously wanting to say something.

"Just say it," I demand.

He glances at the door and then looks at me. "I know you're happy with him, but what happens when he leaves for Louisiana?" he asks with all seriousness.

"What? What are you talking about?" I feel panicked. Josh has never told me he was going to Louisiana.

He sighs, "I guess even the reason for your smile holds deceit. Josh and Collin signed letters of intent with LSU back in February. I'm surprised you didn't know. That was months ago."

Now, it's my turn to open and shut my mouth. The last time Josh and I had discussed college *was* in February, the night he'd found me at the cemetery, after I ran off and skipped school. He told me that he hadn't made a decision. At least, that's what I thought. *But he had?* I try to remember the conversation word for word. It's just hard because I was so stuck in my own damn head of misery that night. *Shit!*

I'm looking at the door where I know Josh is just on the other side of it, and like he knows my thoughts are on him, the door opens, and he walks in. My eyes lock with the hazel ones I love most in the world, wondering yet again if they hold a secret. He looks between Dean and me with curiosity but doesn't speak.

I turn to look at Dean and hate that I see a moment of satisfaction on his face. He has succeeded at once again putting doubts in my head. Dean looks at me, shrugging. "It's something to think about. Maybe you need a Plan B," and then he leaves.

What the fuck? A plan B?

Josh is really quiet after Dean leaves. He doesn't ask many questions, even though I can see them in his eyes when he looks at me. He sits in the chair near the window watching me intently the entire time I eat the shitty hospital food. I can't read him. I just know things are on his mind, and he wants to ask but doesn't. Words sit unsaid inside of him.

My mom agrees to let him take me home instead of her. She needs to run some errands, and he is pretty insistent that he be the one to take care of me anyway. It makes me smile. He always takes care of me, even when I'm pushing him away, he's there for me.

So, here we are—him covering me with a throw blanket on the couch, and holding my head in his lap while he flips through the television. "Are you comfortable?" he asks, as he gently runs his fingers up and down my arms.

"Very," I answer with a deep contented sigh leaving my lips. He doesn't say anything in response. He just places a soft kiss to my forehead and leans back into the couch. He's still more quiet than usual. It bothers me, but I'm so comfortable here with him like this, that I ignore the urge to ask him. I must have fallen asleep, because the next thing I remember is opening my eyes to find I'm alone on the couch. A waft of something yummy hits my nose—spaghetti and garlic bread—my stomach immediately growls in response.

I sit up and stretch my limbs. I walk into the kitchen, and freeze when I see Josh helping my mom cook. It's so cute. I stand unnoticed for a few minutes while I watch them. My heart grows warmer and more his with each second that passes. He stirs the sauce, and then holds the colander for her as she drains the pasta in the sink. She puts the pasta back into the pot and carries it back to the stove, where he pours the sauce in and mixes it together. While he's getting the plates from the cabinet, she gets the bread out of the oven. They do this while carrying on a friendly conversation and not noticing me in the doorway. It really is so completely adorable. I hear the front door chime as Tatum and Joey walk in. Of course. The heads in the kitchen turn to the doorway where I'm no longer eavesdropping and unseen.

I must have a goofy grin on my face because Josh lifts a brow, and tilts his head to the side examining me. We just stare stupidly at each other for a few seconds before he walks to me and kisses my cheek. "Hi, sleepyhead," he says cheerfully.

"Hi, chef," I joke and lift onto my tippy toes to kiss his cheek in return.

His shy smile is freaking adorable, and that dimple makes it sexy. "I'm just helping your mom. It's no biggie," he says grabbing my hand and guiding me to the table.

No biggie my ass. That was the sweetest thing ever.

Dinner is nice, and Josh's dad actually comes over as well, so we can all eat together. Something about that warms my heart, as well. It is like we are a joined family already.

After dinner, Josh's dad and my mom are in the living room talking about work stuff. Josh and I are in the kitchen cleaning up, and of course, the brats run off to Tater's room. It feels so normal the way we are all together like this.

"Thank you for helping my mom with dinner. That was really nice of you," I tell him as I load the last plate into the dishwasher while Josh wipes off the counter tops and table.

He glances back at me with a smile. "Really, it was nothing. I just wanted to help her." His eyes look a little melancholy, and it makes me wonder if he used to do that sort of thing with his mom, back when she was alive.

"Did you used to help your mom?" I ask my thought out loud. Shit, that was probably stupid.

He smiles wistfully and walks to put the dishtowel in the sink. He turns and rests his back against the counter as he wraps his hands around my waist, pulling me toward him. "Yeah, she always let Jo and me help in the kitchen. I'm not that good, but Joey is. She learned a lot from her." He looks down into my eyes, tucking my hair behind my ear.

I hook my fingers in his belt loops as I look up at him. "I think you are amazing," I say truthfully.

"Is that so?" He asks in that flirty voice he reserves for me, with that sexy-as-hell-smirk of his in place.

I nod just as a yawn creeps its way out of my mouth. So much for flirty—I have just botched that. I'm so sleepy all of a sudden, though. This side effect is one I could do without. I really don't like sleeping so much. It leads to dreams and dreams lead to nightmares.

"C'mon, let's get you all tucked into bed," he grabs my hand and pecks my mouth.

I'd whine and complain, but I am so tired. Instead, I just follow him to my room. I'm already dressed in my running shorts and a t-shirt. I'm sure I look like a slob, but I'm comfy. I climb into my bed and get under my covers. Josh sits down next to me, and the look in his hazel eyes is full of love and tenderness. He brushes the hair out of my eyes. "Are you feeling okay? Does your head hurt?"

I roll to where my head is in his lap. He gently plays with my hair. "I'm okay. It hurts a little, but it's more like a dull throb. It will go away soon," I tell him. Actually, it hurts quite a bit—like a motherfucking headache from hell to be honest, but having him near me makes me feel better.

He sighs. "I'm really sorry this happened to you," he whispers. The tone in his voice is laced with sadness and remorse. I scoot up on the bed, rest my head on his shoulder and look into his eyes. I smooth the line his frown has made on his forehead.

I love this boy. "Josh, I'm the one that is sorry. I told you to ignore him and to walk away, and then I turned around to listen to his craziness. It's my fault. I have no idea why I turned around. I knew he had nothing good to say. I was only going to go back after you got in the truck. If I would have stuck to that plan, you wouldn't have been involved, and he may not have been so angry."

His eyes are locked with mine, and with each word that leave my lips; I find they grow more confused. "What do you mean you were going to go back to him after I got in the truck? Why?" He asks in a soft voice, but I can tell he is a tad irritated with me.

"The thing is, Josh, he was drunk. I...I just didn't want him to get on his bike, and I thought I could convince him to call someone to come pick him up. That's all. I knew seeing you with me made him angrier. I just thought I had to try, but then I turned around, and none of what I thought mattered anymore." I sit up crisscross and look at him with all seriousness.

He frowns, but nods his head. "I understand that." He pauses for a beat. "You care about him." He isn't asking me. He's making a statement, and he's wrong.

I'm already shaking my head back and forth. "No, no I don't, Josh. It wasn't about caring about him. It was me...not wanting to see him hurt himself or someone else by driving drunk. That's all, Josh."

We stare at each other for a solid minute without words before he asks, "Do you have a plan B?"

"WHAT?"

"Plan B. Dean mentioned you should get a plan B. Is he the plan B?"

Oh, my god! "Are you effing serious? No, he is not plan B. I have no plan B, Josh. I have you, and that is all I have ever wanted or needed. One plan—with you." Why would he think otherwise? And since he's being so questionable, I wonder if I should ask him if he has something to tell me.

I don't get to think it, or ask him, because he seals my lips shut with a kiss so intense, so breathtaking and so thorough that I can't think straight. His hands are cupping my cheeks and mine are in his hair. When he finally releases me, I'm dumbfounded, speechless and a lot dizzy, which I don't think is a side effect of my concussion, but just him affecting me. "I love you, Riley. When I saw you hit your head like that...I panicked. I honestly thought I could lose you. I never...ever want to lose you. You're my pretty girl, *my* girl, my Tink." He is saying this—all the while he is forcing me to lie back down and covering me up.

He kisses my forehead, but I grab his face before he can pull away. I make him meet my eyes. "Josh, I love you more than life itself. I hope you know that. I hope you know how much you mean to me—because you mean everything to me. Before you, I might have been breathing, but I wasn't truly living—I wasn't me. I'm me...*with* you. Do you get that? Do you know that, in there?" I ask, placing my hand to his heart.

His face is guarded, and I don't like the insecurity I see in his eyes. I've never really seen it there before, so why now? I don't think he knows it. He should, but he doesn't. He doesn't answer. He just kisses my lips softly and tells me to, "Sleep."

Yeah, like that's going to happen now. I roll over and snuggle with Tink. "You know I love *you*, right?" She meows and snuggles closer to me.

CHAPTER 6

Clarity isn't always so clear. It was never clear to me that Dean and I were both affected by the blue/green-eyed girl we'd met when we were five. It was never clear to me that when my feelings for her began to shift into something more—that his had, too. It was definitely not clear to me that he would act on them before I did.

Now that everything is clear and clarity has slapped me in the face...I feel a little insecure. I don't do this feeling well. Hearing Plan B come out of Dean's mouth, and seeing the shock on her face makes me nervous. Its crystal clear that he isn't just going to let her go—too bad for him that she is already gone.

Hearing Riley confess her feelings for me is a huge ego boost. I've waited a lifetime to have her finally admit those things to herself—to me. For whatever reason though, I feel uncertain.

I've been in such a bubble that events are happening around me, and I'm not exactly participating in them.

My mind is always on her. *Does her head hurt? Does she dream a lot when she is asleep? Do her dreams become nightmares like mine? Does she miss me? Does she forgive Dean? What did he say to her when they were alone? Did she believe him? Did he affect her? Does she blame me for her injury? What is she thinking?*

It's just one question, following another question in my head.

Before I know it, the last week of school is upon us, but until then we're enjoying flirty conversation and just—being together.

I'm sitting in her room on a Sunday evening, writing the different notes from school that she missed into her notebook from last week. She is in a really good mood, and it makes me happy.

"Josh, you don't have to do that, you know? School is almost over. I don't really care anymore," she tells me as I close her notebook and smile.

"We have tests believe it or not, and it's my job to make sure you don't fail. Besides, you will enjoy reading my notes, they aren't all school related." I hint, winking. I may have or may not have doodled dirty thoughts in her notebook for later viewing and blushing.

She grins and cuddles into my side. "I like having you here with me, Josh."

I kiss her hair, "You like me in your bed?" I laugh when she pinches my side playfully.

"You're so stupid, but yes. I like you in my bed." She cups my cheeks and looks into my eyes.

I forget how to breathe. She *makes* me forget how to breathe. I look down at her and brush the hair out of her face. "You are so beautiful," I say.

Her eyes flick to my lips, and she swallows, "You are, too," she whispers.

I smirk and roll her onto her back, "You think I'm beautiful?" I ask threading my hands through hers above her head.

She giggles and nods her head. "You're nice on the eyes. I mean...kind of good looking. I might just a li'l bit—think you're hot." She bites her lip. Damn, that is sexy.

I kiss her nose. "Just nice? Just.. kind of and a li'l bit? Really, pretty girl? What could I do to make you know for sure that you're hot for me?" I whisper in her ear as I make her shiver while I nibble and lick at her neck. I've come to notice, this makes her hot—this makes her squirm.

"Mmmmm, that. Yes, you can keep doing that. I like it when you kiss my neck." She wiggles under me.

I kiss my way up to her face. "Where else do you like me to kiss you?" I ask knowing I've only kissed a few spots on her body. Something in the way she freezes and stares at me, tells me she is thinking of places she would like me to kiss. The slight blush that creeps onto her cheeks, tells me it's never been kissed before. Ah. My pretty girl is having a dirty thought, and I friggin' love it.

I kiss her eyes as they flutter closed. "Do you like eye kisses?" I breathe.

"Yes," her voice answers all breathy.

I kiss her forehead. "Do you like when I kiss you here?"

"I love that." *Mental note, she loves that.*

I avoid her mouth and move to her ear. I lick it and then whisper, "I already know you like when I kiss your lips. That leaves a few other places for me to kiss. Are you hot for me yet?" I ask breathing heavy in her ear. I am hot for her. God, I'm hot for her.

I push my hips into her, and I know that she knows now just how hot for her I am. She whimpers a little, and I begin trailing kisses down her neck just to drive her wild. She is squeezing my hands tightly as if she is fighting the urge to use them.

She turns her face into mine, her lips begging for mine to touch them. I don't oblige just yet. I kiss the corner of her mouth and then the other corner. I move down to her stomach and place a kiss on her navel. She is wearing one of those-damn-cami's that always tease my eyes with visuals of what's underneath. It sits above her bellybutton, and the frayed jean shorts she has on barely cover her ass. She is unbelievably edible. I want to lick and kiss every inch of her.

The heated way she is looking at me right now, the way her breathing has changed and the way she is squirming under me, tells me she might just let me if I tried. I don't, though. I don't push it further just yet.

"Josh?" she says my name like a purring moan. It's hot.

"Hmmm?" I ask traveling my mouth over her cami up her stomach and to the spot where her cleavage shows. Without intention, and as though my tongue has a mind of its own, it dips itself in for just a little taste.

"I'm hot for you, Josh. I'm so hot for you. Now, kiss me," she demands, pulling at her hands and writhing against me.

I oblige this time. "My pleasure." I lower my mouth to hers. I kiss her softly and sweetly as her body falls limp below me. She whimpers.

That whimper is my undoing. I deepen the kiss and let go of her hands. They immediately tangle into my hair as mine travel her body.

We're basically dry humping each other, and I could probably get off just like this, she feels so damn incredible under me. I'm thinking by the goosebumps that have covered her body and the way she is trembling that she could to. I wonder how far I should take it, but then we hear the chime to the alarm in the house announcing someone walked through the front door. We both jump apart panting and flushed.

We both sit up and play cool, even though inside my body is hotter than fire. She looks at me with lust in her eyes and smiles. "You, Joshua Parker, are definitely beautiful." I love the things that come out of her mouth. I laugh.

"Riley, I've got Chinese. You hungry?" I hear her mom shout down the hall.

I chuckle and whisper, "Yeah, Riley. Are you hungry?" I ask, knowing for damn sure that I am starved.

She grins, knowing just what I implied. "Very," she whispers.

"Oh hey, Josh." Her mom says, leaning in the doorway. "I've got enough to feed an army. If you wanna stay and eat, you are more than welcome. I'll go dish plates." She offers smiling and heading back down the hall.

Riley's eyes are on me, and her cheeks are the prettiest shade of pink. "Where is your head, Riley?"

She sucks in her bottom lip, and I can tell she is hiding a grin. I release her lip with my thumb. "Say it." I tell her.

She diverts her eyes when she speaks, "you can stay and *eat* if you like. In fact, I think I would love it if you did." She swallows and her eyes flick to my lips a few times before she says, "You know—Chinese food, I mean."

Oh hell, she so didn't mean Chinese.

I make her look at me. "You, Riley Shaw, are mouth-watering. I would love to *eat*...with you." I say with all seriousness, climbing off of her bed and pulling her to stand with me. Her face contorts into amusement and shock. I wink, and smack her ass before I turn around, leaving her standing in her room hot and bothered.

When I glance back at her, she has her mouth hung open. *Picture that while we eat Chinese.*

All through dinner, I make sure I keep Riley just on the edge of uncomfortable. At the table, I sit across from her and repeatedly rub my bare foot up and down her calf. Her skin is always so buttery soft. I can tell she is getting flustered because she keeps missing her mouth when she eats. Of course, it is usually just as her mouth opens that I glide my foot up her leg.

I keep remembering how much I love watching her eat sushi. This take-out is no sushi roll, nor is there going to be any conversation of how to make our fortunes dirty with her mom and sister in the room.

After sharing many pleasantries with her family, and heated gazes with just her, I offer to help her mom with the kitchen clean up. I think I got some bonus points from my girl *and* her mom, because they both look at me in surprise and grow that grin that said 'Awww.' Yeah, yeah, yeah! I'm a sweet guy. Maybe I'm embracing it. After all, the last time I helped Riley and her mom in the kitchen, I happened to enjoy seeing the happy look on Riley's face.

I have just finished loading the dishwasher when Riley wraps her arms around my stomach, clasping them in the front, and resting her head against my back. I let her hold me like this for just a minute, and then I remove her hands and turn around to face her. She is looking up at me with an odd expression on her face. Wonder maybe? A little bit of curiosity? It could be—definitely a lot of adoration. I see it now— that look that others told me about when they see her look at me. She adores me. She looks at me with those gorgeous blue eyes, with those green glitter flecks that make my world become completely centered on her. Seeing it kind of makes the insecurity I've been feeling seem foolish. I hung her the damn moon—that's what they said she thinks. At least I would if I could. I'd bring her every fucking star in the sky, and grant her every damn wish, as well, just to make her happy. At least, I'd try to.

She reaches onto her tippy toes and runs her hands along my hairline before she wraps her arms around my neck and lays her head on my shoulder. Her breath along my neck warms me.

I look down at her and kiss her hair, snaking one of my hands around her lower back as I let my fingers brush the sliver of skin I feel on her back. With the other hand, I wind a curl around my finger and then place it behind her ear. She sighs a contented sigh, "I just want to stay like this forever," she whispers. I glance down at her face and tilt her chin to look up at me with my index finger. I place a gentle kiss to her lips.

"Then it's settled. I'm yours to keep forever, pretty girl," I say, with a hint of humor.

She smiles softly and bites that bottom lip. "Wanna go for a walk?" I ask.

"M'hm," she answers nodding.

We're outside walking on the sidewalk of the neighborhood. I'm careful to go the opposite direction of Dean's house—uncertain if he is back in town or not. He's been AWOL for a few days just like he said he would be. I hate that he lives so close by—just a few houses down—just a few houses too close.

I interlace our fingers and look to Riley glancing up at the sky. "Wanna know what my favorite thing is living here, besides you of course?" she says suddenly.

"What?"

She continues to look up, "The stars. They are so bright and visible here. When you're in the city at night, it's like the stars disappear, but not here. Here, they are so beautiful," she says. *She is beautiful.*

I smile. "Yes, they are beautiful," I agree as I pull her hand to my lips and kiss her knuckles. Not once, do I look up to the sky to see the beauty in the sky. My beauty is right next to me. She glances at me with a happy smile. It's been so long since I've seen this happy side of her. It really warms my heart, but then a sudden realization hits me in the gut, and I choke on it. I will deal with it tomorrow. Tonight, my world centers on her, and the desire to keep that smile on her face forever.

After a few moments of comfortable silence, I feel the urge to get something off my chest. "Can I ask you something?" I ask as we cross the street finding our way to the tiny playground on the edge of the neighborhood. This one isn't as nice as the one by the lake—it's more for toddlers, with its tunnels, slides, swings, and the climbing structure.

"You can ask me anything," she answers, sitting down on top of one of the little tunnels with her feet dangling off.

I drape my leg over the side of it and pull her body in between my legs, closer to me. I rest my back against the play structure, and she rests her back against me—the stars become our nightlight.

She pulls her legs up and her hands fist around mine on her stomach. I kiss the top of her head and take a deep breath. "I don't know why I want to ask this, or if I really want the answer, but I wonder about it."

She squeezes my hands gently and slowly says, "O-kay."

"It's just, I know why you thought you and I could never be together. I never agreed with you, but I got it." Her body goes rigid, and her eyes shut. "But I guess what I don't get...is why you were with...him." Her already shut eyes squeeze tighter, and a deep sigh leaves her chest. I've succeeded in removing her happy smile just as I thought to keep it there forever. *Real smooth, Parker.*

She opens her eyes and sits up. I feel bereft without her close to me. She runs her hands through her hair and then swings her leg around to straddle the tunnel and face me. She places her palms on the tunnel between her knees and tilts her head to the side.

"It's complicated, Josh."

I study her eyes, looking deeply to see if she is angry. I don't see it. All I see is a lot of confusion. "Can you try to explain? Because, I keep thinking that you were with him for two years, Riley. That's a long ass time not to feel something for someone. Do you still have feelings for him?" Like I said, I'm asking, but I don't know if I really want her answer.

She shakes her head back and forth saying no. "Josh, I...I...I don't know how to explain what I felt for, Dean. He um, he confused me all the time. I'd be lying if I said I didn't feel something at some point along the way, but that is where I get confused about it because I don't know for sure what it was that I felt. I just know that it's nothing, and I mean NOTHING like what I feel for you."

She looks away from my eyes and up to the stars. "It's like the stars I mentioned before, like when you go to the city, and they disappear. Everything becomes noisier and less peaceful—less beautiful but still full of nice scenery. You like it, though, because it's distracting, because it keeps your mind on something else besides the beautiful stuff you want and can't have. So you settle on the noise and the view. It's a little of a rush because it's a puzzle you try to fit together, but it doesn't fit, because you really don't love the city, you love the stars. It's all the wrong pieces."

Her eyes look back at me, piercing into my very soul, and my heart constricts in my chest. "See, that one missing piece is always still in the picture, lingering in the shadows, mixing up the puzzle, showing you glimpses of the stars. He's the very reason they never fit together."

She scoots closer to me placing her legs on top of my own and meshing our bodies tightly together, putting her hands on the tops of my thighs. "Because see, he held the piece that matched hers perfectly. That's when the rush comes, and all the stars reappear. The rush isn't the mixed up puzzle. The rush is...knowing his piece is the one she needs to be complete. She wants what she can't have."

I'm sitting so very still, hanging on her every word. I even have to remind myself to breathe. She is gliding her hands under my shirt, touching my skin. It ignites my desire. Then she inches closer, as if we weren't close enough yet. "You had the missing piece, Josh. You helped me put the puzzle back together, and the stars have never shined brighter."

She begins tugging my shirt up over my head, and I let her. She is practically sitting on my lap with her hands running up my arms and her eyes admiring the view. I just want to mimic her moves and feel her skin on mine.

She leans down and kisses her rose on my tattoo. I watch her with deep concentration. She kisses up my arm, over my shoulder, up my neck and to my ear where she whispers the sweetest words. "I've never wanted anything more than I want you, Josh. You have nothing to worry about."

I glide my hands up her ribcage and to the nape of her neck where I pull her mouth to mine. I kiss her so desperately. It's almost painful, as I thoroughly taste every part of her mouth. It's like our tongues are making love. Our bodies are completely aligned, completely in tune with each other. Her hands are moving like she can't decide what to do with them. One minute, they are tangled in my hair, and the next minute they are gliding along my chest, my arms and my back. Jesus, the sounds she makes—the soft little whimpers—I just want to take everything she has. And the way she is arching into me, and rolling her hips like she loves the feeling of the pressure there, tells me she wants me, too.

Her head lolls back, and I take this time to kiss down her neck, tasting the saltiness that is mixed with her sweetness. All the while, one of my hands inches under her shirt to feel her up, and the other is gripping her waist tightly. When her head snaps back, she is breathing heavy, and her eyes are on fire. "Josh, I've never felt this. This moment...like this. It scares me so much because I keep thinking it's all a dream. I'm going to wake up and not have this anymore. All the stars will disappear."

She is dead serious. God. "Baby, I'm not going anywhere. I'm here with you. You're my missing piece, too, Shaw." And then we are all hands and lips again until red and blue flashing lights color our skin. "Shit, we've been busted molesting each other in a public playground," I whisper against her lips. We both break out in laughter and climb off the tunnel just as the officer gets out of his car.

"Sorry, we um...we're going home." I stutter putting my shirt back on. He flashes his flashlight between us, and an amused grin breaks across his face.

"Yeah, you do that. This is a kid's playground and not *that kind*. Okay?"

"Yes, sir." We both reply in unison.

As we walk back toward our houses, she starts laughing out of the blue. I look to her puzzled. "What's so funny?"

She throws her thumb over her shoulder, "Back there. He said this is kid's playground and not *that kind*. It's just funny. I wonder how many kids they catch um...ya know...actually playing." *Hmmm...I wonder if I can let her be my playground and play some more.*

"Yeah, well I'd love to have you be my playground." I say the thought out loud accidentally and realize how forward that was. She missteps and goes tumbling to the ground as I catch her. "You okay? I didn't mean to trip you all up," I say, grinning at her and helping her to her feet.

She is all flustered, and I love it. "Yeah, I, um...it wasn't you. Uh, I'm just clumsy." This is true. She averts her eyes, "yeah, um...it's getting late. We have school tomorrow. I should get home. I need to shower and um, stuff." Of course, images of her and I in the shower fill my brain almost immediately and the wonder of what 'stuff' means.

I clear my throat, "Right. Let's get home. Stuff to do and all."

I kiss her at her door, and refrain from deepening this into any more PDA offenses for the night. It's just enough to leave her tingly.

"Goodnight, Josh."

Her coy smile makes my heart hammer in my chest. "Goodnight, Riley."

 *Riley*

CHAPTER 7

Who knew innuendos could make my heart flutter and my knees feel weak. I sure as hell didn't. I am so excited and anxious to be getting back into my normal routine. Although, my brain seems to be constantly thinking about other routines I could be doing with Josh. In fact, he is all I think about. Was there ever a thought before him?

Sleep didn't come easy last night. I am so nervous about stepping back into the halls of hell. I'm just ready to be done with it. I'm still confused on if I should confront Josh with what Dean told me at the hospital. It's been days and I can't. I just want to enjoy him, and after last night's public display of affection, I think he wants to enjoy me, too. What did he say? That he isn't going anywhere—that he is here with me. I wonder if that means Dean has his facts incorrect, but I know it to not be the truth. Em told me they'd signed. I just think he may have backed out. *I hope he backed out.*

But I doubt it, considering he just told me he was going to see his coach. Josh just left me standing in the hall with Em, neither of us realizing the high school world had just stopped and focused in on us.

"Em, why is everyone staring at me?" I ask her.

She looks around the halls just as curious as I am, that is until her phone pings, and she looks at it. "What the damn hell?" she mumbles under her breath.

I look at her as she is looking down at her phone. Everything in her expression, tells me that these stares probably have something to do with whatever is on her screen. "What is it?"

She hands me her phone, and on replay before me is the fight between Josh and Dean. What is odd, though, is this video is being recorded before Dean ever approaches Josh and me. There is a close up of us kissing and of us talking (no sound). Thank God. The video rolls all the way to me flying in the air and hitting my head on the concrete. "What the damn hell?" I whisper with the same response.

I hand her the phone back. "Who sent that to you?" I ask, positive that shit will hit the fan when I go have choice words with them.

She shakes her head and shrugs. "It's a blocked number. I don't know." She starts looking around the halls and pulls me by the arm into the empty music room. "Riley, someone was watching y'all." The way she said it—well, it sent a shiver up my spine.

Who would be watching us?

Who else, besides Dean, would even care one bit that Josh and I were together?

Who would share that with everyone and why?

"I know, Em. That's um...kind of..." I trail off as my entire body shudders.

"Creepy and fucked up?" she finishes my train of thought.

"Yeah. Creepy and fucked up." The first bell rings and we leave the room. I've realized now that nothing about today will be normal or routine.

As we walk to our lockers, the whispers have already begun.

Slut.

Skank.

Cheater.

I heard that Josh sneaks into her bedroom window at night. She was screwing them both.

What a whore.

That was just the girls' opinions. The boys were vastly different. Their whispers weren't whispers behind my back at all. They were in my face, flirting and eyeing me like their new flavor of candy. It disgusted me. Obviously, they believed the rumors and got the impression I put out. Little did they know, I never had sex with either of them.

Emily squeezes my hand, "fuck em, Riley." She heads off to class leaving me to my own defenses. As if the day needed to get any worse, Dean also chooses today to be the day he returns to school—making it suspicious that both of us missed the same amount of days of school last week. It was a coincidence obviously, but teenagers are wired to believe nothing is coincidence, and everything is suspect.

It doesn't help matters that he walks right up to me, grips my chin and kisses my cheek while I stand shocked and unable to move. He doesn't speak, not a show of expression on his face. He just implies with actions that we are together. We are not. WTF? I just stand there, like a complete idiot. I just stand there, and watch his retreating frame in complete confusion.

More whispers follow me after I grab my stuff and head off to class.

I wonder if Josh knows that Dean has been playing doctor with his girlfriend while he's been at school.

She has some nerve bouncing back and forth from them both.

Personally, I'd take Dean. He has that badass bike. I never understood what he saw in her anyway. She's so blah, and he's so yum.

Oh nuh-uh, girl, Josh is way hotter than, Dean. Those eyes, those abs—Holy hell...I just want to lick every inch of him, and I don't mean his abs, if you know what I mean. I'd let him lick me, too—if you know what I mean.

OH, FOR THE LOVE OF GOD, I know what she means. I have the urge to do the toddler thing and stick my fingers in me ears and shout, lalalalalala.

Ugh...I have one week. One fucking week and these walls will become part of our past. I'm sick to my stomach by the things I am hearing. Inside, the words are clawing at my veins, and I'm bleeding a slow death. Outside, I act like I don't hear them. It's brutal.

The halls are cruel, and the classroom is no safer.

During first period, someone places a condom on my desk. I discreetly shove it in my backpack and ignore the laughing.

In second period, my phone receives a text from an unknown number. *Hit me up, I can show you a good time, too.* I don't even want to guess what that is about.

Now, in the halls before third period, when I see *her*—I'm over it.

Preslee walks right up to me with her crew of followers, smiling wickedly. She is such a bitch. "So, Riley. I hear you have been a very busy girl." She says while her 'followers' laugh. *Such puppets.*

I snort, *"That* is none of your damn business," I retort as I switch out the books in my locker, rolling my eyes dramatically for emphasis.

She laughs and places a hand over her stomach. I flick my eyes to her hand and then back to her face. She notices and is pleasingly aware that I know her secret.

"Well, since one of your boy toys played a little too carelessly with me, I would say that it is part of my business." She states it as though it still could be, Josh. That bitch has lost her ever-loving mind if she thinks I am still buying her shit. I know the truth now. Josh never touched her.

I smile sweetly back at her. "Well, since only *one* has played carelessly with you, I would say that is between you and him. I'm over your willingness to *share* so much with...everyone. And to think, they are calling *me* the slut."

I slam my locker and walk off. I don't get far before she catches up to me, losing her followers in the process. "Only one? Really. Only one? I've played with both of them, Riley. Don't kid yourself into thinking they like your sweet innocent act. Dean likes it rough and dirty, and Josh likes it in my mouth. I've played with both of your boys. If that means I'm a slut, then so be it. I'm good with that, and I am definitely good *at it.* Just ask them. At least, I don't pretend to be something I'm not."

I'm momentarily stuck on her words *in my mouth?* What did she mean by that? "I don't pretend anything," I snap back at her.

I'm aware a few are crowded around us, and I really don't care. I'm over this chick.

"No? You pretended to be a virgin when obviously you were doing Josh at night. You pretended to be this sweet innocent girl incapable of love, but now that Dean's gotten tired of your bullshit, you suddenly have shit all figured out, huh? You just play games," she says, judging me.

I stare her straight in the eyes. "Why do you care so much about what I do, Preslee? What is it to you? You don't have any of your facts correct, but you mean so little to me that I couldn't care less to correct you."

She went to move forward, to say something further to me, but Dean grabs her by the elbow as he locks eyes with mine.

"That's enough, Preslee. Back the fuck off," he whispers harshly into her ear. She listens to him.

He pulls her back with an expression on his face that I can only perceive to be remorse. I don't stick around to listen to them, or the backlash she begins to yell at him.

I take off in the opposite direction, deciding to take the long way to class, scribbling a note quickly as I walked.

I pass it off to Em on my way to class for, Josh. "You look like you are ready to claw someone's eyes out, Riley," she says, concerned.

I don't have time to explain everything, so I tell her quickly that I hate everyone, and that if I survive the rest of the school year without murdering someone—*without murdering Preslee*—it will be an effing miracle.

She just laughs, takes the note and says, "Screw em, they are all just a bunch of fucktard twatwaffles."

Yeah, whatever that is...they are all a bunch of that.

"Can you believe we will be going to school here soon?" Em asks, as we walk around the UTA campus like we already live there. She wanted to take an impromptu drop by after school on Tuesday, and I declined. So here we are, on Wednesday, scoping out our future surroundings—her with excitement, and me with apprehension.

I look around a little overwhelmed all of a sudden. "No, it's still a little surreal. Now, what I really can't believe is that you are enrolling during the summer without me. Why do you want to do that again?" I ask. I mean it's the summer.

She sighs, "Because, it's just one semester early, and my dad already rented our apartment and I'll be living here. Hey, you should move in with me. It has two bedrooms," she says full of excitement. Em's dad is loaded. Her parents are divorced, and to keep her happy, he gives her anything she wants, buying her love. With the exception of the car she wants, that is. She's still driving around a POS. He told her if she quits smoking, only then will he buy her the car of choice. She still smokes, so...

"I don't have a job, Em. I couldn't pay my half," I explain.

"Pay? I'm not even paying. C'mon it will be so much fun. It's the apartment just around the corner. Ohmigawd, when we went to talk to the leasing office, there were so many cute ass guys, my eyes were confused at who to visually molest first."

"I don't need a guy, Em."

She sighs and averts her eyes. A wave of unease sets in. "Why did you do that?" I ask.

"Do what?" she asks, fiddling with an imaginary chip on her nail polish.

"That. Why did you get all weird just now, when I said I don't need a guy?"

She huffs and turns with her hands on her hips. "It's just that...I was talking to Collin yesterday about some stuff, and um, he said he was really excited about being in Louisiana...with...Josh. He um, made it sound like Josh was kind of excited too."

I tense. My entire body goes rigid, and my blood turns to ice. But he said he wasn't going anywhere. I knew it was all a dream. "Oh."

Her eyes look sad, and her shoulders slump as do mine. "Hey, you two belong together. You're like kismet. It will work out."

I wrap my arm around myself, and a physical feeling hits me in the gut as I feel the dark hole widen. "Yeah, um, let's walk. K?" I don't want to talk about this. I'm so stupid. I knew he wouldn't be here at UTA with me. He hasn't mentioned it one time, not one time. But then again, he has never mentioned signing his letter either.

As we walk, I feel like someone is following us, so I look over my shoulder, but I don't see anyone that stands out—just college students walking freely. I release a shiver still because the feeling doesn't go away.

We do a little more sightseeing before we head back to Em's car, but I freeze dead in my tracks when I notice the motorcycle parked next to it unattended. My eyes begin darting around like a lunatic.

Em opens her mouth. "Hey, isn't that—,"

"Dean's bike," I finish. "Yeah, but why is it parked there?" I ask, spinning around to look at our surroundings. I still can't shake the feeling that someone is watching us. Oh God, what if it's him? Why would he be here? I shiver again and grab her hand.

"Let's go," I say as she nods.

Once in the car, I still scan the crowd, but I don't see him. That is definitely his bike, though. "You don't think he is going to college here. Do you?" I ask, as the unpleasant thought occurs to me.

Her eyes dart to mine and she shrugs. "I honestly don't know. We're not exactly friendly company. But good God, I hope not."

Ugh. I hope not too, but why else would he be here. Just freaking great. I don't get to have Josh with me, but as always Dean will be there. No, no, no. I'm not having this.

 *Josh*

CHAPTER 8

My fingers were crossed for another chance at happiness with, Riley. I was so excited to have her back at school this week. But as with anything involving Riley and me...happiness is just a tease, and anything school related just becomes a migraine without relief.

What a hellish week this has been, from start to fucking finish.

So let's backtrack a bit. Monday it all began just like this..."I have to go talk to coach about something. I'll see you at lunch." I told Riley, as I placed a peck to her lips in the hall before first period—trying my best to ignore the strange expression that flashed across her face, or the way her body tensed for a beat.

Of course everyone around was nosey and watching our every move. News of break ups and new relationships traveled fast in those halls.

She smiled sweetly, but it almost seemed forced—not genuine. Once I stood in coach's office, I thought how much I hated the way her smiled appeared like that. I reined in my nerves. Nerves for his response, nerves for the consequences of my action, nerves for why her smile was insincere...*nerves, nerves, nerves.*

Because there I sat—a meeting with my coach to gather information on how to get released from my commitment, since I had another commitment—one I really wanted to keep.

I tried and failed to get him to understand my desires the prior Friday, so I just thought I would try again. I didn't need his blessing, but for some reason I wanted it. I needed to know that I was not making a horrible mistake.

Coach came in, and he frowned as soon as he saw me. "Josh, I already told you last week that this is a bad idea. Why do you want to give up this opportunity?" he asked in a disapproving tone.

He told me to sleep on it over the weekend and to give it some real thought. I had, and more than ever I believed staying in Texas with Riley was the right decision. Seeing her in that hospital bed and thinking about losing her—well, I didn't want to ever let that happen. I knew I couldn't leave her, not after spending the past few days with her—we'd worked so hard to get here. Not to mention, when she admitted all of that stuff to me at the park, and I told her I would be there with her—I knew it would be impossible to go.

"Because Coach, sometimes other opportunities are more important." I admitted, hoping he'd understand but when I saw his expression, I knew that he hadn't.

His mouth set in a straight line, and I was pretty sure he wanted to kick my ass. "Look, boy...I know about you and that girl. Your head has been preoccupied for weeks, but you need to pull your head up and get it back in the game. Balls to the wall—own up to your commitment—you signed that scholarship, and it's a damn good opportunity for you, not to mention this school. A year fully paid to do jack shit but learn under some of the best. I don't support any of this nonsense, Parker. I don't think your dad will either. A pussy is a pussy whether here or there. So man up," he growled at me, slamming his hand down onto his desk.

I stood up, feeling angry at his assumption about Riley and me. "Coach, I came to talk to you because I wanted you to understand, but I don't need your judgment, or for you to agree. I can call the recruiter myself, and I will. This isn't just about some piece of ass. I love that girl. I know well and good that long distance relationships don't work. If I keep my football commitment, I might as well say fuck it, to the one that matters the most to me."

He stood, as well, and again I thought he would punch me the fuck out. Coach is known for drilling sense into his team with harsh language and verbal slander, no one questioned him. "You are throwing away your future, and there is no going back on this," he said sternly.

I nodded my head. I realized that would be the thoughts of many—just not mine. "Coach, if I leave her—I am throwing away my future. *She* is my future."

He sighed, sat down and began to circle his thumbs around each other. "Parker, you've got real talent…a real shot at going to the pros one day. You're willing to just throw all of that away for a high school crush?" he asked.

"She is not just a crush. That is what you're not getting." I threw my hands up and groaned in frustration.

He shook his head disapprovingly. "You're right. I don't get it. If you do this, I can guarantee you will regret it." He pointed to the door—dismissing me.

I headed to the door, fucking happy to oblige, but before I did, I turned around. "I don't want you to think I'm not grateful for everything that has been offered to me, and all the hard work you instilled in me while I was becoming who I am. I am so grateful, but…I believe if I don't do this…that will be what I regret." He frowned and picked up his phone probably to call my old man.

With that, I left.

I'd like to say I didn't have doubts about the decision, and that I knew for sure that I was making the right one—that I knew for certain that one decision would keep my future (our future together) intact.

I don't know any of those things, though. I do have doubts. I do wonder if I am making a mistake by choosing to stay. I do wonder if Riley and I will be okay if I still leave. Could we make it work? Could I have her and the scholarship? A free ride—it was a necessary evil. I didn't have a scholarship to UTA, and A&M is still far away if I choose their offer instead. My dad very well could refuse to pay out of pocket for fees, and all of those feelings make me feel like an asshole, because I desperately, irrevocably and without question love that girl with every breath I take, and every fiber in my being.

My thoughts are all over the place as I sit in second period barely hearing any of the words being lectured to me. I feel conflicted. When I made the decision to sign, I knew the ramifications of it. I knew it meant leaving her, but part of me had been excited, at least, at the time it was. She was with Dean, and for two years I'd watched him have the life with her I wanted. It was painful, so yeah…a little bit of me was excited to start over, make anew. Collin was excited, too. We had discussed that very thing a little later that week.

Back to Monday—after class I was walking to my locker, and I could hear the whispers around me. They ceased when I walked by, so I didn't hear what they were saying, but I knew it was about Riley and me. I heard her name.

One week. One fucking week and these walls become part of our past. That became my mantra to survive the bullshit that surrounded me— surrounded us.

I never understood why those asshats couldn't mind their own damn business. All anyone wanted to do was gossip about shit. In the snap of a finger, the gossip flew from one story to the next—no one really cared about its truth. Tomorrow they would be discussing how Brad was rumored to be having an affair with his girlfriend's mom, just like last week they were bitching about some other lame ass thing— that's just how shit went in those halls.

I hated the way Riley's classes didn't line up with mine. She was on a complete different hall, so I didn't see her until lunch, and of course my favorite period when we had class together—but that wasn't until the end of the day.

Collin came up to me with a note. "Dude, what the fuck is this?" he said handing me a piece of paper.

I took it from him and read, *for a good time call,* and it listed Riley's phone number. "Where the fuck did you get this?" I snapped.

He looked at me just as shocked as I was. "They are being placed inside guys lockers. I have no fucking clue where they are coming from. That is Riley's number, right?" he asked.

"Right." I shoved it in my jean's pocket, and my eyes started eyeing everyone in the hall speculatively. A realization set in that the whispers were probably about that.

"Have you seen her?" he asked.

"No, she doesn't have classes on this end." I said, thinking that the day had just got shitloads <u>worse</u> with each passing second. Then he pulled out his phone, "This is also being shared."

I took his phone, and on display was everything I wanted to forget. In small text scrolling across the screen, *what happens when she can't decide between two lovers?*

You have got to be kidding me? She has decided. Two lovers? Those were all words that ran through my mind. I looked to Collin just as the bell rang, "Find out who is behind this shit," I demanded.

"I'm already on it, Parker," he said.

Emily sat down next to me in third period, placing a note on my desk. I looked at it and over to her, if it's another 'for a good time note' I may have lost my shit right there in that room. Thankfully, it wasn't. "What's that?" I asked, a little harshly.

She frowned, "it's from Riley. People in this school are complete fucktard twatwaffles," she whispered, glaring around the room.

I couldn't agree more with whatever it was that she had called them. I placed the note in my book and discreetly read it.

I might not make it another week without murdering someone.

I texted her my reply, ME NEITHER.

The worst day had to have been Thursday. I was sitting in fifth period, not able to concentrate on a damn thing the teacher was mumbling on and on about. I knew Riley was dealing with shit from the drama at school, even though she wouldn't open up to me about it. I didn't blame her. I was being quiet—unintentionally pulling away again. I didn't know why I did it, but when my head gets fucked up, I retreat into this shell to sort it out on my own. I hated it, because I needed her—I just didn't know how to open up to her about my own issues without hurting her. Not just that, but she genuinely seemed to be freaked out about something. She had been doing a few things that bothered me. One, she was always looking around and over her shoulder. She would shiver, and her frown line would deepen like she was thinking deeply about something. And the second, she would stare at me a little deeper, like she was trying to climb inside of my mind and read it. It was unnerving, but then again I wasn't giving her much to go on.

I wasn't in the mood for school or lectures, but the teacher called on me to answer him. "Mr. Parker, I asked you a question. In chapter twenty-four what was the purpose behind—,"

I stood up and grabbed my backpack, ignoring the gasp from my classmates, or the glare from Mr. What's-his-face. "I don't know the answer. I don't know the purpose behind anything. I didn't read the damn chapter, and I'm out." I stormed out the classroom with him yelling after me.

I was clearing out the rest of my locker, and restraining myself from punching a dent into the metal, when a voice that sounded like nails on a chalkboard screeched in my ear.

"Josh, are you okay? I mean like that was some scene back there. It was kind of hot," Preslee said. I rolled my eyes. *What is up with this chick? Can she not get the hint?* I wondered for n'th time.

"Look, Preslee, I'm not in the mood for any bullshit right now, so just go back to class," I told her.

She grinned at me and ignored my request. She moved to stand directly in front of me and placed her hand on my arm. I looked down at her hand on me with disgust. When I looked back at her, she tilted her head to the side. "No, bullshit, okay. I know ways to make you feel better. It will feel good. I promise." She said in that sugary voice that she liked to use, thinking she was flirting. I knew exactly what she was implying—it wasn't the first time she'd offered to suck me off. As always, I turned her down. If I were any other teenage horny guy, I would have probably taken her up on her offer. Most guys would look at her pouty pink lips and would love them wrapped around their dick. I wasn't like most guys, though. Her pouty pink lips and everything that came out of them pissed me the fuck off.

I tore each and every finger off of my arm and dropped her hand. "No, thanks." I turned away from her, finding Riley standing in the hall—watching.

If looks could kill, she would have stoned Preslee to death. I stood motionless just looking at her until her eyes met mine. She held up her phone, "Em texted me. I came to check on you."

She stated it as though that explained why she was out of class— every word dead of emotion. I forgot Emily had been in my class. I should have known that she would alert the troops of my blow up. I moved closer to her, and her eyes darted back and forth between Preslee's and mine. I didn't know how much she saw or heard, or what she was thinking right then, but I knew that I didn't like it—the unasked question in her eyes—the little visible sliver of doubt always lingering beneath the surface. I reached for her cheek, and she flinched just slightly.

However, then she turned her cheek into my touch, and squeezed her eyes shut. "I hate her, Josh," she breathed. I wrapped my hand around the nape of her neck and pulled her to my chest. I kissed her forehead and inhaled the coconut smell of her hair.

"Me too. I hate her, too," I muttered. When we pulled apart, Preslee was already gone.

Riley looked up at me. "Are you okay?" she asked.

I shook my head. "I'm just in a bad mood. I'm good now, but I'm going home for the day. I'm not feeling this right now." She nodded. It wasn't long before the bell rang, and she went one way, and I went another. The irony of that wasn't lost on me.

I didn't know where I was going, and I also knew the school would call my dad soon. I just didn't care right then. I needed to clear my head, so I left the campus. I drove around aimlessly not really sure where I should go, or if I should go back. Somehow, I ended up in the spot where most confessions and realizations have been made for me. I ended up at *our spot* by the lake.

I sat there at the dock imagining Riley sitting in the same very spot alone, crying and hating me for leaving her. I sat there imagining Dean coming in to dry her tears and to fill her head with doubts and more confusion like he always did when a window of opportunity came. I just imagined all sorts of scenarios, and each made me crazy mad.

I didn't know how long I sat there. It could have been a few minutes, a few hours—an entire day. I wasn't sure. I knew it was long enough for her to realize I wasn't at home and to come looking for me.

"Josh?" *Riley's voice. Jesus. Just her voice alone made me want to cry.*

I didn't turn around. I couldn't look at her. I just couldn't, so I stayed right where I was—facing the water, and imagining my life without her—and hating it.

She knew me well enough to know I was upset, and to know that when I was that upset—I remained quiet. She sat next to me and stared out at the water, probably imagining our future together and embracing it, while my image of us was falling away.

I could feel her look at me, but she didn't pry. She just put her hand on top of mine and interlaced our fingers. We sat like that in quiet silence because she apparently knew it's what I needed. *She* was what I needed. I fell in love with her even more that day—just for being everything I needed and for being her—my love, my life—everything. With her head on my shoulder and without a word being said—she had me.

I offered to give her a ride home, and she agreed. The entire drive was quiet—not a peep—just breathing. She would never forgive me for doing this. We wouldn't survive it. I drove the block, and a million different thoughts sped through my brain at lightning speed.

When we got to her house, I thanked her. She gave me an odd look, but I truly was thankful. And then I told her, "I love you, never forget that."

Her face contorted into various phases of emotion: confusion, high alert, sadness and then panic. She didn't say anything. Then again, I turned away and left her standing in shock in the yard—not really giving her an opportunity.

CHAPTER 9

I'm lifted higher and higher—seeing the world in beautiful colors, until I'm falling and scared as shit. The first weekend as Josh's girlfriend is like a roller coaster ride. One second, my head is stuck on my worries about rumors, and then I'm thrown for another loop, my head becoming consumed on the potential loss of everything I want—again. Not just that, but I get a creepy feeling someone is always watching my every move.

Some words are like torture to my ears—and I hope are lies. I'm lying in my bed replaying what Preslee had said to me, 'Josh likes it in my mouth.' I may be virginal, but I know what she meant. It's been on my mind for a week. Imagining her on her knees for him is torture. She has to be screwing with my head, because he told me he never touched her, and even if technically she was the one doing the touching, it's still a sexual act. I just keep remembering the time at Collin's party, though, when they went in the bathroom together, and he joked with me about her doing him a favor. He'd seen my reaction and told me he was kidding and that they just made out. Surely, he wouldn't have lied about that just to spare my feelings. She's just always there—making me uncomfortable about them.

Everything in my mind is one big cluster fuck, because not only am I stuck on her implications, but also, I'm worried about Josh. He kind of has me freaked out this week. He's been extremely quiet but then he kisses me, and it's a different kind of kiss—a desperate kind of kiss. Yesterday, he flipped out at school, and when I found him at the lake he couldn't even look me in the eye. He didn't talk the entire ride back to his house, which wasn't that long of a ride. It wouldn't have bothered me as much except that he'd gotten out of his truck, and then he'd hugged me tightly and told me 'thank you.' *Thank you?* He'd looked directly into my eyes and told me he loved me and to never forget it. After that, he went inside and left me in his driveway wondering what the hell had happened and why he'd said 'loved' like it was in the past tense.

I have suspicions about what's going on with him, but I'm not 100% positive on any of it anymore. I'm pretty sure nothing is thrown under the rug. Something is definitely bothering him, and he won't open up to me about it. It's a bit of unwanted déjà vu, because the last time he got this quiet and shut down on me this way, was three years ago when our lives had been changed forever. I can only think he just isn't ready, but the fact that he isn't telling me puts my nerves on high alert.

It's the last day of senior year—big friggen' deal. It's done, kaput, O.V.E.R.—over. I should feel bliss, but I only feel on edge. I barely even saw him today to question any of it. At lunch, I had to make up things I'd missed last week just to complete my grade. It's been one hell of a week, to say the least, one I barely survived, but it's over. My nerves are shot. I'm ready to explode. Then there is the thing that Josh and I have yet to discuss—the elephant always in the room— his scholarship, among the other things that seem to be weighing heavily on him, which could very well be one and the same.

Today is the first day I turned my phone on in a few days. I'd been getting random texts with dirty messages from unknown numbers, some also known—all guys. I had to delete my Facebook page just so I wouldn't see the mentions of us in the newsfeeds. It's so ridiculous. I'm tired of hearing people talk shit about me—about us. Their words make Josh and me sound ugly and debasing. We are beautiful—like a sweet symphony of music.

My phone alerts me of a text message right away, pulling me out of my reverie. It's from, Josh.

Josh: WANNA GO FOR A WALK – OUR SPOT?

I do. We have so much we need to discuss

Me: YES. MEET YOU OUTSIDE

I feel frazzled as I slip on my flip-flops and pull my hair into a ponytail. As soon as I step outside though, I'm suddenly calm. His eyes meet mine and we both freeze—just staring at one another. He is still a distance away from me, leaning against his truck. My eyes study him to memory.

His hair is messy on the ends like he has just run his hands through it. He just stares at me. He doesn't crook his finger for me to come to him. He doesn't smile or smirk. He's just watching me. Waiting.

I can't read his expression. His eyes tell several stories, all at once. I slowly walk to him, and when I do, I have the sudden urge to cry, but I don't.

I won't give that school the satisfaction of hurting me. I won't give Preslee the ability to put those doubts back in my head. I won't give Dean the power to confuse me any longer. Their opinions—just shit I need to cover with dirt and keep on moving. Real life hurts—the potential of being apart hurts.

And now that I am up close to him, I see it—he is sad too. *Why is it so hard for us to just open up to each other? We're always walking on eggshells—afraid to crack the other.*

"You okay?" he asks, looking at my eyes.

I shake my head and shrug, "I hate everyone. I hate life."

He tucks a curl behind my ear. "Me too," he whispers as he pulls me into a hug. "Let's walk," he says holding my hand and pulling me to follow him.

We start walking to the lake together, admiring the stars in the sky. I love that part of living here. The stars are always so bright. *I wish Josh and I could just have peace—no thoughts of leaving or of change.*

"I'm sorry about yesterday. I know I probably freaked you out. I was just having a bad day," he says.

"It's okay, Josh. I'm just worried about you—about us." I admit.

He stops and turns me to him. "You never have to worry about us, Riley. Ever. I'm..." he runs his hand nervously behind his head, "I'm going to fix this."

"Fix what?" I ask my voice barely above a whisper. *Just tell me.*

His eyes never waver away from mine as his mouth opens and shuts, and then he pulls my body to his and crashes his lips to mine. It's *the* kiss—the desperate kiss. He pours everything into it—the words he can't seem to say out loud—he tells me like this, and I take it because I feel the same desperation.

He pulls away and leaves me breathless. "What was that for?" I ask, touching my lips as they tingle.

He reaches his hand out and pads his thumb along my bottom lip. "Not that I need a reason to kiss you, but I missed you, and sometimes I can't help but kiss you. I need to."

I stare at him unable to ask the things I need to—to form the sentence that needs to be said for us to finally break this cycle of holding things in.

"I know we haven't talked about this all week, but I saw the video. Are you okay?" he asks out of the blue.

I sigh and put my head down. "Not really. Everyone is saying that I was cheating on Dean with you, and then I cheated on you with him after it. They are saying that I'm a slut, and that you would climb in my bedroom at night so that we could...well, you know. But they are saying I was, or that I am sleeping with you both."

And then Preslee...god, I hate her. I hate her so fucking much. I don't tell him what she said—I can't handle the truth if he let her do that to him.

He places his index finger under my chin and lifts my face to his. "Look at me. Nothing they say or think matters—we know the truth. I can guarantee you that when I find out who started this shit, and who put those notes in the guys' lockers, I will raise all kinds of hell."

"What notes?" I ask. I hadn't heard about any notes. I notice his mouth set into a thin line and his eyes harden.

"It doesn't matter. It's all behind us now. We write our story—not them," he says.

"Oh, and then the text messages. I'm getting weird text messages with um, dirty things...from guys at school," I say.

"That would be because of the note. Do you know who's sending them to you?" he asks.

"Some—not all." I flip through my phone and show him the numbers that are visible. He reads a few messages and his eyes harden instantly. I'm afraid he is going to break my phone by how hard he is holding it. When he looks back up to me, a thousand things are hidden in the depths of his hazel eyes.

"It's behind us," he whispers more to himself than to me. It's almost like he needs the mantra as much as I do.

"And then what? What's next for us, Josh?" I ask, and in an instant, I see his fear. I regret the words instantly as the realization hits me that neither of us knows what might happen next. That's the truth. That is the wall between us.

Surely he won't still go to Louisiana, not now, not when we are finally together. Right? I mean, there is no way I could follow him there. I had barely got into UTA. My grades are shit, and my mom can't afford out of state fees. What if he has no choice like I have no choice, but to stay here?

Shit. Shit. Shit.

How could we never have discussed this again? Why didn't he tell me?

I can feel his eyes on me as a thousand and one thoughts and questions race through my mind. I don't ask them all—the one asked was enough. I'm not sure he has the answers, or if today I could handle them.

As if Josh knows what I'm thinking or what I'm feeling, he embraces me. He pulls me to his chest, and he holds me like he understands I need him to. It's always been like this—my pain is his pain. Our veins are connected to the same artery like that. Like when we were kids, and I skinned my knee, he would always put a Band-Aid on his own knee so I would feel better. Or when he was sick, I would only eat chicken noodle soup for dinner because I knew it would be what he ate. We mentally sympathized with one another.

His arms are wrapped around me, and I'm squeezing his shirt tightly in my hands as tears threaten to escape my eyes. He squeezes me tightly in return.

There is something to hugs—like some hugs are meant to comfort or console. Some hugs are short and friendly, and then there are these kinds of hugs—the kinds of hugs that answer unasked questions...we will be okay. We have to be.

I don't know how long we stood like that...just embracing one another. It may have been just a moment or several long minutes. Either way, his arms around me make me feel better. Both of us are clearly on the edge, with our fears circling us like a whirlwind. The air is suffocating, and yet I need desperately to just breathe him in. I don't want him to let me go—ever!

He walks me to my door, and I turn to look at him hoping he doesn't see all of my questions hiding. He places his hand on my cheek, and I lean into his touch, "Nothing matters more to me than you. I thank god every day that we finally made it here—together. You asked what happens next for us," he says in a hushed whisper.

I squeeze my eyes shut and brace myself for what I fear. His breath feathers across my face as he kisses each of my shut eyelids. His hands glide along my cheeks and to the nape of my neck where he pulls me closer to him. I can feel his breath on my lips, which part just a fraction. He breathes the words against my lips, words I want so badly to believe. "We just get better baby—stronger." His lips press against mine, and this very kiss steals the breath right out of my lungs—slow, sweet and beautiful.

"Yeah?" I whisper against his lips.

"Yeah," he says before that soft tender kiss becomes so much more—more demanding, insistent, desperate, and raw. He presses me to wall next to the door, caging me in as his tongue makes love to mine. His hand slips just under my shirt by my waist. I moan at the smallest touch on my skin and wish he would move it north. One of my hands are tangled into his hair, while the other is touching his face. I want him so badly. Eventually, the kiss ends, and he rests his head against my forehead while we both catch our breath.

I have my window open listening to the wind howl as the clouds form various patterns in the sky. A storm is brewing. I love watching the clouds roll and the colors change as the storms near. We frequently have storms here—mostly around spring—some even severe enough to fear tornadoes. I have never been afraid. I like to stand outside and watch it—curious and intrigued.

Tonight's storm frightens me, though, because it isn't one in the sky. It's a storm brewing of words in the window across from mine. Josh also loves the sound of rain, and he too has his window open. I'm sure he doesn't anticipate my hearing this altercation between him and his dad. I know I don't.

"Joshua Michael Parker!" His dad shouts.

"Sir?" Josh says, with all his manners in place.

"Care to tell me why your coach called me at work to inform me that you are wishing to withdraw your letter of intent?"

He changed his mind. Oh shit! That must be what he went to talk to the coach about, what he meant about fixing things.

"And then I get a call that you yelled at your teacher and left campus without permission. What is going on?" he asks.

"Isn't it late for that dad? Joey would be giving you an ear full if she saw you eating ice cream this late." Josh says, evidently trying to deflect the conversation. Joey is like little mother hen and rides his ass lately about his diet and keeping him healthy.

I'm trying to see inside his window without being noticed. I see Josh's dad sit a bowl down on the dresser and cross his arms over his chest. "That's why I'm eating it. She isn't here to nag me. Now quit ya bitching about my ice cream and tell me what's going on with you, kid."

Josh has his guitar in his hand. He had been humming a melody that I was enjoying—his voice always soothing me to the core. Now, I am aware of how much I don't like this conversation or the tone in Josh's voice—no longer soothing.

"Dad, Louisiana is hours away from Riley. I don't want to go anymore. I signed in February, and a lot has changed since then. I can stay here and not play football. You know? Just focus on school." *Yes, please.*

"Listen, I know you and Riley have a good thing going on, and I don't want to mess that up. It's not that simple, though, Josh. UTA didn't offer you a scholarship, and you already missed your chance with A&M when you signed with LSU. I'd have to pay out of pocket or get grants, Joshua. I can't afford to do either. I have Joey to think about soon, as well. Louisiana offered you a full ride, son—for a year. You need to take it. It's the best decision. You signed an agreement, and you need to follow through. Maybe Riley can transfer next semester and be with you."

No, no, no. Now, what? My heart is beating erratically in my chest, my palms feel sweaty and I'm aware now of how much I'm scared of this. He has to go. He doesn't have a choice.

Josh stands up and begins pacing his room. His fists are balled, and for a second, I worry he is going to hit his dad. He doesn't. He runs his hands through his hair and looks to the ceiling as if the answers are written there. He takes a deep breath and sits back down. His voice is so low that I have to strain to hear him. "Dad, this could ruin us. Do you know how hard it was to get where we are? Do you?" He asks, and his dad nods—I can see his face falter, he is aware.

"That girl means everything to me, dad. Everything. Nothing matters more to me than her—not even football—and you're telling me the best decision is to leave her? That isn't an option for me. I won't go to college then. I'll just get a job. I'll figure it out some other way." Josh explains.

He's willing to give everything up *for me?* I can't let him do that. As much as my heart is shattering into a thousand tiny pieces, I know I can't let him do that.

His dad's shouts make me jump. "You will do no such thing, Joshua! College isn't optional. You.will.go."

Silence follows where I hear nothing until Josh's dad speaks again—this time more composed. "Look, I'm sorry this situation is shit to you. But it is what it is, and you and Riley will figure it out. You need to realize that you are being handed an opportunity, son—one that could lead to something great. You are a quarterback, a damn good one. They signed you to take the place of Jessie Bridges when he graduates, which is in a year, son. That leaves an open college career for you. You can't pass that up. Period. Now I'm going to bed. This decision is final. No more talk of releases. Do you hear me?"

The sound of thunder and a crash of lightening in the distance filter out Josh's response. I'm staring at him through our open windows—wanting to just go hold him and tell him *we will be okay*. He must feel my eyes on him, or maybe he feels the need to do the same, because he turns his head—almost catching me watching.

I fall back on my bed as a sob overtakes me. My heart is crushed. I love him enough to let him go. I know he has to go, but everything in me is worried about what this means for us now. Life is unfair and cruel. Why give him to me just to take him away again? So much time has been wasted and now it's slipping away—becoming borrowed and limited.

CHAPTER 10

Another damn roadblock, and another hurdle for us to climb—life is shit sometimes. I'm not sure why fate hates us so much, but she is a bitch. To every truth, every decision comes a consequence or action. What happens when your action tells the wrong truth, or your decision causes the worst consequence imaginable? How am I supposed to handle this one?

I can hear Riley crying through her window. I'm not sure why, but I have a sickening feeling in the pit of stomach when I realize her window is open, which means she could very well have overheard the argument with my dad. *FUCK!*

After a few hours, the silence becomes deafening, and I can't stand it. It's past midnight, and I can't sleep. I toss and turn restlessly— worried about her. I look out the window and see that her window is still open, so just as I have many times before, I decide to climb through it.

I fall into her bed, wearing nothing more than my running shorts. Her breathing is shallow, and I assume she is sleeping. A sharp hiss escapes from her blanket as I climb under her covers and pull her back against me. "Shhh....," I say to Tink moving her to the floor. Riley is wearing a t-shirt that has risen above her waist. I can feel her bare legs touch my skin—warm and soft. I fight the urge to touch her. I bury my head in her hair, and inhale the scent that has become my addiction. "I love you pretty girl, so much," I whisper into her ear.

Her breathing changes, her body begins to shake and she sniffles. *Shit!* She is crying. She rolls over and wraps her arms around me and buries her head into my chest, which slowly becomes damp with tears. I rub her back and her hair as she softly cries. I can't take it. It's killing me. I pull her face into my hands and use my thumbs to wipe away her tears. I kiss her forehead, "I love you, Riley." She shakes more. I kiss her cheeks, "I love you so fucking much, baby." The need to hush her tears is overwhelming. I crush my lips to hers and she whimpers. Her body falls limp into the bed within my arms. The taste of her salty tears mixes with our kiss as one of my own meets them. "I love you, baby." I can't stop telling her—the need to reassure her is so strong.

"I love you, Josh. I love you so much it hurts." I know why it hurts her, because it hurts me, too.

Our kiss deepens as emotions take over. She glides her hands over my skin as I kiss down her neck. She wraps her leg over my waist, and I let my hand travel down her leg to cup her ass. She moans, and either willingly or just by reaction she pushes her hip into me. She applies pressure on the hand she has on my chest to roll me onto my back and then she straddles me. *Oh fuck!* This is going somewhere I'm not prepared for—somewhere we can't go tonight. We're emotional—she's emotional, and this decision can't be made like this.

I'm talking myself off the ledge, and she is removing her t-shirt bearing her breasts to me. *Oh, for the love of all that is holy—give me strength.* I glide my hands up her stomach until she fits beneath my palms. She is perfect—so fucking perfect. *Damn.*

I flip her to her back in one quick motion causing her to gasp. I love the sound of it. I kiss her lips fervently now and full of the passion I feel. I lick a path down her neck and begin to kiss her in places my lips have never touched before.

She squirms as I suck her nipple into my mouth, and then the other. She grabs my face and pulls me to hers, "I love you. You love me. Make love to me, Josh."

And here we are again—her begging me for the second time to do something I feel we can't do because the situation is...all wrong.

The first time, she was drunk and pissed, and now she is upset and scared. *No!* Why can't we get this right? I want to make love to her when the time is right. Not like this. Not because we are both scared.

I swallow the huge lump in my throat. "I love you. I want to show you just how much I love you, baby. But not now—not like this. You're upset, emotions are high and we have so much to talk about before we take this next step. Please, baby, believe me when I say I want you so much. God, how I want you—but not tonight."

She falls back into her mattress on a sigh, "I know."

"What? You aren't mad at me?" I ask.

She wraps her arms around my neck, "No, you're right."

I roll us back to our sides as we hold each other in silence—the sound of our breathing becoming so loud—until she breaks it. "I'm scared," she says into my chest as she slowly strokes small circles over my stomach.

I pull her tighter to me feeling the same fear inside of me. I kiss her hair, "Me too, baby. Me too."

She means too much to me to lose her over some game that I didn't care about anymore. I care about her. I didn't see the same future my dad saw for me—coach saw for me. My future is the brunette with eyes that reminded me of vacations at the beach—the girl in my very arms yet slipping away. My future is with Riley. I knew I had to do this, be away from her, though. I've feared it from the beginning. I have a plan B in play. I will do this for a year and transfer back home, I will get a job, shit I'd get two if I had to. We were going to have to discuss this soon. I'm just not sure either of us is ready. That is the last thought I have before I fall asleep.

I don't know what time it is when I jolt awake and hear Riley obviously suffering from a nightmare.

She is whimpering and mumbling incoherent words, but I distinctly hear her say, 'Josh how could you?' My stomach twist with what she could be dreaming about.

I flip the lamp on her nightstand and try to wake her. "Riley? Baby, wake up, you're having a bad dream," I speak softly in her ear.

She gasps for air and sits up startled.

"Josh?" she asks blinking her eyes rapidly.

"Yeah, baby. It's me. You're shaking, and you're drenched in sweat. Jesus, that must have been some dream. Are you okay?" I ask her concerned.

The strangest expression crosses her features when she looks at me. For a second, she looks angry, but then she wraps her arms around my neck and squeezes me tight to her. She is shivering, and a sheet of dampness covers her skin as I hold her. She doesn't explain—her breathing slows and before I know it—she is asleep again. Rest for me doesn't come as easy.

CHAPTER 11

Nightmares come in various ways. The kind where you are haunted lying in REM slumber—shaken to your core—waking up drenched in sweat, then the other kind—where an event in reality is so bad—you swear it is a nightmare. You wish someone would pinch you, and it all just go away.

It's just a fact—Josh and I will be apart for college. I have so many fears about this. I can't even count them all. So many questions are swimming in my mind, my insecurity making me crazy. The worst one of all—what if Josh meets someone else? We haven't had sex. We haven't done anything sexually—and my fear is that he may have with Preslee—not sex, but other stuff. If I'm not satisfying him—just like I didn't satisfy Dean, then he will find other ways. All I know is that I need to be stronger now than I ever have if I have any way of saving us and keeping him. But what if I can't be?

It must have been the last thing I thought, because my nightmare was about that very thing.

I called Josh as I drove to his dorm to surprise him. I needed to hear his voice. I needed him.

"Heeelllooo," he answered slowly on a slur.

"Josh?" I said, in a questioning tone feeling my throat tighten.

"Oh baby, it's you. God, I mish...miss you. I wish you were here." He stuttered, and his speech seemed off.

I could barely hear him over the loud music in the background. "Are you at a party?" I asked.

"No, I'm in my truck. That is the radio. Just a sec and I will turn it down."

I heard a female giggle. "Shhhh..." Josh said, muffled away from the phone.

"What was that?"

"What was what?" he asked.

"Don't do that?" I snapped.

"Do what?" he answered my question with a question again.

"That. Answering my question with a question. I heard a girl giggle, Josh. Is someone with you?" I asked, feeling the pit in my stomach growing wider.

His breathing was heavy and labored in the phone. "No, I'm alone, baby. It's just you and me. God, I love your voice. Keep talking to me, baby," he told me groaning in his throat.

I wondered why he had made that sound as nausea swept over me.

"Are you drunk?" I asked feeling pissed off and scared, because he just said he was in his truck, which meant he was driving. Didn't he realize that was how my dad died, the reason his mom was gone?

"Just buzzed...I'm good pretty girl. Tell me something sweet," he said, with a heavy sigh.

"I miss you, Josh." I told him sweetly, but I wanted to scold him for driving intoxicated.

"Ahhh...shit. I miss you too, baby." He paused, and when he withdrawals a breath making a seething sound, my unease was intensified to the max. "Damn, just like that. Mmmm...Don't stop," he said groaning. My only thought was, 'What the fucking hell?'

"What? Who are you talking to?" I asked, feeling my skin prickle and the bile rise to my throat.

"Huh? What?" he asked. I didn't answer. I just listened—listened to his breathing as it increased in heaviness and intensity, listened as he threw me away. I felt sick. It just got worse with each wicked thing he said. "Oh yeah, baby, just like that. Jesus Christ, Riley. I love your mouth, baby. You're so fucking good." He rambled and then groaned loudly before he stopped. That pit swallowed me whole.

My mouth? He was fucking my mouth? But I was in Texas, and he was there—in Louisiana. OH GOD!

The darkness invaded me when an unfamiliar female voice that was definitely not mine was heard. "To get you to smile like that, baby, I will let you call me any name you want."

"Josh, what the fuck? Are you going to tell me you're alone again? How could you?" I shouted into the phone, pulling over on the side of the road with silent tears streaming down my cheeks. My vision was blurred.

"Riley? Baby...I...OH, SHIT!" he shouted, and I heard a crash as the phone went dead.

"JOSH? JOSH? Are you there?" I shouted frantically.

"JOSH? JOSH? JOSH?" He didn't answer. Everything went black. My heart stopped beating. My heart just died because he was my heart. My world had ended. He'd cheated on me, and he'd driven drunk—he'd crashed. It was every fear wrapped into a dirty little box with a tainted bow of lies and betrayal.

"Riley? Baby, wake up. You're having a bad dream," Josh says.

I gasp for air and sit up startled.

"Josh?" I ask blinking my eyes rapidly.

"Baby, you're shaking and you're drenched in sweat. Jesus, that must have been some dream. Are you okay?" he asks me concerned.

I feel discombobulated and bewildered. My heart sees him and is relieved that it was just a dream—my mind though—is pissed as hell at him for what he just did in my nightmare. Normally, my mind would win out, but my heart needs him. My heart loves him. I throw my arms around his neck, and I wrap my body around his, squeezing him tightly to me.

He just gently rubs my back and holds me. His heart beating—reminds me that he is here, and we are together—and that wasn't real. The thumping beneath my cheek and his touch soothe me back to sleep where no more nightmares haunt me this time.

"A'hem" I hear a throat clear, and realize the sun is filtering into my bedroom window. "A'hem" I hear the throat clear a second time, so I start to wiggle around, but I find that I can't move.

I'm too warm and feel a little smothered. I notice a muscled arm wrapped around me and feel that my legs are tangled with Josh's legs. My shirt is still off, and one of his hands is on my breast under the blanket while the other has my back pulled to his front. *Oh shit!*

I blink my eyes lazily as the third cleared throat alerts me that this throat clearing is definitely not that of Josh. I nudge him, and he groans in his throat, pulling me tighter to him. I feel him harden into my back and—*oh.my.god.*

"Five more minutes. I'm so tired," he mutters. Just damn—his voice in the morning is hoarse and sexy as hell. Involuntarily, I squirm which makes him push into my back and squeeze my breasts. *Ah hell*. I almost moan at the feel of him.

"Your five minutes is up." My mom's voice booms from the door of my bedroom, causing Josh to jump up. This movement simultaneously removes my comforter completely from my bed, and exposes the fact that my shirt is off, and all I'm wearing are my pink panties.

My mom's eyes widen at the sight of her daughter like that. I hear giggling from my sister in the hallway. "To your room, Tatum," she snaps at her.

In between glaring at me, my mom frantically pulls open my dresser drawer, throwing several shirts of any kind at me to cover myself.

Josh is wearing his running shorts, his chest heaving—it's distracting. His eyes are wide like saucers looking back and forth from my mom to me. Every time he looks at me—he really looks at me and then looks at her apologetically. He is trying and failing so hard not to notice my practically naked body in front of him. My breasts were on display for him last night, but it was in the dark—I am one hundred percent visible for his eyes right now.

I stand up and put one of the shirts on. Unfortunately, it isn't a t-shirt and only covers my top. My panties are still very visible. "Jesus Christ," my mom mutters.

"I'm...I, uh...I'm sorry, Mrs. Shaw. This looks bad. Oh God, this looks bad. I swear we didn't...ya know...we didn't do...that." He has his hand over his eyes so he can't look at me. I can't help that it makes me giggle a little at him, which of course makes my mom's eyes cut to me immediately with a warning glare. I shut up.

"Out!" She shouts at him, pointing her finger to the door.

He pulls his hand down, and his eyes meet my lower half before looking to my eyes apologetically. He clears his throat. "Yes, ma'am," he says, his voice croaking, and he practically runs out the door.

My mom's eyes are locked with mine in silence, until the front door shuts and the alarm chimes—then all hell breaks loose on me.

"What in the world do you think you are doing, young lady? I find that I am a pretty reasonable mother when it comes to most things. I don't give you a curfew. Your sister and you come and go as you please all the time. But I draw the line at boyfriends sleeping over, Riley Evelyn Shaw. I know he said y'all didn't...do that...but you had no clothes on, and I'm no fool."

"We didn't, Mom. I swear." I try to interject her rant, but she isn't done.

"And in my house? For the love of all that is holy—if you end up pregnant like I did—I'm going to kill you," she says.

Now, I'm pissed. "Look, Mom, I'm sorry. We didn't have sex. I promise, and no one is getting pregnant in your house," I explain.

She nods her head and stares at my bed with loathing. "So, you didn't have sex last night? You were practically naked, Riley. I'm sure you did...something."

I shake my head and frown slightly. I'd be lying if I said I didn't wish that we had done something. I do want to do lots of 'something's' with Josh. "No, we didn't. We kissed. We held each other—nothing else." I tell her. Everything in her eyes tells me she doesn't believe me and she isn't at all convinced.

"If you didn't have sex last night, did you um...have sex any other night before last night?" she asks. She shifts her weight uncomfortably—and *cue the talk*.

I walk to my dresser and bend over to pick out a pair of shorts to put on, when I turn around I see Josh sitting on his bed looking right into my window. He saw me bend over just now. My cheeks flush on the spot, and I clear my throat as I step into my shorts. When I look back up, he is no longer there. *Did I imagine him watching me just now?*

Thankfully, my mom hadn't seen him, but our windows are both still open, so if I didn't imagine him, then I know he can hear every word we are saying unless we whisper—and we aren't whispering.

"No, mom. I've never had sex. I'm still a virgin, and I've never done the other 'something's' I assume you are referring to. So stop worrying. Besides I'm eighteen today, so if I wanted to——,"

"Do you want to?" She mutters in a soft voice, ignoring the fact that it's my birthday.

My eyes dart to hers, "Huh?" I ask, glancing at the window to see if Josh is listening. I don't see him.

"Do you want to have sex, Riley? It's a simple question. Because if you are thinking about doing that...then I'd like to know, so I can talk to you about it. I know we have had many sex talks, and you know based on my own experience how one slip up can change your entire future, but I don't want that to deter you from talking to me about it. I don't want you to have sex, but I was your age once. So, answer me. Are you thinking about having sex with Josh?"

Oh God. This is awkward.

"Yes," I answer truthfully. I know he is listening because I saw movement in his room, even though I can't see him physically—he is there. "I want to have sex with Josh. Like I said, I'm eighteen, today. I'm on the pill for my period. I love him. He loves me. Our future *belongs together.* I don't see me ever being with anyone else. So, yes, it's weird telling you this...but it's true. If the timing were right, and it felt like the right time, he would be the guy I want to share my first time with."

She smiles, and it confuses the hell out of me. "I appreciate your honesty. I'm not ready for you to be ready, sweetheart. I'm not ready for you to be graduating tonight, or for any of these changes to be taking place, or for you to be eighteen, today. OH, MY GOD! You're eighteen today! It's your birthday?! I forgot your birthday. What kind of mother does that?" Her eyes glass over, and she rubs her temples, wobbling a little to sit down on my bed.

"Are you okay?" I ask her. "It's okay, Mom." I mean, it really isn't but um, okay.

She nods, "Just a little dizzy spell. I haven't had breakfast yet. That's all." I notice she looks pale, and I begin to worry about her. She's been getting dizzy a lot lately, suffering from headaches and bouts of nausea. It concerns me. "I can't believe I forgot it's your birthday," she whispers, forlornly.

My mom looks around my room like she is finally paying attention to something. She looks back at me and sighs. "You're a strong girl,

Riley. I just worry because I'm your mom. I can't stop you from growing up. I always said when I became a mom that I wouldn't react to these things the way my mom did. So I'm trying here—but this is hard."

"I know, Mom," I whisper.

"And, I forgot your birthday, so I'm going to go remedy that." She pats my knee and goes to stand. She doesn't move right away as she looks to be gaining her balance—again it concerns me. I just nod in response.

After she gets to the door, I stop her. "Mom?"

She turns to look at me, "Yes, dear?"

"How will I know if it's the right time?" I ask her. I genuinely wonder.

She glances at the window and then to me as she shrugs. "You just will. It's hard to explain. I'd prefer it be on your wedding day, and then it's just obvious, because that is what happens next. But if not...just follow your heart—and be careful." Then she leaves me sitting in my bed with a case of whiplash.

My phone pings almost immediately.

Josh: SORRY :(

Me: NO WORRIES

Josh: I'M GLAD YOU AREN'T IN TROUBLE

He just gave himself away. He was listening which means he heard everything. I text him back.

Me: ME TOO :)

Josh: HAPPY BIRTHDAY PRETTY GIRL x

I smile and type my response.

Me: AT LEAST YOU REMEMBERED :(

Josh: :(THIS SHOULD CHEER YOU UP. I CAN'T GET THE IMAGE OF YOU OUT OF MY HEAD. YOU ARE BEAUTIFUL.

Damn.

Me: *BLUSH TY - MY BED SMELLS LIKE YOU. I LIKE IT.
;)

Josh: I LOVED WAKING UP TO YOU IN MY ARMS (FOR LIKE 2.5 SECONDS THAT IS LOL)

Me: I LOVED BEING IN YOUR ARMS FOR THOSE 2.5 SECONDS. YOUR SKIN TOUCHING MY SKIN FELT INCREDIBLE. BEST BDAY GIFT EVER

Josh: DAMN, BABY! YOU ARE INCREDIBLE. I HAVE MORE 4 U

Me: HMMM...I'M CURIOUS. YOU MAKE A HABIT OF WATCHING ME THROUGH MY WINDOW???

Josh: I WAS WORRIED ABOUT U. I DIDN'T EXPECT TO SEE YOU BENT OVER. THAT WAS JUST A PLEASANT SURPRISE. :) YOU HAVE A NICE ASS BTW.

Me: OH, MY GOD. UR CRAZY.

Josh: 4 U! x

He kissed me. He text kissed me.

Me: xoxo

My morning is spent in a happy yet sad bubble. I'm happy because it's my birthday. I'm happy because Josh thinks I'm incredible, but I'm sad because of everything I heard last night. The feeling that this will end soon makes me not only sad, but also I feel the onset of a full-fledged panic attack on the horizon.

After breakfast, Em texts to tell me she is on her way over, so I shower quickly and get dressed. I have a few things I want to do today. One, we're graduating high school tonight so I'd like to go talk to my dad. Two, I want to go print some photos for something I've made Josh. I'll give it to him tonight after we go to dinner with our parents. Just in case he is leaving me soon then he can at least take this with him and remember how much I love him.

The doorbell rings, and Emily practically attacks me in a giant bear hug when I open the door. "Miss me much?" I joke as she squeezes the life out of me.

She laughs and releases me. "Well, yes, actually. We haven't hung out as much since you've become Mrs. Joshua Parker."

Oh, I like that. "Funny, funny...but I kind of like that," I tell her as we walk to my room. I notice she has a small box in Tinker bell wrapping paper.

"Tinker Bell?" I ask, tilting my head.

She smiles handing me the box. "I know we weren't friends back then, but it's cute so...just open the damn present." She pushes me gently to sit on my bed.

I unwrap the paper, reach into the box and retrieve a small black velvet pouch. She snatches it from me. "Okay, let me explain, first."

I nod, and she says, "I don't do this mushy love stuff. I mean...I know nothing of it. I change my mind about boys constantly. It's just that I've never experienced what you and Josh have. So um, this is really cheesy and very unlike me, but I saw it and thought it was sweet. The pixie was reunited with her music," she says. I'm confused.

"M'kay," I drawl as she hands me the pouch back. I pull the little threads that hold it together and my breath catches. "Oh, wow!" I breathe. I dangle the delicate silver necklace from my fingers and admire its beauty. Small lime green crystals shaped like a heart surround two tiny charms. I touch the charms and smile widely—a little fairy and a guitar. Suddenly, I understand the tinker bell wrapping paper and her statement.

A tear falls down my cheek, and I swipe it with the back of my hand. "This is...wow...just wow! I love it, Em. Thank you." I wrap my hands around her neck.

"Yeah?"

I nod against her head. "Yes, it's perfect."

She helps me put it on, and I stand in the mirror admiring it. It's so beautiful and so perfect. I feel the sudden weight of what it means. What if the pixie loses her music? I've waited all my life for him. I knew his heart would bring warmth to my cold one. His music would breathe life into my lyrics, and now that it has, I can't—not have it. I won't survive losing him. I just won't. I begin to cry.

"Riley, what's wrong?" Em asks, coming to hug me. I explain it to her in a blubbered mess of words.

"Oh," she whispers. She knew all along. It's just confirmed now. What is there to say? I get the boy I've spent my lifetime loving, only to lose him as soon as I have the courage to let him in. It sucks. It one hundred percent sucks, and yet, he still hasn't opened up to me about it, or told me the truth. It's like he is in denial or something. Like he thinks he is staying with me. We need to talk about this, though. He can't keep kissing me to avoid saying what needs to be said. We can't avoid the real possibility that this could be the end of us. *Please don't let that be true. Please!*

Em and I go to lunch together at a local deli that has the best baked potatoes ever. We get manis and pedis spontaneously because the shop is next door, and then we stop and get Coke Icees to cool off from the heat outside. She drops me off at my house and tells me to think positively and not let this silly fear of mine ruin my birthday and graduation/birthday dinner tonight with our families. I wish she were coming, too, but being as though it is graduation night that is impossible. Her family wants to celebrate with her, as well.

I have a few hours to kill, so I get in my car to drive to the cemetery and talk to my dad. I'm unsure of what I will say, but knowing today I really wish he was here with me. I'm eighteen, an adult now, and I'm no longer in high school. It's a major milestone, and he isn't here to celebrate it with me. *I miss him.*

 *Josh*

CHAPTER 12

For the love of all that is holy and good—give me strength. Riley feels unbelievable in my arms. She is right. Her skin on my skin is incredible. The way she looks wearing nothing but panties, and bent over in them...Damn—it's burnt in my mind. I am unraveling. I want her badly.

I have no answers to give her about our future. I don't know them. I can't figure out what is right and what is wrong for us. My mind knows my dad and my coach are right, but my heart is screaming at them to shut the fuck up. My heart belongs with her.

So, here I am at a place serenity sometimes happens. I am with my mom—at her grave. I've sat here in silence, replaying the past weeks, months, hell—years in my mind. I'm graduating in a few hours. Riley's birthday dinner is after and my mind is overwhelmed with thoughts about her—thoughts of taking us places neither of us have ever been, and then thoughts of losing her all over again—so many thoughts and fears.

"Hey, Mom. I'm graduating high school tonight. I wish you could be there to see me grab that diploma. I miss you so much." I tell her as I place a rose on her grave for the third time this week. "I wish I could say I'm happy that today is the beginning of the bigger part of the rest of my life, but I'm not. I get the feeling that everything is going to change now. I hope I'm wrong about that, but I don't think I am," I say feeling melancholy.

"Did you know that Riley and I are finally together, like you always thought we would be? I feel like I'm about to jeopardize everything we have fought so hard to have. What sucks more than that, is there isn't a damn thing I can do to change it. Shit, sorry for cursing." I sigh, and lie on the grass looking up to the sky, wishing it would give me the answers I so desperately need.

I don't find the answers. I just find more questions and more concerns. "I made a mistake, Mom. Well, it wouldn't have been a mistake if Riley hadn't become so crucial to my heart remaining intact.

It's just...I made a decision without her—it wasn't like I had a choice—but I did it, and now things are going to change between us. That scares me, Mom. It scares the living hell out of me. I don't want to do this. I know how fragile she is—how untrusting she still is. It's not her fault. It's just the way she is. I just don't know what to do, or how to tell her I'm leaving here, soon."

I suddenly feel sick about going to her birthday dinner this evening. The thought of breaking her heart today of all days is killing me. My heart feels like it's coming undone in my chest.

I tell my mom how much I love her and miss her at least three more times. I've come here more than usual this week, just hoping somehow a piece of her will wrap its arms around me, and tell me this will be okay. Instead, I leave with a chill and a pit in my stomach that it won't be.

I climb in my truck and grab my cell, debating on doing the coward thing and telling Riley what I need to over the phone. It would be easier to do than watch her expression—watch her eyes as they show me her disappointment. I'm sure she wouldn't find that as the best birthday present ever. I sigh, put the phone down and lay my head on the steering wheel. *I don't know what to do.*

I hear a tap at the window and turn my head to find the vision of what keeps my heart intact. She steals the breath right out of my lungs. I roll the window down, and Riley tilts her head to the side studying me. I'm sure she can see the storm brewing behind my eyes. "Hey, birthday girl." I try to smile convincingly. *I know I don't because she frowns.*

"Hey, yourself." We peck on the lips. "You okay?" She folds her arms on the door, resting her beautiful head on top of them.

I contemplate just telling her, but I don't want to do it here and now, and definitely not today. I nod instead. "I just wanted to talk to my mom today—it's a big day for us. You went to see your dad?" I ask, and she nods.

Her mouth thins into straight line. "You've come to see her a lot this week. Um...are you all right? You know you can tell me anything, right?" she assures me.

Not liking where this conversation is going, I go to grab her face and kiss her, but she pushes me away

"Don't do that?" she says.

"Do what? Kiss you?" I ask.

"No, try to distract me. You're using kisses to avoid saying something. Just tell me, Josh." She says in a hushed whisper as her eyes become glassy.

"No," I reply.

"No?" she asks

"I need to kiss you, and it's your birthday, and I just want to kiss you, Riley. Can I kiss you?" I admit. Her eyes climb inside of me, seeing through to the deepest part of my soul. They flick to my lips, and she begins to take shallow breaths. She feels this, too. The constant pull—the magnetism between us—it's impossible to ignore.

She slowly nods, but I find myself already leaning over to kiss her nose and then each of her eyes. She doesn't stop me. She inhales a deep breath and slowly releases it. I kiss the corner of her mouth as her lips part. I kiss her bottom lip, pulling it gently between my teeth. She softly moans, and I will never get over the way her sounds get to me. I reach my hand to cup her cheek, and she leans her face into my touch. I kiss her because I have to, because if I don't kiss her right now—I can't breathe. I kiss her because even though I feel lost and confused in this moment, she is here. Out of nowhere, she appeared—as if she were a sign sent to tell me it's going to be okay—like an angel before me. I kiss her, and she kisses me with the same passion—embracing the same moment.

Her tears are falling onto my fingers, and I can taste the salt in my mouth as it mixes with our kiss. I rest my head on her forehead, as we both stay silent—just breathing each other in.

"Josh?"

"Don't, Riley. Don't say it. Not yet. Just let me love you, please." I beg because I know what she wants to say. She keeps trying to start this conversation, and I'm just not ready.

I hate that she has tears on her cheeks. I hate that she knows more than I want her to. I hate that I can't explain it, and I hate that I don't know what she is thinking.

After I pick up my dress shirt and pants from the cleaners, I make my way to the boutique where I ordered Riley's gift. I'm sitting in my car contemplating giving this to her. Will she understand it? Will it break her heart or make her happy? I just don't know to be honest.

"Oh, my god, Josh. That is the sweetest gift ever," Jo says, touching the silver box. And then she cries. Yep, this will break her heart. Sweet gesture or not, she will cry. Dammit. Riley said she loved the stars, then she referenced to me being her stars. I can't give them to her, but I can try.

Graduation is one of those things that either you are super excited about, or you don't really give a shit about it—I kind of sit in the gray area of both excitement and not giving a shit. I'm excited for the fact that it is over. I'm no longer in high school. I don't really give a shit about it because a special woman is missing in the row of my family members, and also because it's just moving on from one piece of baggage to another set.

Two people separate Riley and me in the pew—Ashley Roberts and Kevin Randall. I lean forward to glance at her, but she isn't looking at me. She is fiddling with something on her neck and looking lost deep in her thoughts.

"Psssst," I'm trying to get her attention. Kevin nudges Riley, and she looks over, blinking her eyes a few times.

"Hmm?" She says to him, but he nods his head to me. As soon as her eyes meet mine they instantly warm. "Hey," she whispers.

"I just wanted to say hi. Don't trip going up the stairs." I joke and she glares. Honestly, it's funny because when we practiced this yesterday, she did trip. Her face was beet red, and she was afraid it would happen again today.

"Ha Ha, Parker." I grin and wink. Her face flushes, and she bites that damn lip.

Okay, so maybe now I'm a little more excited about graduation.

CHAPTER 13

Silence is a peculiar moment. It can either be calming, refreshing and just perfect—or it can be the loudest moment of confusion with unsaid words and unheard fears. Some silent moments are scary as hell.

I'm sitting in Josh's truck, both of us silent. So many things need to be said. It's just ironic that *Say Something* by A Great Big World is on the radio. We're both just listening, probably thinking the same thing. We are sitting outside the restaurant, not ready to leave this space yet. We've already taken one step into a new future. We're no longer high school students, but what now? Neither of us is saying it. He knows I heard his dad. He has to know, but we aren't talking about it—we're just kissing and holding onto each other like we are the others lifeline.

"Riley?" "Josh?" We both say at the same time when the song is over.

"You go first," he says.

I take a deep breath and slowly puff it out. "I love kissing you and even though we've been doing a lot more of that then we have done talking—I think it's time we talk about stuff. Don't you?" I look over into his eyes.

He is sitting so still, his breathing becoming labored. He punches the steering wheel and curses.

"I can't, Riley. I hate what needs to be said. I'm not ready to say what needs to be said. I love you. I just want to feel this, not think about it and not face what's next. I know we need to talk. I do. I just— FUCK it. I don't know how to do this and not today, okay?"

"Okay. I get why you don't want to talk today because you think whatever it is will upset me, and you don't want to upset me on my birthday. But Josh, do what exactly? Tell me the truth? Are you breaking up with me?" My voice just a slow whisper.

His eyes dart to mine. "What the fuck, are you talking about? I'm NOT breaking up with you. I'm just...we will just be. No! I don't want to do this right now. You want to know how serious I am about you. I will show you." He then he turns off the truck and comes around to my door.

He opens my door, his eyes lock with mine as he unbuckles my seat belt. I'm wearing a white sundress. He reaches under my legs to pick me up—it makes me squeal.

"My legs aren't broken you know?" I joke to him as he carries me from his truck to the restaurant. I'm not complaining at all. I mean, my hands are wrapped around his neck, and my head is nestled on his shoulder. So obviously I am content right where I am. Besides, he looks downright edible in his black slacks and white button down shirt, with one side loosely un-tucked and the top buttons undone.

He kisses my head and chuckles, "Maybe I'm practicing."

I lift my head to look at him, "Practicing for?" I ask with piqued curiosity.

He stops and his eyes lock with mine with such intensity that I feel the need to squirm, or look away, but I can't move because he is holding me, and I can't look away because his eyes have cast a spell on me.

"For walking you over the threshold one day as, Mrs. Parker. Not anytime soon of course, but one day. That is what I see for us in the future—not us being apart." He graces me with a tempting dimple.

"I like practicing," I whisper, biting my lip to hide my grin.

"Yeah?"

I nod, "M'hm. Maybe we could practice what happens after you walk me over the threshold later?"

"After? Is that when you cook me dinner, baby?" He laughs when he sees my face scrunch up. "I'm kidding, Shaw. We can share the cooking skills."

I shove at his chest, "That's better, Parker. Keep undigging your hole, jerk face. Besides, we're eating dinner here, so that leaves dessert only."

He grins playfully. "Hmmm you do make the sweetest brownies." He leans down to whisper in my ear, his breath tickling me. "I looove the taste of you and brownies—perfect fucking dessert."

Holy Shit. How many times is he going to make me say that in a day?

He lifts his face up, and his eyes land right on my mouth. He ever so slowly leans down and licks the corner of my mouth just as he did that day when he kissed me for the first time—that day where we tasted each other—and brownies.

How many effin girls get kissed for the first time with chocolate goodness incorporated?

Chocolate and his lips...yum—my favorite.

He licks my lips, and I forget how to breathe. Our brownie kiss is definitely not something I could ever forget either.

He smirks seeing my eyes stare at his lips. "So, you are responsible for dessert or just be dessert. I'm not picky." He waggles his eyebrows suggestively, and it's like his words have a direct connect line to something we haven't explored yet, something I want to explore—so badly.

"I like brownies, but I think I'd like being your dessert, too." I smile sweetly up at him.

His eyes search mine, looking for something, and his face turns serious all of a sudden. We are no longer moving. He slowly sets me down leaving my hands tangled around his neck and his tightly around my waist. I'm confused by his sudden change in playfulness. I'm aware that we are both distracting each other again and ignoring what needs to be discussed.

His eyes flick to my lips and then bounce back and forth from each of my eyes. "We have plenty of time to get to dessert, Riley. How about we just enjoy our...brownies...until you know for sure you're ready for...um, dessert."

I think he just made my heart melt. He is so adorably sexy. I never knew adorable and sexy could be the same thing, but he totally is both of those. He knows the way Dean was with me, and he is clearly worried we are moving too fast. He wants to be sure I'm ready. I am.

At least, when he is looking at me like that and touching me the way he does—I think I am.

I let my hands slide down his neck and chest until I reach the bottom of his shirt. I place my hands inside of his shirt so I can feel his skin. He takes in a breath, and his heart hammers underneath my palm as I glide them up. He is warm, and his muscles are artfully sculpted just for my hands—to explore.

I look up at him through my lashes and smile coyly. "I enjoy brownies with you...very much, Josh. I'm tired of wasting so much time, though. I've had years with the wrong guy, years doubting love and everything about it, years without dessert with you. I'm ready for dessert with you. Okay? I want to have dessert, Josh. When I felt your skin on my bareback this morning, I knew it then. I knew I wanted to feel all of you pressed against me." I bite my lip.

And then he is on me. Hands in my hair—tongue in my mouth. We kiss desperately. Pouring everything we want with each other into that kiss—releasing years of longing, of desire, of want.

When we pull apart we are both panting for air and staring at each other, and then we are at it again. "I haven't been able to get the image of you like that out of my mind," he says between our kisses and breaths of air.

"Let's get this over with." He smiles devilishly at me.

When we get to our table, my mom is already in tears. Josh does that guy pat and hug thing with his dad, then he leans down to kiss his sister on the cheek.

"I can't believe you're eighteen. Y'all are leaving the nest, soon. Can you believe it, James?" she asks Josh's dad.

I cringe thinking about what it means for Josh and me to leave the nest. Josh's dad looks a little pissed. He gives Josh a look that tells me he and Josh are still at odds.

"Nope, I can't believe it," he replies a little miffed, masking his irritation with a forced smile. They stare coldly at each other, which is so unusual. I hate that they are doing so.

Our parents are across from us, and our sisters are together at the other end. I try to overlook the fact that my mom has a margarita in her glass. I've lectured her more than once on not drinking with her medication. I hate when she drinks in the first place. It's like this coping mechanism we all seem to suffer from, but this is a celebration, so...

Dinner conversation flows freely, and laughter fills me with a sense of thankfulness as we eat together. Even with the unspoken fear looming in the air—I feel extremely happy—excited about the summer ahead with, Josh—excited to finally be eighteen.

I open a present from my sister. It's a new notebook that says, *You're a little weird. I like it.* It makes me smile. Joey gives me a scrapbook with lots of photos of Josh and me, from childhood to now. I love it beyond words. My mom hands me a book full of poetry. It actually shocks me, because it means she pays attention to the small things I love, and as a last minute gift, it's pretty darn generous. Josh's dad grins and tells me that he paid for Joey's gift, so that is from him, too. Josh says he is giving me his gift in private, which makes our sisters giggle and my mom glare. Josh's dad remains in the grey tonight.

A group of the wait staff makes me wear a sombrero as they sing in Spanish. Because it is my birthday, they give me a free sopapilla with honey. The entire time I eat it; I'm thinking about what dessert will be like with, Josh. Will I be good at it? He watches me lick the honey with *that* look—that one that says he wants a taste. That one look turns my insides into mush.

Conversations continue around me, but I'm having a hard time concentrating on who is saying what, though, because Josh keeps brushing his knuckles along the outside of my leg. Perhaps, wearing my sundress wasn't the best idea. My head is already clouded with...ideas of us naked and the taste of brownies on my lips.

"So, Riley...your mom said your headaches have finally gone away. That's good. I bet you were excited about not missing the last week of school?" Mr. Parker asks with eyes so much like Josh's, twinkling friendly at me.

I nod and shrug at the same time. "If I could have gotten away with missing, I think I would have taken it." I laugh lightly. I most definitely could have done without the rumor mill and the bullshit of last week.

He nods. "I remember the way it was. So eager to leave it all behind, but then you become a grown up and miss it. Right, Claudia?" He glances to my mom slowly working on her second margarita. He adds, "Kids these days are so quick to grow up." I don't miss the flick of his eyes toward, Josh.

My mom gets a look of irritation, but composes it into a friendly smile before replying. "Well, I can't say much. I was one of those kids that grew up too fast. But yeah, you kids should just enjoy being young while it last—NOT be in a hurry to *experience* everything." She smiles, but it doesn't reach her eyes, and again I'm reminded of why she grew up so fast, and even if she says she wanted me, I think the slightest regret does exist. I also know what she meant by not being in a hurry to experience everything. She doesn't want me to move so fast.

It's just, I feel like I need to grab this moment, take it and never let it go. The truth is, I might lose it. It may slip right through my fingers, and I need it.

Josh turns to whisper in my ear at the same time he places his hand onto my knee. "I like this dress," he says, as he slowly inches his hand higher up my leg.

I bite my lip—hard. I'm trying not to react to his touch, to his voice and to his breath in my ear. I can't help it, though. Thankfully, the table is covered with a long tablecloth, and we are sitting so close to each other, no one would guess his hand is traveling up my thigh.

He licks my ear discreetly and turns back to the conversations. He is totally composed, carrying on a conversation with our parents as if he isn't inching his hand in between my legs now.

The blood is roaring in my ears, and my breathing is shallow as I intentionally slow it so not to pant and writhe in this chair. My heart is pounding in my chest with nervous energy shooting throughout my body. *What should I do? Let him touch me?*

I don't even realize I'm doing it, but I'm inviting his touch when I slowly part my legs for him. He side glances at me, as if for just a moment he needs to see my reaction to him or make sure I'm agreeing. His eyes hold the unasked question—smoldering with want for me.

I meet his gaze as I bite my lip and reach under the table to place my hand over his. I make sure the tablecloth covers my entire lap, and

I sit back in my chair. If anyone were to look at me, they would just assume I am comfortable. *I am so comfortable.*

I open my legs just enough for me to guide his hand where I want it. He cups me over my panties, and I almost gasp at the feeling. My hand is still over his, and I feel him move one finger along the edge. He is slightly moving the soft fabric to the side. It's all so deliberate, so slow—so unbelievably torturous—and completely wrong as we are in a restaurant full of people, full of our families.

Holy shit! I was so nervous about today, but now I am in love with it. If this is an appetizer to dessert, I so need dessert with Josh.

He touches me just a little. I guess just to feel my desire. I apply pressure to one of his fingers to beg him to enter me. *Oh God, please touch me.*

He very gently pushes one finger inside of me, and I am coming done. I am focused on his movements, on his now two fingers as they push into me when I'm suddenly shocked back to my surroundings.

My mom's voice filters into my ears unbidden. "Honey, are you alright? You look flushed. You're not getting a headache, are you? Coming down with something?"

Oh hell. No, headache...but I am coming down with something. I feel Josh's eyes on my face, and the smirk on his face makes me want to climb on top of his lap and give everyone here the shock of their lives.

I'm shaking my head back and forth as I'm incapable of speech. At the same time, I am wishing for him to go deeper into me, he isn't moving anymore, and I need him to. I want to move so badly, but I can't. He feels so completely delicious, and my body is craving something I don't understand. I need something. I need him to move faster. I need more of this.

I don't get it though. Evidently, the bills have been paid, and everyone is beginning to stand, as goodbyes must have been said around me unnoticed. He withdraws his fingers and smiles. "You kids have fun tonight," my mom says as I watch in a daze as they all leave the table.

I have to gather myself. I adjust my panties and push my dress back down. I'm not even sure that I am even capable of standing. I am completely dizzy and beyond shocked.

Josh must not be aware of this because he places his fingers into his mouth as he locks eyes with my wide ones—shocking me further. With his other hand, he reaches for me to place mine in his. I do, never looking away from his eyes, as he tastes me on his fingers. It does something strange to me. He releases them with a pop and places both fingers to my lips, where I kiss them because I don't know what else to do. His eyes darken and dilate right before me. *Damn.*

Can anyone else see that we are completely undressing each other right now?

I hear a throat clear and realize we are blocking the aisle. I blink my eyes a few times, and move out of the way.

"Sorry, I uh...we should go. That um, was...dinner was...yummy," I stutter. Josh laughs a full-on belly laugh. I watch even more mesmerized with him in this moment. The way his cheeks get rosy and his eyes light up. It really is a sight and sound to experience. He's tugging at my hand to follow him as his guffaws soften, and I realize that this night has just taken a sudden turn I hadn't expected. *Happy birthday to me!*

When we get outside, the sudden rush of fresh air cools my warm skin. I take in a lungful because I've been holding my breath for so long. I head to the truck door with my back to, Josh—unable to look back at him. I go to open it, but he puts his hand on the door and presses his chest against my back—depleting me of air again. I lower my head, and he moves the hair out of my face. He kisses that spot between my neck and shoulder as my body reactively tilts to the side to welcome it. He's unraveling me. "You smell so good," he whispers against my ear as he inhales my scent.

My mouth parts as a rush of air escapes, when he releases me from his spell. He backs away—the distance allowing me to breathe again. He opens my door for me. I'm having a hard time looking at him. I'm sort of embarrassed by what we just did, what I let him do, what I encouraged him to do. Even if it was just a tease—we did it.

He lifts me into his truck as always, and reaches for my seatbelt—just barely brushes his knuckles across my breast as he reaches across my chest to buckle me in—I'm unsure if done by accident or intentional. I still haven't spoken or made eye contact, but I softly gasp involuntarily when he touches my boob. I can feel his eyes on me, but I don't yet meet them.

He stares at me for a moment before he shuts the door and comes around and gets in on his side. He turns the ignition and *Bloodstream* by Stateless comes through the radio. It's hypnotic and very suiting for what I feel right now.

I have my hands folded in my lap, and I'm just staring down at them. I don't know why I feel shy, but I do.

He turns in his seat as he fully un-tucks his shirt, and with his index finger under my chin he guides my face to look at him. My eyes slowly lift to meet his, and I find him intently looking at my face. I turn to look away.

"Why aren't you looking at me, Riley?" His voice is a mere husky whisper.

I answer so quietly I don't even know how he hears me, "I'm embarrassed."

He tucks a curl behind my ear. "Why? I'm not. That was so fucking hot, Riley."

My eyes cut to his, and I couldn't look away even if I wanted too. "I've never done anything like that before. I felt out of control, Josh." I admit. I lean my head to the side of the seat as I mirror his position, pulling my legs up on to the seat.

He mimics my move by resting his head on his own seat—his face just a few inches from mine now. "I never have, either. Did you like the way it felt?" he asks.

My mouth suddenly feels dry, and I lick my lips just to wet them. His eyes watch its path. "Yes. I liked it...a lot. I wanted..." I trail off, unable to say what I wanted, what I felt.

He moves his face closer to mine—just a breath away now. "You wanted what?" He whispers the words almost against my lips.

"I wanted more. I didn't want you to stop. That is crazy. People were there and I...I just wanted...you," I admit.

His eyes twinkle sinfully. His smirk deepens the dimple I love so much. I want to lick it, but I don't.

He releases my buckle and pulls me to the middle of the seat. His finger trails down my cheek, down my neck, down my rib cage, and to the hem of my dress. He moves underneath the fabric, placing his hand firmly on my thigh and up to my waist. I jerk a little. His eyes never leave mine as he moves his mouth closer. I can't help it. I lick his dimple, and he groans. He licks my lips, and I moan. He glides his hand further up my dress until his hand begins to feel me up, as our lips finally touch and begin a wicked dance together.

"Josh?" I breathe between kisses.

"Mmm?" He replies in between kisses as his thumb twirls around my nipple over my bra.

"What are we doing?" I ask pulling away, breathlessly.

He grins and moves his hand back down my stomach, and down the outside of thigh and around the curve of my ass. "You're not the only one feeling out of control. I haven't been able to think straight since I saw you practically naked."

He leans into my neck and begins licking and kissing me there. Once again, I'm nervous someone is watching. I've never been more thankful for his tinted windows and that it's dark outside because I need him to keep doing what he is doing. He pulls away just slightly catching a glimpse of my necklace. He moves his hand back to the top of my leg and touches the charms with his other hand. His eyes warm and his lips curl up into a smile.

"Where did you get this?" he asks.

"Emily. It's my birthday present. Something about the pixie reunited with her music."

His soft smile is now wide and just beautiful. His eyes lift to mine, and they heat instantly. "I love that," he says tracing the line of my lips with his thumb.

"I love you," I mutter.

He gently presses my legs down onto the seat, turning my body to the front. He has his hand sprawled out on the top of my leg as his thumb caresses the inner part of my thigh. "I love you, too. I love that necklace, and I love this dress," he breathes the words hot in my ear, then gently nibbles on it.

"God, Josh." He's slowly coaxing my legs to open for him, at the same time he is licking the spot behind my ear that makes me shiver.

"Do you want more?" He whispers into my ear as his hands slides into my panties.

I can't control my breathing now. I can't *not* pant or writhe. I can't control what my body wants, and it wants more. "Yes, please. I want more." I am shocked at how my own voice sounds when I speak—breathy and needy.

He cups my sex and his thumb pushes on the spot that has me throwing my head back in ecstasy.

He feels me again just like before. "You're so wet for me," he whispers.

"Please, Josh." I beg.

He kisses my lips, his tongue seeking permission to enter my mouth. I part my lips, and as if the timing were crucial, his tongue moves into my mouth at the same time his fingers enter me. He moves slowly...in and out. And his kiss deepens at the same time I roll my hips into his hand, leaning further back into the seat.

Moans and whimpers are embarrassingly coming out of me, as I've never felt such pleasure before. I can't hold them back. I try to remain quiet. I try to be still. But I can't do either. I'm shamelessly rubbing myself against his hand. He groans deep in his throat as I do. He begins to move faster and deeper and whatever I need—whatever this feeling is tightening inside of me—I know it's about to be unleashed with delicious force.

I can't breathe. I try to break free of his lips just to catch my breath, but he doesn't let me. He catches every moan and every whimper with his mouth. His thumb pushes down on my spot again.

This is it.

I understand now why girls get addicted to this. Easy or not, it's hard to not want this feeling, once you've had it. I'm in love. I'm on fire. It's all in perfect symphony to the music filling the cab of his truck. It's beautiful—he is beautiful. What he is making me feel is beautiful.

I'm grabbing his hair with one of my hands as he kisses me senseless, and the other hand is feeling him explore me. He is right...it's so hot. Feeling him touch me for the first time is a heady mix.

I bite his lip, and the sound he makes deep in his throat sends me over the edge. My head falls back and my back arches. He licks a path down my neck and begins to circle his thumb and move in and out as my body squeezes deliciously around him.

"Oh God, Josh. Ah...that feels..." I say between pants and moans not even able to finish my thought before all I can do is feel.

I've never felt an orgasm before. Not like that. I've touched myself, but it has never, ever made me feel...that. When I'm done shaking and trembling under his touch, he removes his hand.

Once again, he shocks me by placing his fingers onto his tongue. This time, I shock him, as well. I move my face right to his and grab his wrist. I pull his fingers away from his mouth and take them into my own. It's so unexplainable...how it affects me, and then his mouth devours mine. Tasting me on his tongue is a heady concoction and makes my mind wonder how that too would feel. He is amazing with his fingers, and his kisses make me crazy. Kisses *there* would damn near kill me.

When I pull back, his eyes are clouded with lust and love. I smile and bite my lip. I'm not sure if I should thank him. I'm not sure what the protocol is for what he just did to me. But I feel completely sated and like I should thank him. I don't though.

"Better?" he asks, smirking at me.

I nod. *Dessert is going to be delicious.* I think to myself but then realize I've said that thought out loud.

Shit.

He laughs, "Damn straight. But playing is just as much fun." He winks at me, and turns to put the truck into reverse.

What the hell did we just do? Wow...like I have no other words but wow.

I spend the rest of the ride listening to him sing the chorus to *Bloodstream* and thinking that I will never listen to this song again without remembering how he felt.

Josh takes us to our spot. I'm completely shocked when we get there. My eyes dart to his in response. "How did you do this?"

He shrugs and drapes his arm around my shoulder. "A guy never tells his secrets in that department, baby girl." I'm speechless.

By our tree, lies a blanket surrounded by a few tea light candles and a small basket. It's so beautiful. Once we reach the spot, I feel all teary eyed. I just don't know what I did to deserve him. I just can't believe he is truly mine after all these years—after everything my family has cost his. I wipe a stray tear as it falls and turn to find his eyes watching me carefully. "I love you, Josh. I completely and without a doubt love you." He smiles the softest of smiles. He's so gorgeous under the moonlight and the candles that flicker against his olive skin. "I never thought we would be together, you know? I just knew it was impossible after everything, but somehow I got lucky."

"I'm the one that's lucky," he says.

"Not a chance. I'm nothing special, but you...you are so beyond special it almost seems unfair that you would be stuck with me."

His smile falters. "You have no idea how special you are. Do you?"

I don't reply. I just stare at him—uncertain. His hands cup my cheeks as he squats down to look into my eyes. "You are the most beautiful girl I have ever had the pleasure of laying my eyes on. Your heart, although you think is cold, is so full of love for everyone in your life. You care more about the people around you than you do yourself. The fact that you don't know how special you are makes you that more special to me, and makes me want to spend every day for the rest of my life showing it to you until you believe it. I have never in my life loved someone as deeply as I do you, besides family, of course. I need to see your smile, to hear your voice, to just be anywhere in your presence just to breathe. I wasn't fully living before you. I've only just begun now, and now that I have you, I don't ever want to lose you."

I brush my fingertips across his cheekbones. This moment—this one moment between us—it's so completely beautiful. I almost think it's a dream, but then his lips touch mine, and I know. I know that, for the first time, I'm not dreaming about him. I'm not wishing he were mine, because he is. He is actually with me. Loving me, kissing me, and I never want this moment to end.

He coaxes me down onto the blanket as he kisses my mouth. I am addicted to his lips. He pulls away, and I whimper in protest. "I didn't bring you here to make out." He smiles as I adjust my dress and sit up.

"Okay."

He reaches over to the basket and pulls out a small box with a bow attached. "I want you to have this because it's your birthday present, but I don't want to explain it completely just yet. Okay?"

I meet his eyes, unsure of exactly what he means by explain it completely. I nod my head, remove the bow, and lift the lid off of the box. Inside, I find a silver box with various shapes of stars on the top. It's beautiful. I'm unsure what it is, but it's beautiful. I delicately touch the box all over as I feel the indents of inscription in the front of it. I turn it into my lap, but I can't read it in the dark. I move to where the candles are brighter and read, *For each star in the sky, I have a reason why I love you. When you look up at night, never forget this truth.*

I look up at him, and he takes the box, flips it over and presses a button, which illuminate the stars. My breath catches as light comes out of each star shining on the blanket. I flip it over and realize it's a nightlight of stars. "The idea is that no matter where I am, the stars will shine for you...to remind you of all the reasons why I love you. The reasons are endless. The stars will never disappear."

Wow. No matter where he is? I don't miss it, and that is what he means by not explaining it completely.

I don't want to discuss his not being near either. "It's beautiful, Josh. I love it." I put it down and climb to my knees to give him a kiss. "No matter where you are, know that I'm looking up at those stars thinking of you and wishing we were counting them together."

He stares at me for a long time, just touching my face, tracing around my features like he's memorizing them. He sighs deep in his chest as he leans into my face. I meet him half way as we kiss, slow and deliberate. It's not the desperate kiss. This kiss is passionate and full of the love we have for each other.

We spend a lot of time lying back on the blanket stargazing as he tells me just a few of the reasons why he loves me. Of course, I have many reasons in response. He's right...the reasons are endless.

My phone pings from inside my purse. "Sorry." I reach in and find a text from Emily.

Em: AT COLLIN'S. COME PLEASE. *PUPPY EYES

I laugh, and Josh looks at me puzzled. "Em went to Collin's, and she wants me to come. Party time as usual I guess?"

"We can go. I told him that we might. I just didn't want to commit since it's your birthday."

He's lying back with his hands behind his head looking very comfortable. I crawl on top of his stomach, fold my hands under my chin and smile. "I think attending a party at Collin's for the first time as Joshua Parkers girlfriend would be a ton of fun."

He smirks. "Is that so?"

"M'hm. Perhaps you could take me upstairs, and we could have dessert." I bite my lip and wait for my statement to click in his brain. There it goes... 3, 2, and 1.

He rolls me onto my back, pressing his hips into me. A soft moan escapes my lips. "Baby, I'm not making love to you in Collin's bed. That's like sharing you with other people, and I am not sharing you. Besides, when I love you for the first time, I want to take my time, to remember every sound you make as you respond to me...for it to be just us, no inhibitions and for our eyes and ears only."

I smile, and tug his shirt to pull him to me. "I love you. I don't care where it is, as long as I'm with you."

He tucks my hair out of my eyes and studies my face. "I love you too, Riley. I want you...badly. I'm sure you can feel that." I *can* feel him. "Not tonight, though. Okay? Not at his house, not in my truck, not here on this blanket. It needs to be special because you are special, and you deserve that."

I nod and once again, wonder how I managed to get so lucky. Most guys don't care where or how it happens, just as long as it does. Josh wants to cherish me.

"Let's go before I try to change your mind," I wink making him laugh.

He kisses my forehead, and we gather our stuff, blowing out the candles.

CHAPTER 14

On replay in my mind is the way Riley looked and felt last night in my truck as she shivered. The sounds she made when I touched her for the first time have me high. A high I never want to come down from.

I wake up on Collin's couch feeling slightly hung-over. I have Riley's body on top of mine. She wriggles a little, and I smile as I snuggle her tighter to me.

Collin walks in the door with a grocery bag and a smirk. "I'm glad y'all are dressed," he says grinning.

"I heard that," Riley says, groaning.

I laugh. She climbs up off of me and stands. I watch mesmerized as she stretches like a feline. I clear my throat and look away. It's getting harder to breathe around her without taking everything she has.

"I'm not one of the skanky hoes you let roam this house at your parties, Collin," Riley says.

Collin eyes flick to the balcony where his room is. I try to remember whom he took up there last night, but I don't.

"I know that, Riley. I was just joking with y'all." Collin says defensively.

"I'm going to the bathroom," she says walking down the hall.

Collin actually looks sheepish all the sudden. It's weird, and suddenly I care a lot about who he took upstairs last night. His eyes keep flicking up there. "Why do you look nervous?" I ask.

He looks at me and sets down the bag full of breakfast burritos. "I um, I sort of hooked up with someone that I'm sure I shouldn't have." He frowns and sits on the recliner with his head in his hands.

"Who? I already know it wasn't Preslee, thanks for that by the way." I say.

Last night, we were well on our way to having a kick ass graduation party when like the bitch she is, Preslee tried to crash it.

We were all standing in the yard drinking and having a good time when Preslee arrived with Laiken. Time froze and all eyes were on Riley. Turns out the head of the rumor mill had a name—Preslee. She was the one that had videoed us, then sent the video around. She apparently was also behind all of the notes. Needless to say, shit got real, and Riley wasn't holding anything back with her anymore—not that she had before.

"You shouldn't be here," Collin said, "Only my friends are invited, and you aren't on that list," he added.

Preslee laughed. "Oh, I'm not your friend? Just a quick fuck when you need it? Real nice, Collin," she snapped.

Riley was tipsy and a lot bolder. "Oh, my God. Is there anyone you haven't fucked? You are such a slut," she said.

"I'm a what?" Preslee shouted as the group of us laughed our asses off.

"Should you even be partying in your condition?" Riley asked her, ignoring her last question. I couldn't agree more with her terminology for Preslee.

Preslee's gaze raked up and down Riley with disgust, and she rolled her eyes. "And what condition is that exactly?" she asked full of irritation.

I debated on intervening, but it was entertaining seeing Riley handle her own. "Um, well let's see...you being with child, bun in the oven, preggers or just plain fucked. However, you consider it? It's a condition," Riley said, gesturing to Preslee's stomach.

Preslee smiles and bites her finger, "Oh that. Well, come to find out it was just a false positive. I'm good to do whatever I *want*." She actually looked at me when she said *want* as if it were a possibility. That chick was crazy.

"WHAT!" WHAT!" Riley and I both said at the same time.

"Does Dean know?" Riley asked. Of course, that pissed me off. I wondered why she would care.

Preslee snorted, "Tsk tsk, Riley. Should you care about how your ex-boyfriend feels? I was kidding. I'm pregnant, but you know what's good about that. I can fuck whomever I want—slow or hard—all fucking night—and I don't have to worry about getting knocked up because your boyfriend already handled that. Oh, ex-boyfriend I mean."

"You're a fucking bitch!" Riley shouted throwing the remains of her drink in Preslee's face.

Preslee squealed, and all of us stood their speechless with wide eyes.

"Preslee get the fuck off my property and leave Riley and Josh alone!" Collin gestured to her car.

Preslee ringed out her hair and wiped her face. "Seriously? You are choosing her over us, Collin?" Laiken asked, finally piping in.

Collin walked right up to both of them, "Yeah, I am. You're right, neither of you were ever my friends. You were both just quick fucks that a lot of us enjoyed from time to time, but I'm done. Now leave!"

They did. The rest of the night was less drama. Just a few close friends having a good time together.

"Hey, what time did Emily leave last night? I don't even remember her telling me bye." Riley says, walking back in the room, not allowing enough time for Collin to tell me who he hooked up with.

Collin's eyes dart to mine, and in an instant I know.

Riley has her phone in her hand. She clicks a few buttons and then puts the phone up to her ear. The ringing starts—the ringing we all hear—because it's coming from upstairs.

Her eyes cut to the shut door above the balcony and then widen. She looks back to Collin, "You didn't?"

Collin looks down. *Oh damn.*

"Hello?" She says into the receiver. "Hey, Em. Sleep well?" *Pause* "I'm not yelling. You never told me bye last night. I got worried since Josh and I crashed on the couch."

"OH, MY GOD! Where the hell are my clothes?" We hear Emily shout from upstairs.

"She hung up on me." Riley says dropping her phone to the coffee table. "Is this breakfast? Awesome. I'm starved," she says grabbing a burrito.

Collin and I exchange a look, as Riley acts nonchalantly as she bites into her breakfast burrito.

"You're not mad?" Collin asks.

Riley's eyes harden, "Oh, I'm fucking pissed, Collin. But Emily is a big girl, and she makes her own decisions." She sets her burrito down and leans forward, "But if I hear you refer to my best friend as a quick fuck in any future conversations with anyone, I will cut your balls off and hang them for the pit bulls next door to devour. K?"

Holy Shit!

Collin just stares in disbelief at Riley as she picks up her burrito and devours it. "Thanks for breakfast. I will be upstairs helping my best friend find her clothes before she does the walk of shame." Then she leaves.

"Damn, dude," Collin says.

"I know, right. She is amazing," I say.

"What are you going to do in a few weeks without her?" he asks. We got our schedules, and we have summer drills in July that I haven't yet told Riley about. Shit, I haven't told Riley anything about any of it yet, even though I know she knows.

I run my hand across my face, "Go crazy," I answer truthfully.

It's been an amazing two weeks for Riley and me, even with the looming fate nearby, as I have to leave in a few weeks. We've been actively doing things outside of her bedroom and mine, purposely avoiding the temptation of going further. I'm not sure what we are waiting for, but it's just not the right time yet. So we hang out. We go to the movies, and we swim at the lake, which let's face it—seeing her in a bikini is distracting and just as tempting, but we've been good— until today.

Her mom and sister left to go to Sugar Lake earlier today for a weekend away. Riley stayed behind due to Beau's wedding tomorrow.

We get the weekend to ourselves in a hotel in San Antonio, separate of course. We leave tomorrow and for tonight we are behaving.

"I hate my hair," she gripes staring at herself in the mirror as I watch her try to tame her curls. She just took a shower, and my mind starts imagining what Riley looks like wet and lathered in soap. *Shit!*

Clarification—trying to behave.

I reach for the brush and come to stand behind her. "Let me." I meet her eyes in the mirror. She smiles. I love her smile.

I take to brushing my girlfriend's hair, and it's the best damn feeling in the world. I don't know why. It just gives me a warming sensation in my chest. So does the way she breathes shallowly when I'm this close to her. So does the way she stares at me in the mirror with a look of wonder. I love that she is affected by me.

"There. You're beautiful and tangle free." I say as I place the brush on the dresser in front of her. I rest my chin on her shoulder and stare at her in the mirror. "We look great together, huh? We are so going to make some awesome looking babies together one day." She laughs. I love her laugh, too.

She rolls her eyes. "You're so crazy." She wiggles away and starts putting away folded clothes from the basket next to her dresser. I laugh, as she seems flustered.

I lean against her dresser with my ankles crossed and ask amused, "Watcha doing?"

"Laundry," she says grabbing a handful of undergarments to place in the top drawer next to me. I visually begin exploring the lot of them.

"Nice," I say as I reach in the drawer to retrieve ivory silk and bring it to my nose. She gasps and snatches them out of my hand.

"Oh, my God, perv. Give those back. They probably smell like downy soft not pussy."

Holy shit! As soon as the word leaves her mouth, her cheeks flame the sexiest shade of pink and her hand covers her mouth. My eyes dart to her in surprise. "Oh hell, you said the p word."

She puts her head down and starts fiddling with the laundry again. "It wasn't on purpose. I just...ugh...go over there," she says, shooing me with her hand.

I can't help but chuckle at her innocence on some things. I love it...a lot to be honest. I sit down on her bed and rest back comfortably with my hands behind my head. She can't meet my eyes. She's embarrassed. "What's the big deal with you and saying stuff like that? You say fuck all the time, and that doesn't bother you."

As if her cheeks couldn't get any sexier with her blushing, she turns to glare at me. Her hands on her hips and her head tilted to the side. "For your information, Josh, I say fuck in a different context—like you're so fucking stupid or what the fuck? I don't say, fuck like, I want you to fuck me, Josh," she says in one deep breath. *Damn.*

She looks away. Everything in her statement and her body language tells me that it is what she wants though. "But you do, though?"

"Do what?"

I reach out and grab her hand, pulling her to the bed, where I flip her to her back and breathe in the scent of her by her neck. She shivers. I breathe the words into her ear, "Want me to fuck you. It's written in your eyes. You might not have said it...sober that is, but you do want it. Don't you?" She whimpers as I reach my hand under her shirt and feel her skin.

"Yes," she answers breathlessly.

I pull back to study her eyes, and I see her answer. That edge of decision is no longer there. She wants me. She is ready to take this step, but am I? I claim her mouth, cherishing it, tasting every bit of her sweetness. She is so damn delicious. I can never get enough. When we pull apart, out of breath, I lock eyes with hers and grin. "I guess we have a problem then," I state full of mischief.

Her eyes lift in question. "Why's that?"

I roll off of her and feign unaffected, "Because, I'm not that easy."

She laughs, and the sound of it is like music—a symphony of angels singing. "You are ridiculously crazy, Parker." She snuggles up to my shoulder as I wrap an arm around her. She drapes her leg over my waist, and we both sigh in contentment.

"I can't help it. You make me crazy, but in a good way, of course." I admire her eyes. Today, they are more green than blue. Gorgeous.

She begins to rub circles on my stomach under my shirt. "So, tomorrow will be our first wedding together. You promise to try not and propose to me? I know it's going to be tough being as though you love me so much and stuff." She grins.

I smile and shake my head, "Now, you are crazy." I peck her lips. "For now, you are safe, but I make no promises on the future of non-proposals. We have a forever future to plan, remember? A wedding is just another moment of practicing for us."

She smiles and nods, and then we spend the next several minutes reminding each other's mouths of how crazy in love for each other we are.

Moments later, we are lying on her bed listening to music. She has my shirt lifted, and she's writing something on my chest with a pen. It tickles, and I'm curious about what she is writing. She places a soft kiss to where my heart is and then she lowers my shirt and climbs back into her spot. "Done," she says.

"What did you write?" I ask grinning at her.

"You will see it when you get undressed later. Don't peek until then. Promise?"

"Promise."

She rolls onto her back and places her head into the crook of my shoulder and neck. She lifts my hand into the air and interlaces our fingers. I pull our intertwined hands to my lips and kiss them. She begins to hum along with City and Colour.

I have my other hand dangling off the bed, and Tink is rubbing her body against it. I decide to be stupid as I scoop her up onto the bed.

I open my mouth and wait for her horror, "I never thought I'd be the kind of guy to say this but...I really love your pussy—,"

She jumps up and stares down at me, "WHAT?"

I laugh because she didn't let me finish, and I knew that would be her reaction. She can be so predictable about some stuff. Tink meows and I point to her, "Cat, Riley. I was going to say I really love your pussycat." I tap my index finger to her nose. "You have such a dirty mind, pretty girl." I laugh at her shocked face that is a pretty pink color again. I love it when she blushes. I don't know what it is about that word and her.

She takes Tink, puts her on her chest and begins to pet her fur. "Whatever, Josh. Who says pussycat? She is a cat or a kitten. Only in nursery rhymes are they called pussycats. You know you were being perverted by saying pus—by saying that word." She ignores my rolling laughter. "I still can't believe you bought me a kitten. She's my best friend," she says, deflating the joke.

She's so right. I'm totally being perverted, and hearing her say the P word isn't helping my mind climb out of the gutter. Not.at.all. Her shyness only makes her more adorable to me.

"Hey, I thought I was your best friend?" I mock offense.

She puts Tink down and rolls on top of me and begins kissing my neck and up to my jaw. "You know what you are to me," she whispers.

I shake my head. "No, I need convincing. I'm not so sure. What am I to you?" I run my hands down her back and cup her ass.

She licks my dimple and makes me intake a breath of air.

"You are my best friend, my boyfriend, my addiction, my obsession. You, Joshua Parker are everything I crave. "

And then she convinces me in the sweetest way with her lips. I'm addicted to her, too. Her mouth. Her taste. The sounds she makes. The way she feels—everything about her. I crave her just as much.

I roll on top of her and kiss along her neck, "You, Ms. Shaw, are equally addicting. I love the way you smell and taste."

But knowing this tangled web of limbs and lips, and talks of pussy and fucking, is going to get us in heaps of trouble, I climb off of her and stand.

She flutters her lids open and sits up. "What are you doing?" she asks pouting.

I laugh. "We can't hang out in your bed anymore, Riley." *What the hell am I saying?*

"Why not? We're all alone—finally." She pouts, climbing onto her knees on her bed. Her head tilted adorably to the side.

I move forward and cup her chin. "Because, baby. You're tempting."

She lifts up and puts her arms around my neck, tangling her fingers into my hair. She licks the corner of my mouth and pecks my mouth. "Tempting how?" She asks in a sultry and seductive voice. I know she isn't naive. She knows what she is doing.

I wind her hair around my hand and tug just a little causing her to gasp. "You know damn well what you're doing, baby."

She bites her lip innocently as she glides her hands down my chest. She puts one leg on either side of me and pulls me towards her. My stomach is lined up with her mouth, and for a moment I can't breathe.

She lifts my shirt and kisses my stomach. She lets her hands explore my chest...and *shit*, she is killing me. Her delicate fingers begin to trace certain lines and ridges, until they land on the button of my jeans.

She looks up at me as if she is asking a question. I'm not sure what my response should be. No one is home, and we could very well play and have dessert. I just don't want to push her. I want her to be sure, so I don't reply. I just watch her as she slowly unbuttons them and lowers the zipper.

I wonder what her intentions are, how far she is willing to take this moment. I don't wonder for long though, because she pushes me back with one hand until my back is pressed against her dresser. She reaches into my jeans and wraps her hand around me. I grab her face and kiss her desperately. She is unraveling me. We have been getting pretty damn close for weeks now, but it's never been the right time, someone's home, we're in my truck, in a public place—but now? We're alone. *FUCK!* She is moving her hand, and it feels so good.

And then she does the fucking hottest thing I've ever seen and also the one thing I least expected from her. She gets on her knees. *Holy hell.*

She looks up to me with her wide beautiful eyes, and it does something crazy to me. "I never thanked you for what you did for me in your truck."

Damn.

"You don't have to do this, Riley." I take a deep breath as she ignores me and does whatever it is she has her mind set on doing.

I have never been inside someone's mouth before, and having Riley's pretty mouth wrapped around me is the sexiest sight. I will dream about this at night—more to add to the list of things I lie awake remembering. She licks and twirls her tongue around me. She moves her mouth up and down on me, and then she moans as though this brings her pleasure. It's hot as hell.

I'm letting her control this, whatever she can handle, as much or as little as she wants. I'm gripping the edge of her dresser as to not grab her head and thrust into her throat.

She makes a gagging sound, and I fear she is going to stop, but she doesn't. She just readjusts herself and somehow gets me deeper into her mouth. I hit the back of her throat, and she swallows slowly. *Oh, fuck* that motion creates a tightening sensation around me. Then she slowly glides up and down—repeating the delicious process. Lick. Swirl. Suck. Swallow. She begins to move faster, and I begin to push into her further—my hips unintentionally doing their own thing. "Baby, I'm fixing to come. If you don't want to swallow then you need to stop. Okay?" I warn her.

She doesn't let up. She just sucks harder, and I don't know if that is her answer. Just in case it isn't, I push her back gently, and pull free of her mouth just in time to release in my hand.

Once my breathing has slowed, she stands and places me back into my pants. She buttons and zips my jeans and then places a sweet peck on my lips.

I stare at her with a little bit of shock and wonder. I didn't expect that from her. I don't even know where that just came from.

I guess she isn't always as predictable as I'd once thought. Then another thought catches me off guard. *She was pretty damn good at that, what if she already did...that...before. FUCK!*

"Um, let me go take care of this. I will be right back." I tell her as I head to the bathroom to wash my hands.

I meet my reflection in the mirror, and mentally scold myself for letting my head go there just now. Riley spent two years with Dean. It's foolish of me to think they never did anything sexual together at all.

Riley keeps moving us forward, taking steps in that direction. *Why do I keep stopping us?* It's not that I'm not ready. I'm so ready to go there with her. I guess I'm just afraid she will regret it once we do, or that it will change us somehow, and knowing that I'm leaving in a few weeks to Louisiana, I'm just afraid to ruin us.

I don't want her to think I'm like Dean or that sex is all I want from her. I want her to know I'm content with things the way they are between us—that I'm in it for the right reasons. That I see forever for us.

When I head back to her room, Riley is sitting on the edge of the bed looking deep in thought. When I open the door, her eyes look up to meet mine, and I notice them glisten. I think she is about to cry. I don't understand it, or what could have happened in the few seconds I've been in the bathroom.

"Are you okay?" I ask closing the door behind me out of habit. I walk and sit down beside her on the bed.

She sighs, "Did you like what I just did to you? I mean did I do it right." Her voice is small, and her eyes are looking away from me.

Wait! What?

"Riley, look at me," I demand.

Her eyes slowly meet mine, and the insecurity I see in them rips me open. "Why would you ask either of those things?"

She shrugs and attempts to look away again, but I keep her eyes locked with mine by gripping her chin.

"Something made you think that just now. Tell me," I plead.

"It's just that I never have...ya know...and I didn't know if I did it right." I sigh in relief realizing that I was her first blowjob. I can't picture her mouth anywhere but where it was just now.

Then she blurts out, "It's just...Preslee said you like to be in her mouth," and my heart stops.

I stand and look at her as though she has lost her damn mind. "SHE WHAT?"

She stands. "She told me that she has played with both of my boys even if I think she hasn't. She told me Dean likes it rough and dirty and you like it in her mouth." She throws her hand over her mouth and the tears begin to fall.

What the fuck is Preslee talking about? I've never. Why would she say that?

Riley continues to ramble and cry as I try to wrap my head around this. "I don't want you to think I did that to you because of what she said. I did it because I wanted to. But then I sat down, and her words were in my head, laughing at me. I realized that I didn't even know what I was doing, and she may have already done that to you. Then what if you were picturing her or what if she did it better? And the thoughts wouldn't shut up Josh, and the image of her like I was just now with you makes me sick on the inside. I'm sorry. I shouldn't have said all of that. I should just shut up, but I can't shut up, and I can't stop thinking...and I—,"

I grab her shoulders. "Stop it. Stop. Okay?" I pull her to me, and I feel like the biggest asshole to ever live. Of course, she doubts this. It was Collin's party, and I was totally wasted. I remember making out with Preslee. I remember her pulling me into the bathroom, and her intentions were to go down on me. I was wasted enough to probably let her, but I couldn't get it up. I was too drunk, and when my mind realized what we were doing, I stopped her anyway. Her mouth never came near me. I even joked with Riley about it after, made some lame ass comment about favors. I didn't realize. *Shit, I didn't realize it.*

I pull her away and make her look at me. I wipe her tears with my thumbs and sigh. "Baby, listen to me. I don't know what Preslee is talking about. I have never been in anyone's mouth but yours. You are my first everything, Riley. I promise you that."

She visibly relaxes until she tenses again when I say, "But...there was that time at Collin's party. Truth is...she propositioned me in the bathroom, but I didn't accept her proposition. I was too drunk anyway.

I remember kissing her and joking with you after. I'm so sorry for making a joke out of it. "

"Too drunk? What do you mean? Like you couldn't...ya know? Are you saying if you weren't so drunk...you would have let her?" she asks, wiping at the tears that are falling.

I promised to never lie to her. I hate that I'm about to admit this. "I don't know. It's not that I wanted to. But I'm a guy and the girl I loved was with someone else—at the same party as me. I might have to be honest. I don't know. But still, it's not because I wanted to share anything with her. I promise it's not like that."

She has her eyes squeezed shut and is shaking her head back and forth. It guts me.

"Stop. Don't say anything else. I hate her. I fucking hate her. She ruins everything," she says between sobs.

Dammit it all to hell. She is right. Preslee ruins everything. I fucking hate her, too.

I try to pull Riley close to me, but she pushes me away. *Fuck!*

"I can't right now. I just...I'm not mad at you. It's just...I need a breather."

I nod. "Riley, don't do this. Don't give her the power to come between us. I would never intentionally hurt you. What you just did to me—it was beautiful."

Her eyes are cast down, and she slowly lifts them to mine. "She won't come between us, Josh. But hours apart will."

"What?"

"If I'm like this now with a girl I've seen you with, how do you think I'm going to handle the things I can't see? My imagination is already the biggest bitch in the world."

I swallow down the sickening feeling in my stomach. We still haven't talked about this. I shut it down every time she brings it up. And right now, I think if we discussed this it would end up in an argument.

"We're not doing this now," I snap.

She looks at me confused, "Are we ever? When are you going to tell me the truth, Josh? I appreciate you being honest just now with me about that, but you've been keeping me in the dark for months about our potential future. Were you ever going to tell me that you signed with LSU in the first place? When are we going to face this? On the day you leave me here?"

I feel sick. She sighs. "I hated that I had to hear this from Dean, only to confirm it for my own ears through that window. Why didn't you tell me the truth back in February?"

"FROM DEAN?" I shout.

"Yeah, he told me at the hospital. Imagine my shock to find out that after you told me you weren't sure what you wanted for your future that you had already made a decision."

I sit down on her bed and put my head in my hands. I can see her feet move to in front of me. I slowly lift my eyes to hers and find hers full of pain. "I didn't purposely keep you in the dark. I didn't lie when I said I hadn't made a decision. I just had to make a choice that day or the choice would be gone. We weren't together, Riley, and I didn't know if we ever would be."

"And we are now," she mutters.

"We are," I reply.

"So, will we be when you leave?" she asks in a soft voice.

"Of course." I stand and wrap my arms around her.

"I love you, Riley. I will always love you. I've been trying to tell you for weeks now that nothing changes." I am rubbing her back and her hair.

"I love you too, Josh, but everything changes. You have to know that." She pushes off of me to look in my eyes.

We stare at each other, knowing the truth—everything changes.

"I have to go to dinner with my dad and sister. Can I come over later tonight and we'll talk?" *Please, let me.*

Her voice becomes soft, "Of course." I hate the sadness I see in her eyes. I fucking hate all of it—change, life, all of the years we were robbed of when we should have been together.

CHAPTER 15

I feel empty—jaded, like a pit is swallowing me whole, and someone is spitting on me for kicks. For weeks, Josh and I have been ignoring the truth—postponing the inevitable—our heartbreak. Now, it's all I feel—all consuming.

How am I supposed to go to a wedding tomorrow with him and not imagine what I wish for him and me one day?

I have my ear buds plugged in my ears, and *Get Around This* by Safetysuit is playing. I feel like I am in a trance. I'm focusing on the words of the song and not the ones in my head replaying endlessly.

It is a part of the night where the sky is in between colors— changing from orange to pink to violet, and it is just breathtaking. I hate running to be honest. My lungs burn, my legs cramp and it tires me, but tonight I need it. It's cathartic. Writing is my escape, but even that has me stuck in the dark parts of myself that I don't like. So I'm running. Running to be free. I'm running harder than I ever have before when Rise Against starts blaring at the same rate as my heart beating.

What do I do with everything I'm thinking? Josh is leaving. We will be hours apart. What will that mean for us both? Could we survive it? Why wouldn't he have told me sooner so I could have followed him? Even though I know I couldn't have, the question is still in my mind. Why is life so unfair? Everything about losing him consumes my thoughts.

Holy shit, I can't breathe. I stop for air, and I don't even realize it, but somehow I end up near the lake—near our spot. I walk a few yards feeling the chilly night air cool my damp skin. The stars are so bright out here. The stars. *For every star in the sky, I have a reason to love you. When you look up at night, never forget this truth.* It's beautiful, and I understand the gift better. He's leaving me, and he wants to leave the stars with me, see them and remember that he loves me. He knew I'd said the stars here meant something to me, and that, without him, they disappear. He listens so attentively to the things I say. God, I love him.

I walk to the pier and sit. The sounds of nature are soothing and calming me slightly. I lie back, pulling my ear buds out. I rest my head on my arms and admire the view of the night sky hoping just one of those stars will take my wish and grant it.

All is quiet with the exception to crickets, the tiny splashes in the lake, the wind rustling the trees, and my racing thoughts about Josh. I hear footsteps, and for a second, my skin prickles, but as though his presence has a direct connection to my heart, I sense him before I even turn around. When I look over my shoulder, my breath catches at the sight of him.

He is glowing under the moon and breathing fast as though he'd also just stopped running. His bare chest is slightly damp with sweat. The words I wrote on his chest visible. *Thank you for saving this for me. You have saved mine.* His heart is mine; his heart gave life to my own when it wanted to quit beating. I let my eyes drift lower seeing him in his running shorts that hang in that uber sexy way I love so much. Dear God, that V. I just want to lick his chest and taste the sweat beads off his muscles. He is beautiful.

He smiles and runs a hand through his hair. "I thought that was you. What are you doing out here all alone?" He asks in a raspy voice as though he hasn't caught his breath yet. Does he even realize that his walking up like that has damn near stolen my breath away?

I stand up and stretch my arms above my head. His eyes rake over my petite body dressed in a sports bra and yoga pants. "I went running," I say, suddenly feeling self-conscious about the way I look in front of him. It's ridiculous considering he has seen all of me already—almost all of me.

"You hate running," he states, knowing me so well.

"I needed to think." I tell him and feel the butterflies in my stomach flutter madly with the way he is looking at me.

He steps closer to me, "About?"

I swallow, "Stuff."

He is standing right in front of me now, and his eyes are full of curiosity. He is close—so close. My hands twitch to touch his chest and feel his muscles. He looks down at my stomach unapologetically and smirks. He reaches up trailing his index finger along my rib cage causing my skin to break out in goose bumps. "What kind of stuff?"

Seriously, I can't think. I can't form a single thought. I can barely breathe with his nearness, his eyes, his skin taunting me, the temperature, the way he is breathing, his finger even feather light on me like that. Oh, my God and he smells like heaven. "I don't remember," I breathe.

"I missed you." He puts his hand around my back, pulling me closer to him—our skin now touching. He looks down at me, and his dimpled grin is about to be my undoing.

"You just saw me. You miss me already?" I ask jokingly.

He gives me an Eskimo kiss. "I always miss you, baby."

He gave me a noozle? It's so cute. I let my hands do what they've wanted to since I laid my eyes on him moments ago. I glide them up his chest and intake a breath at how perfect he feels. I wrap them around his neck and tangle them into his hair like always, and now he inhales. We are taking turns in breathing the same air—our breaths dancing sinfully between us. He ever so slowly lowers his mouth to mine, and when our lips meet it elicits a moan from my chest. It doesn't matter how many times we kiss. It's always like the first time. It always moves me to lose my balance and forget everything else but his lips on mine. He lifts me up effortlessly and my legs naturally wrap around his waist like they belong there. I let my head fall back as he licks and kisses down my neck and chest.

"Ah, Josh," my voice is a hushed whisper. I move my mouth back to his, and our kiss is no longer sweet and soft. It's rough and fast as though neither of us can get enough of the others taste—needing to taste more—just a little more. I don't even know he is walking until I feel him lower me back onto the grass by *our* tree. Our legs are tangled, our bodies moving against each other—our hands gliding along each other exploring the others skin. Something about him without a shirt makes me want to do anything and everything he ever asks of me. I can't help but lose myself in the moment.

"I love the way you feel, and God...you're sexy, Riley," he says between kisses. He reaches into my pants and begins touching me. I'm slowly coming undone, and then he stops. I whimper in protest making him laugh. He rolls to his back and sighs heavily in his chest.

"Why did you stop?" I ask him breathlessly. He turns his head to mine and smirks.

"Because, baby I need to, before I can't."

"Maybe I don't want you to stop, Josh. Maybe I—,"

He rolls back over and grabs my face kissing me fiercely again. He pulls back and pecks my forehead. "Shhh...I know what you need, baby, and it's not here by a tree."

I sigh, "Fine. Now I'm hot *and* bothered."

He laughs as he sits up and reaches for my hand. "C'mon, let's go cool off."

I look at him confused but still place my hand in his. "Where are we going?" I ask.

"To the lake," he deadpans.

When we get to the lake, his smile is gone. His playful nature becomes unreadable. "Riley, you know I love you more than anything, right?" Everything in the way his face is serious, and the statement he just made makes me uncomfortable. I don't answer him with words but with a nod of my head.

"Tonight, I just want us to feel...not talk about everything. Okay?" He speaks into my hair as he pulls me close to him. My heart breaks a little.

"Now, get undressed," he demands out of the blue.

"What?" I shout, shocked. *What the hell?* He is all over the place. He just said—and now he wants me to get undressed?

"We're gonna skinny dip. It's a first for us both. We're both hot and bothered. Let's cool off," he says, grinning at me. I'm looking back and forth from the lake to him in contemplation.

"Um, Josh? I don't think getting naked is going to help us not be hot and bothered. Right?" I'm pretty sure we are just digging a deeper hole of temptation to climb in.

He doesn't answer. He just turns his back to me and begins to take his shoes off, and then he lowers his shorts and boxers in one fell swoop gracing me with his ass.

Holy Shit! Oh, my God.

He is naked.

Outside.

And he wants me to do the same.

That ass, though.

Oh, damn.

He doesn't turn around. He dives in the water from the pier, and it splashes. Oh, my gosh, he is obviously serious. "What if someone sees us? We could get into so much trouble!" I shout over to him.

"We're good, baby. Now, c'mon. I'm going to turn around. I won't peek. Promise." He does turn around, and I watch him constantly as I undress until I bend down to remove my socks. I can't believe we are doing this. I'm naked—outside.

I jump in and tread over to him grinning like an idiot. "Did you peek?"

He laughs and says, "Maybe."

I splash him making him laugh harder.

Jerk.

CHAPTER 16

Beautiful and tempting. She is quickly becoming my obsession. I don't want to think about how anything may change, or about what we should and shouldn't do. I just want to feel. Fuck the rest.

After we chase each other, laughing and splashing over and over again, we both swim to the spot under the dock where we can both touch without treading water. Rocks line the bottom and the walls around this hidden nook. Riley and I have come under here many times before during the summer, but never has it felt like this—intimate and private. No one can see us here at all.

I have her pressed completely against my chest and the edge of the rocks. Her skin on my skin is about to damn near kill any restraint I have left. She has one leg wrapped around my waist, and if I moved just an inch to the left I could slip right in and we could move together, but I don't do that. I just run my hand up and down her thigh and around her ass and taste her lips. She moans and begins to writhe against me.

I pull away, and it's not because I don't want to do this with her. I know she keeps hinting at taking this last step together. I just don't want to and then leave her, and have her hate me. I also don't want her to hate me and walk away never having had her. I'm conflicted. I want to do the right thing. Tonight was about just feeling. I want to feel every inch of her.

I hadn't planned on literally running into her tonight. I planned on going over to her house and talking things out, but there she was looking the way she did, and looking at me the way she did. Now, here we are pressed against each other in the warmth of the lake.

"Josh, look at me," she says turning my eyes back to hers. I listen and meet her eyes. I know she sees my struggle, and she doesn't understand it. She doesn't know why I'm holding back. I can sense the difference in her breathing. I can sense the change in her when we touch. She *isn't* holding back. She told me tonight she wants me. She is urging me to go further, and I'm stuck between what is right and what is wrong without the faintest clue as to which is which.

"What are you thinking about?" She reaches up to smooth my frown line.

"Stuff," I repeat her answer from earlier.

She nods and looks away sighing, "You said no thinking, just feeling—remember?"

"I know. I'm sorry." I say as I rest my head against her forehead and sigh. I can't do this. She is in my veins. She is in my bloodstream—a necessary piece for me to breath every day. I need to feel her daily—to see her daily. And I'm torn in shreds.

"So, stop thinking about what comes next. We're here in this moment...now," she says touching my face.

"Baby, God... I'm so sorry," I whisper against her lips. I feel her chest rise and fall. I feel her body become limp beneath me, and then she begins to breathe fast and shake.

"Stop, please. I can't hear it. It hurts. Please," she begs and begins to cry. Damn it all to hell. Fuck my life. Fuck it all.

I pull her to my chest and hold her. I lift my eyes to hers and squeeze her cheeks, rubbing my thumbs underneath her eyes to catch her tears. "I love you, so much. We will figure this out –just like we always do," I say.

She nods, wraps her hands around my neck, her legs around my waist and presses her lips against mine.

Our kiss is slow, meaningful as her hands tangle in my hair and my hands glide along her back.

Her head falls back as I trail kisses down her neck. Our eyes meet, and the decision is there for us both.

"Just feeling?"

"Just feeling," she whispers and nods her head. She bites her lip as she pushes up on my shoulders to line us up, and then she slides down, and everything beautiful happens.

Fuck! She feels perfect—better than I ever imagined. It's slow, and she winces just a little, so I freeze. I don't want to hurt her. I've heard that can happen with your first time, but then she grabs my face and begins to move, coaxing me to continue.

"Show me, Josh. Make love to me." She arches her back, pushing me deeper.

"Fuck, baby." I growl as I push her back gently against the rocks. I hold her up with one of my hands as the other feels her perfect breast in my palm.

"This isn't how I wanted to do this. This isn't making love, Riley. This is fucking. I wanted to take my time, to feel every inch of you shiver, but I can't think straight. I picture you like this—naked all the time. I feel you around my fingers at night. The sounds you make, I hear them in my sleep." I say as I begin to thrust deeper—faster—harder.

"Oh, god, Josh. I picture you, too. The way you feel—the way you make me feel. The way you look at me, touch me, and kiss me—it drives me crazy. I need this—to feel this. You are perfect. It's like we fit perfectly together."

I swivel my hips, and she moans loudly. Her body begins to tremble, her breaths causing her breast to peek in and out of the water. I'm not going to last much longer.

She rolls her hips into me, and I must hit a spot because she squeezes my shoulders and whimpers my name. I'm ruined. She has ruined me. We have to figure out a way to make this work because I won't be the same after her.

I look her right in the eyes as we both embrace this moment. Together.

"I'm freezing now," she says as we walk back to our houses with our clothes back on and our hair wet.

"I'd be a gentlemen and give you my jacket, but I'm a tad underdressed myself." I explain putting my arm around her and trying to warm her with a hug.

"So, I guess we can't go steady, huh?"

I raise my brow and look at her. She shrugs, "Sorry, that was corny."

I laugh at her, "You're cute."

When we get back to her house, she kisses my lips and for the first time I feel a sense of peace. Maybe we can do this. Maybe we will be just fine. I grip her chin, "Hey, you saved my heart, too, you know?" I point to where the ink is smeared on my chest.

She leans forward and presses a kiss to the spot on my chest. "This heart is beautiful and will always be mine."

"You will always be mine." I tell her, rubbing my thumb along her bottom lip, and then we are at it again—kissing and making love to each other's mouths.

CHAPTER 17

Marked and changed. Sex is something peculiar. It's like the act of it is something we are wired to know how to do. Because when we first started it—it hurt, but then something happened—it began to feel good. Even inexperienced, our bodies knew what to do, knew how to move together—to bind us forever. Something primal took over, something necessary and now I want more of it—more of him.

I woke up this morning feeling the effects of my exertion last night. Not just the loss of my virginity but the running that I *never* do. My body is sore and reminding me of it. Oh, my God. Josh and I had sex. It wasn't how I imagined it would be, or in a bed, but yet it was intimate and passionate. At least, it wasn't in the back seat of his truck, or in the grass by a tree. Wow! We did it. I smile as I curl up remembering the way he felt inside of me. At first, it was painful, but then it's like my body took over and knew just what to do to turn the pain into pleasure. Josh is blessed—very blessed!

I'm not sure what I thought I would feel after. Part of me wondered if I would feel guilty or less innocent, but I don't. I just feel happy, and like for the first time, I made a decision in the moment that was right for me—right for us. We needed each other. We needed to be connected in all ways, and now we are. I wonder how he feels. I wonder if he feels the same way as I do, or if he is regretting what we did.

I continue to wonder as I pack my suitcase for the weekend in San Antonio for Beau's wedding. Em will be here in an hour to pick me up, and we are supposed to meet Josh and Collin for breakfast, but plans may have changed since Em went and did the unthinkable with Collin—can't change too much since we are riding together anyways. She will have to get over it.

I need a shower to relax my muscles, and then I need to bring Tink to Josh's, Joey is going to kitty sit for me. I undress and stretch as the steam fills the bathroom. I hop in the shower and the second the stream hits my back, I intake a seething breath. "Ow!" I squeal jumping out of the shower to look at why my back is burning in the mirror.

"OH, MY GOD!" I breathe, looking at the slight bruising and abrasions that colored up my back. I never even felt that when Josh had me pushed against the rocks last night. I was just so lost in the depths of his eyes, in the feelings of him moving, the emotions that were pouring out of me as he took me somewhere beautiful. He started slow and sweet—gentle, but as our emotions became more tangled, more intense—so did what we were doing. It wasn't just making love anymore, it became desperation to claim the other, the need to crawl inside and possess them. It became raw, passionate fucking against the rocks. Our bodies knew how, magically—knew exactly what we craved, what the other desired.

My shock slowly becomes...a smile. He marked me. Something about seeing it there makes me feel beautiful.

I carefully shower and wrap a towel around my body. I brush the mess that is my hair and run some curl lotion through the many layers of it. I leave to get dressed, but the doorbell rings, so I take the detour down the hall to let Em in.

"Hey, bitch," she greets me with her pleasantries.

"Hey, ginger."

She frowns, "Stop calling me that."

I grin as we walk back to my room, careful to not expose my marked back to her. "Why? You call me bitch." I whine in good humor.

She places her hands on her hips, "Well, you are my bitch."

"And, you are my ginger," I retort.

She huffs and walks off. We will never get anywhere because she will always hate her hair and will always be my ginger and well, I am a bitch.

"Oh, my God. Are you ready to spend the weekend with, Josh? Y'all are so going to do the nasty." She grins like an idiot, and I tense. I'm not going to tell her that we already did. It's private—for just us.

I shrug like it's no big deal. "Maybe, but I'm sharing a room with you, and he's sharing a room with Collin. That could be an issue of privacy. That is unless you want a repeat with Collin." I state with a lifted brow. We haven't discussed her spur of the moment decision in all that much detail just yet.

Her eyes flick to mine as she tenses. Hmmm...Interesting. "I uh...we um would obviously let y'all have privacy, Riley." She says, looking away almost immediately. She isn't telling me something.

"So, you know I'm going to examine your suitcase. I need to make sure you are bringing the correct necessities." She unzips my small suitcase, clicking her tongue as she throws it all over my bed.

"Hey, I had that all organized neatly," I complain.

"I've got you a gift in my car. I'll be right back." She ignores my complaint.

I tilt my head, "A gift? What for?"

"Um, just consider it an additional birthday present," she tosses over her shoulder as she walks out the door.

I take the moment that she is outside to dress quickly. If she sees my back, she will want to know what happened. I don't want to share that moment with anyone other than Josh. Just as I slip on all my clothing, which is nothing more than an Aero t-shirt and my frayed jean shorts, my phone pings.

Josh: MORNIN PRETTY GIRL

It makes me smile. I reply immediately.

Me: HEY x

Josh: HOW DO YOU FEEL?

How do I feel? My legs feel sore, my back burns, and everything else just feels... WARM.

Me: LIKE I HAD THE BEST NIGHT EVER

His text isn't right away, and it makes me nervous. Maybe he does regret it. Maybe it was amazing to me, but not so much for him. Maybe's fill my head but then he texts me back.

Josh: BEST EVER. NO REGRETS?

Me: NOT EVEN THE SLIGHTEST. YOU?

Josh: NEVER. JUST WISH I HAD BEEN GENTLER AND TAKEN MY TIME

My heart melts. We couldn't do gentle—not last night.

Me: WE HAVE NEXT TIME ;)

Josh: IN A BED WHILE I TASTE EVERY INCH OF YOUR SWEETNESS

Geez. Just his words have my belly coiling deliciously, and the spot between my legs aching.

"Why are you are smiling like that? And your cheeks are all rosy," Em inquires as she comes back into my room.

I climb up on my bed atop the clothing that was once organized neatly in my suitcase. "It's nothing." She hands me a pink bag. Victoria's Secret? My eyes dart to hers with question, and she shrugs. Really? I reach into the bag and find not one, but two sets of lingerie—one is black silk and lace—very exotic, the other more delicate—soft pink. I like the soft pink one best, which is odd for me because I love black anything. The demi bra is gorgeous, soft pink cups with intricate lace detail in the center and lace around the back. The panties are pink with lace detail—a dainty yellow bow in the center. It's beautiful.

"Okay, Em, I have a few thoughts here. One, I love matching bras and panties...so, thanks. Two, why did you buy me matching bras and panties?" I ask, tossing them back into the bag.

She reaches over pulling them out of the bag and placing them into my suitcase. "Well, duh. They are ammo."

She explains further when it's obvious I don't understand. "For Josh? You dress sexy for him, and it leads to sex. Ohmigawd you're such an innocent." She laughs, and I cringe.

I'm not so innocent, but she doesn't know that. "Well thank you, I guess."

After repacking my suitcase to meet Emily's approval, we drop off Tink to Joey and head to breakfast with the boys. "So, who will you be spending the weekend with, Em? Collin or Brandt?" I ask her as we drive.

She side glances at me with a frown. "Sheesh, you make me sound like a slut."

Now I'm frowning. "Sorry, that's not what I meant. I'm genuinely curious."

She lights a cigarette, rolling the windows down. "I am a slut. And honestly, I don't know. Brandt only calls when he wants some. We don't go out on dates, and we really don't have much of a relationship. I think he is too old for me."

"Yeah, but he likes you and you like him. At least, it seemed like that."

She laughs and takes a drag. "Honey, that is called lust covered glasses. He doesn't like me. He likes what we do together. I mean I made out with his sister and he didn't care."

I'm in the middle of putting lip-gloss on my lips and straight up jab the sucker at my nose when she says that. "YOU WHAT?"

She glances over at me. "Don't look at me like that. I'm not a lesbian or anything. She kissed me, and I kind of let her, that's all. It's not a big deal. I've kissed you."

"Um, it's a huge freaking deal because Rebel is a lesbian. And for the record, I kissed you because I was wasted."

She huffs, "Rebel's not a lesbian, Riley. We've talked about this. She likes guys, too. In fact, she prefers sex with men and foreplay with woman." She explains it like I don't understand bi-sexuality. I get it.

"Are you jealous that you're not my only girl?" She jokes, laughing at my face all scrunched up.

"Hell no. I still can't believe I kissed you in the first place. But wow...you made out with Rebel. You didn't like...you know...do the foreplay stuff like you just said?" Her eyes immediately flick away from mine. Oh, my God!

"YOU DID?"

We pull into the parking lot and notice Josh and Collin aren't here yet. Thank goodness, because I'm not done with this conversation.

She flicks her cigarette out the window and turns in her seat. "Look, it's not like that. But yes, I fooled around with her. Brandt walked in and didn't even blink an eye."

I swallow hard and try to gather myself, but I'm a little shocked. I had no idea. It's like she is this whole other person I don't know. "O-kay. And what about Collin?"

"What about him?"

"Was that lust covered glasses, or an alcohol induced mistake, or something you want to explore more?"

She sighs, "I don't know. Collin and I are kind of friends, and we talk, but he's a douche. I mean, look who he hooks up with besides me, of course? He's not exactly boyfriend material. I'm not girlfriend material, either, though. Did you know that his tongue is not the only thing pierced on his body?"

I try to think of what else could be pierced and then..."No? Really? His junk is pierced."

"Really." She proceeds to take out her phone and show me a picture of his piercing.

"Oh, my God. I didn't want to see that, Em. How am I supposed to go eat breakfast with him, with that that image in my brain? Do I even want to know why you have a picture of it on your phone?"

She laughs and shakes her head. "I didn't make you look. I'm not one to think penises are cute or anything, but that one has a little magic in it."

Dear Lord. Of course, now I'm thinking about Josh's magic stick and all the ways I want to see it again. Shit. I turn away from her just as *23,* comes on the radio. She blares it, and we hop of out of her car and dance like crazy lunatics in the parking lot.

 *Josh*

CHAPTER 18

A weekend—two whole days with her in a hotel room—the many things I think about it are endless. Collin doesn't know it yet, but he will not be my roommate. I have other plans, and they involve a brunette with eyes that captivate me.

We pull up to the pancake house and laugh hard as we see these two crazies dancing in the parking lot.

"Damn dude, your girl has some moves," Collin says from the passenger seat.

Riley and Emily are both shaking their asses—hands in the air, hair flying around. It's actually refreshing to see Riley be so carefree. "It seems Emily does, too," I say gauging his reaction.

He just watches them, or Emily. "Yeah, she does." Hmmm...that is interesting. I think Collin has a slight crush.

We park on the opposite side of them and climb out of the truck. "Party at the pancake house," Collin says joining their shenanigans. Emily carries on her little show, but Riley freezes and locks eyes with me. It's the first time we've seen each other since last night.

She walks slowly to where I'm standing against Emily's car just watching her. She really does have moves. She stops right in front of me, looking up into my eyes and biting that fucking lip. God, that drives me insane. Every time she does it, I want to pull it between my own teeth. "Hey," she says in a tiny voice.

"Hey." I tilt my head and grab a curl to twirl around my finger. We stare at each other for a solid minute without words—just breathing. "You are so beautiful," I tell her breaking our trance-like state.

She says, "And you are...you are...fuck it." She crashes her lips to mine. Her hands immediately tangle in my hair and my hands roam her body.

I hear whistles, snickers as well as a few scoffs. We're in a very public parking lot, in front of a very crowded pancake house. She pushes off my chest, "Sorry, I um...sorry." She blushes and hides her face in my chest.

I rub her back and whisper in her ear, "Never apologize for doing what you want. If you want me, say so. If you need to kiss me, do it. Never second-guess what you want or need with me. Okay?"

"M'hm."

"Let's go eat, bitches. I'm starved," Em says, hopping up next to us.

Collin clears his throat. "Looks like Riley is too."

"Oh God," she says, hiding her face even further in my chest.

My laugh causes her to look up at me with those crimson cheeks of beauty. "My fave shade," I grip her chin and kiss her colored cheeks.

We're in Collin's 1970 Challenger instead of my truck. He wanted to drive, and I like the backseat—very comfortable. Trust me, I know, because I'm in it with a beautiful girl. She's lying back on the seat with her head in my lap, her eyes shut. One hand is holding mine on top of her stomach. I'm running my fingers through her hair and tracing the features of her face with my eyes. She really is the most beautiful girl I've ever seen in my life. From the pretty pink lips she covered with berry Chapstick, to the cheeks that blush so easily, to the small nose that gets graced with light freckles during the summer, to those eyes. Jesus, her eyes have always been my very favorite part of her. She hides so much behind them, but I see it. I always see it.

Those very blue/green eyes snap open and lock with mine when *Bloodstream* comes on the radio. Emily turns it up, "I so love this song. His voice is so damn sexy." Neither Riley nor I reply. Speech is impossible when the images of what we did to this song fill my head. Her eyes flutter and glass over. She bites her lip and her breathing changes. She is remembering it, too. I can't breathe. I just want to touch her—to feel her respond to me touching her again. She has her knees pulled up in the seat, and I trail my index finger from her knee down to the edge of her barely there shorts and back up. Her skin breaks out in goose bumps and she shivers. My eyes never leave hers. She reaches her hand up and traces my bottom lip. I harden instantly, and her eyes widen. *Damn.* Good thing her head is covering my lap. Bad thing is her head is in my lap—not really helping my problem here. I'm so turned on. *Fuck!*

So, about that backseat—it's a small confined place—and all I can smell is her jasmine and vanilla scented lotion. I'm fucked and not in the way I'm imagining in this backseat.

Luckily, Collin exits the highway and stops for gas, because I'm struggling here with her in this tight space.

I thought I'd be safe from temptation for at least a few minutes, but then she buys a fruit punch Icee, blow pops and skittles. Good grief, I'm in a lust bubble of desire. We're standing outside of the car just talking. I'm half listening to all of her words because I'm watching her sip from her straw and then lick her lips, which are now tinted red from her drink. Opening her bag of skittles, she laughs at something Em says and for the life of me, I can't stop thinking about how much I want to taste the rainbow. And so I do. I grab her drink and candy, passing it to Em who says, "What the..." I don't listen. I grab Riley's face and taste every crevice of her mouth. The fruity taste lingering all over her tongue and sending my senses into overdrive.

"Holy shit! Collin, what are we going to do with these two?" Emily asks.

I hear him laugh. "Uh, I guess move out of the way? Wait in the car? Give em' dollar bills? Hell if I know."

Her hands are in my hair, pulling as always. I have her pressed into the car door, my hands holding both of her cheeks in my palms. I glide my hand to the nape of her neck and into her hair as we deepen the kiss. I don't know how long we kiss, just that I feel better once we do. I release her and step back as she lifts her hands to touch her lips. She always does that. It's like the feeling left on them shocks her. She just stands there, dazed for a few seconds—staring at me. Collin leans out of his window. "Y'all coming, or you gonna stand out there eye and mouth-fucking all damn day?"

Riley blushes and gives him a look, and then gives me a look. Em has her door wide open for us to climb into the backseat. I enjoy the view as Riley climbs in first. Emily smacks me on the back of my head. "Hey, what was that for?"

"For molesting my friend in public, not once but twice today. Jesus, you two are like dogs in heat or something. You seriously need to do it already."

I point my thumb in her direction and look in the car to Riley. "Baby, do you feel molested or just *in heat*? Should we go do it already?" Her eyes narrow and she yanks me in by my shirt.

"Shut up and just get in the damn car. Besides, if I remember correctly I molested you this morning." She grins and blows me a kiss, then leans over the console. "Now, can I have my drink and candy back? I need some sugar."

Collin coughs, "You mean you didn't get enough of that, just now?"

"Ugh, fuck you." She pouts and sits back in her seat, sipping on her drink.

We stop for lunch as our last stop. It's pretty obvious to both Riley and I that something may be brewing between Collin and Emily. They are oddly enough...cute together. *Is that even something I should be thinking?* Because if he fucks it up, then it could make things a little awkward with our group, and knowing Collin, he *will* fuck this up. Then again, Emily is like the female version of him, so we may be okay here. One positive of them maybe liking each other, it will make this sharing a room switch much easier.

We're back in the car, and Riley is bent over in her seat digging through her purse, sucking on a fucking blow pop. I now believe that she is intentionally torturing me. I'm rubbing the skin exposed on her lower back. She tenses, releases the sucker on a pop, lifts her head and looks over the console to Collin. "Er, um...I'm not judging here, and being as though you have handcuffs hanging from your rear view mirror, and I've seen you in flirt mode, this shouldn't surprise me, but seriously?"

I lift a brow wondering what the hell she is talking about. Collin does, too. He glances over his shoulder. "What?"

She reaches under his seat and pulls out a red lacy thong. "This." She has them pinched in her fingers like she may catch something. Her nose is all scrunched up. It's adorable. *Holy shit.* She found panties in his back seat.

"Shit. That's where those went." Collin's eyes flick to Emily's briefly and then away.

Riley notices because she looks between the two of them as Emily snatches the thong and throws them into the front. "Such a pig," Emily mutters under her breath. Nothing further explained from either of them. Hmmm.

Riley turns to look at me with a curious expression, mouth agape. She mouths, "Oh, my God." It just makes me laugh. Obviously, their hook up wasn't a one-time thing.

"You did at least clean the seats, right? Cuz we're like sitting on these." Riley asks, and I cough a laugh.

Collin looks over the seats at us, and then to Emily as he shrugs and looks back to the road. "Who said I fucked in the backseat? I may have just been eating a delicious snack. The only mess that makes is on my face."

Emily curses and Riley sputters, "Holy fuck."

"Nope, the holy fucks happen on Sundays." Collin retorts and earns a punch in the arm.

I am literally dying in laughter at Riley's face. I don't miss the daggers Emily shoots at Collin, or the smirk he is wearing across his face. Collin has always been and always will be crass.

The rest of the ride is pretty uneventful with the exception of me watching Riley suck on the damn lollipop and remembering the way her mouth felt. My imagination runs wild. She isn't paying any attention, though. She is apparently not realizing at all what she is doing to me. She is too enraptured into the conversation Emily and Collin are having, or the flirty looks they keep sharing.

She pulls out her phone and sends me a text. I give her a puzzled look. I'm sitting right next to her, and she texts me?

Riley: DO YOU HEAR HER USING HER SUGARY SWEET VOICE ON HIM?

Me: YES, DOES IT BOTHER YOU?

Riley: IT'S JUST WEIRD, RIGHT? I AM POSITIVE HE JUST ADMITTED TO EATING HER OUT IN THE BACKSEAT OF THIS CAR. DID YOU SEE HER FACE? THOSE WERE HER PANTIES. OMG.

I read the text and imagine eating her. Good God, I need out of this car. "Are y'all sexting each other back there?" Emily asks. *Huh? Now, why didn't I think of that?* That would have made this portion of the trip eventful for sure. Definitely wouldn't have helped my problem of wanting Riley something fierce, though.

Riley throws her phone in her purse. Evidently, we are done texting. "Busted. I can't help it. Ever since this morning when I saw a certain pic, I've felt antsy," she replied.

Emily starts laughing, and I give her a WTF look. We were far from sexting. "What pic?" I ask.

Riley shrugs and leans into my side. "Oh, it's nothing. Emily just showed me a pic of—,"

Emily lunges over the center console and covers Riley's mouth. Riley is laughing and mumbling into her hand. Emily is glaring at her with warning eyes. Now, I'm really curious. Collin smacks Emily's ass and makes her squeal over her shoulder.

"Get your sweet ass back in the fucking seat before you make me wreck, Violet."

"Who the fuck is Violet?" Emily asks, sliding back down into her seat.

"My car. That's who."

Emily asks, "You named your car?"

"Damn straight. Now what pic is she talking about?" he inquires.

Riley leans forward cupping her mouth like she is about to tell a secret, "A penis." I literally choke. A what? She glances at me. "Yep, a penis with a piercing, actually. It was interesting. I can now say I've seen two in my life."

"Fuck!" Collin says, swerving the car as if he is shocked by what she just said. No more shocked than I.

"Two?" Emily retorts, her voice squeaking.

Riley's eyes dart to hers then mine, wide like saucers. "Oh...well, I mean like in pictures. Not up close...or in action...or um...ya know what I mean. *Shit!*" Riley says, blushing and hiding her face as she tries and fails to backpedal.

Collin pulls into the hotel parking lot just in time. As soon as he shifts into park, he turns to look at Riley laughing hysterically, to the point of tears. I think she is going crazy.

"A penis with a piercing you say?" I lift a brow and look at Collin, who looks at Emily, who jumps in the back seat straddling Riley's lap.

"Look at me, you bitch. Look at me, now!" Emily says, prying Riley's hands away from her face.

Riley's eyes are squeezed shut, and she has tears streaming down her cheeks. I'm highly amused and a little perturbed by this information. We all know about Collin's piercing. It's no secret. He'd shamelessly show anyone his junk. Luckily, I have nothing to be ashamed about in the size department. So even if she compared the two she's seen—I'm good.

Riley finally stops laughing and starts swiping away at her tears. She flutters open her eyes to look at her best friend staring at her. "Okay, okay, I'm sorry. I think I've had too much sugar, or maybe I'm delirious. Look we're here. Let's go in. I need to pee now, because you're bouncing all over me."

Emily shakes her head back and forth. "No way, hooker face. You better spill it." She gives me the eye. "You said two. I can see the guilt all over your face and his. Y'all had sex, and you never told me." She leans back and looks between Riley and me. I look to Riley curious as to what my reaction should be. I don't care if anyone knows, but I'm not sharing the details, and I hope she doesn't either.

Riley narrows her eyes and frowns, "And so did you and Collin," she states looking between them.

"You already knew that."

"Yeah, that time. That is your thong up there. I'm not stupid. You two are hooking up. Right?"

They stare at each other as Collin and I look to each other shrugging. A mental high five taking place.

Emily nods her head. Then they hug. *What the hell?*

"I'm so happy for you."

"I'm sorry I didn't tell you."

"Was it good, you've gotta tell me all the deets, K?"

"Did he really go down on you in these seats?"

They speak over each other, nodding and shit—neither ever answering the others questions.

Girls...

Now that the cats out of the bag...to the matter at hand—room arrangements.

"Dude, Riley looks hot," Beau says whispering to me as we wait for his soon to be wife to walk down the aisle to their forever. Something aches in my chest as I look at her and imagine her walking down that same aisle. I can't take my eyes off of her as the image sears itself into my brain. She would be so beautiful. I pray to God we can have that someday. I'd meant it, when I'd told her that I picture forever for us. I do. I see the whole thing.

"I know right. It's distracting." It really is. Collin and I had to be at the wedding early so I didn't know what she would look like until she made an appearance with Emily, and man did she ever make an appearance.

She's dressed in a dark teal silk blouse that make her eyes pop in color, a black short skirt with a slit at her thigh and these silver strappy high heels that make her look tall. Her legs are to die for right now. I can picture them around my waist as I hike up that skirt and press her into the wall, or better yet around my neck, as I taste her for the first time.

Holy shit! My images of Riley *are* getting perverted, and now I'm hard in a church full of people. This is bad—so, so bad. I bite my lip to the point of pain, as I taste the metallic bitterness of blood. I have to look away from her, but it's like I'm trapped in some wicked spell. She has this pull on me.

"Quit picturing sex at my wedding. That is inappropriate," Beau says laughing.

"I wasn't—okay I was, but damn dude I can't help it." I laugh with him, and that's all it needs to break the hypnosis that has come over me.

I meet Riley's eyes and wink. She says something to Emily and blushes. Something tells me I'm not the only one thinking about sex right now. I wish this wedding were over with already. I need time alone with her—a lot, a lot of time.

I turn to look at Collin and catch him completely undressing Emily with his eyes. I've never seen this side of him. I think he actually has it bad for this girl. "Hey?"

"Hmmm," he doesn't look in my direction.

"Thanks for the whole room switch. I'm pretty sure it's to your benefit, too, right? Emily and you seem to um, like each other?" It comes out as a question because I'm not sure if they like each other, or if this is just a casual thing, but he nods his head, nonetheless.

"What? You and Emily have a room together?" Brandt asks with a tone that is not happy. *Oh shit!* I completely forgot he and Emily liked each other? Had a casual thing? What the fuck? I don't know.

Collin glances to Brandt and shrugs, "Yeah, what about it?" Collin doesn't know they are, or were, together. I never actually heard them ever confirm being a thing or not being a thing.

Brandt turns his eyes to Emily's direction as do the rest of us guys. She freezes and shuffles her eyes between us looking at her. Then she turns to Riley and says something in her ear. Riley's eyes widen, and she darts her face to Emily's and begins to speak animatedly with her hands. Emily nods, shakes her head and then puts it down. Riley turns her head to meet our eyes and frowns. Hmmm...this may not be so good, after all.

Collin sees the whole interaction with the girls and turns to look at Brandt. "You seem pissed about this. Do y'all have something going on between the two of you?"

Brandt looks to Emily briefly before he smirks. "Did. But that's over now. So, you two, huh? Good for you. She's a fun girl."

Collin doesn't reply right away. His jaw tightens and he swallows hard. The implications in Brandt's words were there. Finally, he speaks. "We're not really a thing, but thanks." He turns around, avoiding Emily's stare.

This should be interesting.

CHAPTER 19

Kissing I think is my new favorite hobby. I've noticed lately how I haven't been writing as much. I'm not sure if it's because I'm so distracted by Josh, or because I'm finally breaking free from the darkness some, or that I find kissing much more cathartic. What I do know is that I love Josh's lips pressed against mine—they are so soft. It's always like the first time, like he is savoring me. I might need to write about that. An entire poem dedicated to Josh and the many ways he kisses me.

Before the wedding, there was a lot of chatter about who would room with whom. Granted, the original agreement was girls together, boys together. But since I want a night alone with Josh, and Collin and Emily seem to be comfortable with whatever it is they are doing, the plans have been changed. However, Em and I got ready in our room alone, and the guys got ready in their room, because they had to be there early, Collin actually left the keys to Violet for Em to drive us. Just that act alone made me think he likes her. I had no idea what Josh would look like, but just...*hot damn*. He is ridiculously sinful looking right now.

In all my life, I don't think I've ever felt so happy and yet so scared. It didn't happen for us easily, and we had to work really hard to get where we are, and there are still a lot of things that can go wrong for us, but right now we are here. I can't picture ever being apart, and yet I know it's going to happen. It's going to be so hard to be apart. Not having his lips to kiss every day or whenever I want to, or feeling his arms around me all the time, or having his eyes look at me the way they are *right now*.

I'm going to miss him so much. I have an ache in my chest where my heart is, just thinking about our future. College and all its complications, adding more shit to the overloaded baggage we already carry—a total bitch.

"Holy shit, Riley. Your boyfriend looks pretty damn edible in a suit and tie." Em says, staring at Josh with the other groomsmen. Then she clears her throat, "And um, Collin, Beau and Brandt look really, *really* nice too."

Oh my God. It's just dawned on me that she has slept with the groom and all of the groomsmen, all except Josh. "Holy shit, Em. You've had sex with the groom and all of the groomsmen, except for the edible one in the suit and tie." I whisper the words to her hoping no one hears me.

She puts her head down and turns it to me. "This is weird, right? Like all kinds of inappropriate weirdness."

I can't help but think she is right. It's super strange that Beau invited his ex-girlfriend to his wedding. But I can only assume he did it for me, or because Em is or was dating Brandt, or perhaps it's because we were all friends before she started hooking up with them. Whatever the reason, I'm thankful. I love having her around. This weekend wouldn't be the same otherwise.

"Kinda for you, yeah." I look up at Josh and the guys. Collin is staring right at Emily and Josh's eyes meet mine. I hold his gaze and something in his eyes draws me in. His eyes are smoldering hot, and I squirm in my seat. He must notice because he winks at me. He winks at me, and I think I'd do anything he asked me to do right now.

I turn to Emily. "You are so right, though. I just want to take that suit off of him slowly, and wrap that tie around his neck, and use it to pull his nakedness on top of me as I wear some lacy piece of Victoria's Secrets that my favorite person in the world bought for me." I say with all seriousness low enough for only her ears to hear. I've been picturing Josh in all kinds of scenarios lately.

"You shameless slut. You so want to hump his leg right now." She laughs. "I can almost feel your ladyboner from here."

I glare at her, "Shut up. I'm not shameless, and it's not his leg I want to hump." We both crack up laughing making people stare at us.

I lean forward to the people in front of us, "Sorry, sorry. My friend here accidentally let one slip." I cup my mouth, "Silently. If you know what I mean." I laugh as they scrunch their noses at us.

"That was ridiculously mean, Riley Marie Shaw." She glares at me.

"My middle name is not Marie," I state still chuckling.

"What the hell ever." She rolls her eyes and turns away from me.

I turn her head and kiss her cheek leaving bright red lips on them. "You love me. That was funny, and you know it."

"You're so stupid, Riley. I think hitting your head has made you a little nuts," she says giggling at me.

Next thing I know, we aren't laughing anymore, because Emily freezes when she notices all the guys except for Beau staring at her. I'm looking at them when she leans over to whisper in my ear. "I have a problem. I'm not sure if I'm supposed to be at this wedding with Brandt or not."

I dart my head to hers. "What?"

She sighs. "We haven't talked about it. He never asked me, but he looks really pissed right now. You think Collin may have said something about us?"

"Emily, do you like Collin?" She nods her head. "Do you want to be here with Brandt?" She shakes her head, no. "Are you still hooking up with Brandt?" She puts her head down. Oh man. This is bad. This could be bad.

I turn to look at the guys and frown. Well, shit.

The bridal march begins to play, and we all stand. When the bride walks down the aisle, I feel Josh staring, so I meet his eyes. His smile is soft and content. I wonder what he is thinking right now. I hope we are those two people one day. I am fidgeting where I stand because the way he is looking at me with heated eyes makes me feel warm. I want to push the bride out of the way and run to him. I want to kiss him senseless and then say I do.

Wait! What?

"Can I have this dance?" he asks, holding his hand out in front of him.

I smile and hesitate. "I don't know if my boyfriend would appreciate me dancing with someone as handsome as you."

He smirks and tilts his head to the side adorably. "I think your boyfriend was a fool to leave you sitting here by yourself. You are breathtaking. I just might have to sweep you off your feet and keep you forever." He bends and cups my chin, "Now that dance?"

I place my hand in his and let him pull me to the dance floor.

Josh's hand is around the small of my back, and my hands are around his neck tangling into his hair. "You look so beautiful, Riley. I really love those heels."

I smile up at him and glide my hands down to his tie that has been tempting me all night. I grab it and tug a little. "I really like this tie."

He smirks, "Yeah?"

I bite my lip, "Yeah."

And then he pulls me close to his chest and whispers in my ear, "You're killing me." He kisses my hair, and we slow dance together well past the time of the song ending.

A guy walks up to Josh and says, "You ready?" He nods and kisses my cheek.

"It's my turn," he says.

"Turn for what?"

"Bride and groom dance," he says.

Clearly I'm confused. "Okay, then how is it your turn again?"

He laughs, touches his finger to my nose. "Just listen, okay…every word…hear them." He presses his lips to mine, pausing there for a beat, and then walks off.

What?

I make my way to our table finding it empty. I look around, scanning the crowd, but I don't see Emily or Collin.

All of a sudden, Josh's voice booms over the sound system. "Hey, y'all. I'm Joshua Parker…good friend to that man over there." He points to Beau standing with his arm around his bride. "He asked me to sing for y'all as he dances with his lovely wife. I told him I had no idea what a wedding song would be, and he said to pick something that explains love. That didn't help me much." Josh locks eyes with me, and people are laughing. "But I heard this song and realized that these words mean something to me. So, to Beau and Jess, here's to giving your all to each other, and may y'all have a lifetime of lovemaking." Hoots and hollers erupt, and Josh picks up his guitar and starts strumming the chords to *All of Me* by John Legend.

Every word moves me. He's so beautiful—his voice—the way he shuts his eyes when he gets emotional—the way he stares into mine when he wants me to hear him. There is no doubt in my mind that he is singing this song to me. I just want to scream it, that I give all of me to him, too—that every piece of me belongs to him and will always belong to him.

"Thank you," he says, placing his guitar down and walking over to me. He stands right in front of me sitting at the table. My eyes slowly meet his as I stand to look up to him.

"That was the most beautiful thing I've ever heard," I tell him.

He grins adorably and then gets serious. "I meant every word. My cards are on the table. I'm willing to risk it all to have forever with you, Riley. I want this with you someday. You and me…like that." He points to Beau and Jess dancing.

I nod and wipe a tear that falls from my eyes. "I do, too. I want forever with you." I reach up and wrap my hands around his neck and hug him tightly.

After we throw the birdseed, we're all standing in the parking lot together saying our goodbyes to guests we don't really know.

Josh and I are standing next to Collin's car, and we find our lips attached again, they seem to have minds of their own. Emily honks the horn causing us both to jump. "Shit, Emily. What the hell?" I shout into the car at her. Collin's still inside. We have no idea why.

"Let's go. Make out later. Please. Go get Collin or something." Something in her tone and something in her eyes lets me know my best friend is not feeling herself. So I peck Josh's lips one last time and tell him to go find Collin. She hops out so I can climb in, and I can tell she is on the verge of crying.

"Everything okay, Em?" I ask concerned.

She looks at me with tears brimming in her eyes. "I hate guys, Riley. I just assumed that Brandt would want me here, ya know, even if we didn't talk about it, even it were just as friends. I just thought maybe he would, but he was so cold to me." She swipes a tear that falls and looks at me. "He barely looked in my direction, Riley. I tried to talk to him, and he told me to knock it off. He said I was fun, but that he was done playing games with me. I mean what the hell does that mean, anyway? I never played games. He never called me unless he wanted to fuck. And he never took me out on dates. I mean is that what he considers fun?" She says, in one giant breath.

I lean over the console to give her a hug, "Brandt's loss, Em. You're an amazing person. Besides, I thought you liked Collin." She tenses and pushes me away.

I look at her, but she can't meet my eyes. She looks out the window at Josh and Collin talking a few feet from us. "What is it? Why do you look like you're about to throw up? Please don't throw up in his car. He will kill you for sure."

She sighs and looks everywhere but at me, "I'm not going to throw up, Riley. Geez—melodramatic much." She apologizes and then says, "I did something stupid, Riley. I'm sure I'm going to hell now, because you aren't supposed to do what I did before marriage and definitely not in a church utility closet."

"What?"

She shakes her head and glances back out the window and then back at me. "I hooked up with Collin...*again*. It's official. I am a whore." She puts her hand over her mouth and chokes back a sob. "Oh, my God. Something is wrong with me, Riley. I don't even like Collin like that. I don't think I do. I mean he bangs every easy chick at school, and that disgust me. Look at this for fucks sake." She flicks the handcuffs hanging from his rear view mirror. "He's as much of a slut as me. We could never work. I just...God, I'm so stupid, Riley. I'm one of those easy chicks aren't I?" And the sob comes. She is leaning over in her seat bawling her eyes out into her hands, and I have no words to say to her. I just rub her back and look out the window noticing Josh glance back at the car, too.

Wow! I have no idea what to say to this. She is a free spirit and doesn't follow any rules. "Em, it's okay. I mean you can't change it. No one thinks you're one of those easy chicks. Stop talking about yourself like that."

I glance back out the window. I see Josh coming back towards the car with Collin following behind him. They both glance at Emily, who is steadily wiping away tears from her eyes. I know right away Collin just had this same heart to heart with his best friend.

Collin taps on the window where Emily is sitting in tears. She rolls it down as Josh climbs in from the opposite side. "Hey, can I talk to you for a second?" he asks her.

She nods and climbs out of the car. They walk off together. I notice he interlaces his fingers with hers as they walk. She doesn't pull away. If anything she leans closer into him. I don't care what she says. She likes him, and I think he may just like her, too.

So, we're in the back seat of Collin's very sexy car—alone now, and Josh begins kissing my neck and gliding his hand up my bare legs. "Joshua Parker, what are you doing?"

"Being bad," he breathes into my ear. "Something about you and skirts or dresses." He's coaxing my legs open and pushing his hand further up my leg and under my skirt. I glance around the windows and see we're pretty secluded, so I let him. I let him take me back to the place that make the stars shine so fucking brightly. He doesn't kiss me this time. He watches me as I come undone. He watches the way I respond to him. He just watches me under hooded eyes, and I realize I will never, ever have enough of him. I definitely didn't get enough of him this time, because Collin and Em come back to the car and unknowingly break our wicked spell.

I lean over to whisper in his ear, "Behave," and he just smirks. The ride back to the hotel is quiet. Emily sniffles a few times, and I notice Collin glance at her with concerned eyes. There is something different in how he looks at her right now.

We're in the elevator on the way up to our room, and I give a questioning look to Emily. I'm worried about her. But she nods her head and smiles at me. It's a small gesture that lets me know she is okay. She looks up at Collin, and he stares down at her. I notice the brief moment his chest picks up pace in his breathing. His eyes are soft, and he begins to pull his tongue piercing through his teeth. I see movement by their hands and my eyes track downward to see him interlace his fingers with hers. She looks back to me grinning like a lovesick puppy. I can't help but return her grin.

The ding alerts us of our floor, and we as couples, walk to our rooms, which are across from the other. I hug Emily and Josh and Collin bump fist. My nerves are suddenly hitting my system. I know Josh and I have already had sex, but this is something else entirely. We are intentionally spending the night together. The butterflies in my stomach that I always have around him are fluttering madly. Josh halts his hand on the key card by the slot. He looks down at me fidgeting with my hair and just fidgeting in general. He lifts a brow and cocks his head to the side. "You okay with this? If not we can—,"

"No, I'm okay. Just um, nervous I guess," I say honestly.

He slides the key into the slot and pushes open the door, letting me enter first. It's not like I didn't know we would be sharing a room. We'd discussed this. It's just earlier we were getting ready for the wedding and temptation wasn't there just yet. But now? We're standing in the middle of this room with one bed and our quick breaths. I'm staring at it when he walks behind me and moves my hair away from my shoulder. He breathes along my neck, and my breath quickens, the butterflies free falling. "Are you tired?" he asks. I immediately shake my head.

I turn around and find his hazel eyes smoldering with want for me. We just stare at each other breathing the same air. His mouth is so close to mine that I can almost taste the mint from his in my own. He tucks a curl behind my ear, and then trails his index finger down my neck and across my collarbone. My breath hitches and he smiles softly. "I love how you react to me."

That one smile, that dimple and the look in his eyes sets me on fire. My body is covered in goose bumps, and he feels it as he brushes his knuckles down my arm. I don't know what to do with myself. Last night was just a spur of the moment decision. This right here is deliberate. My mouth goes dry, and I lick my lips just to wet them. He makes a seething sound as he sucks his own lip into his teeth. Our eyes are on the others mouths, and we are leaning into each other. He cups my cheek and groans when our tongues touch. The kiss is sweet and full of all of the emotion we feel for each other—so beautiful that I almost weep.

It doesn't take long for our kiss to become deeper, more impatient and our hands to begin removing the barriers that are between us. He lifts his shirt over his head with one hand, and I let my eyes trail down his chest. His muscles are ridiculous. I trail my finger along his V, and he sucks in a breath. It makes me smile. When I look back to his eyes, I find them dilated and dark.

Like a jolt of electricity has shot through my body, I become all nerves and butterflies on speed. I feel my hands shake, and I have to mentally talk myself into a state of calm.

This is Josh. Your best friend. Your boyfriend. Someone you have been with forever in your mind. This is nothing to fear and everything to desire. You love him. He loves you. Let it be beautiful.

It's crazy. We have already done this, but I feel scared as hell. He's unbuttoning my blouse and watching me. His hands glide under the fabric on my shoulders as he removes my shirt. He admires me and trails his index finger along my chest and down my rib cage. He lowers his lips to my neck and that spot by my ear. My hands are on his chest, his heart hammering against my palm and then his eyes lock with mine. Next thing I know he gasps, and looks over my shoulder into the mirror above the dresser.

"Oh, my God. Your back?" I look over my shoulder smiling, but when I look into his horrified eyes, I know his reaction is not the same as mine, not the same at all because he looks on the verge of punching the wall. "Did I do that to you? Oh, fuck. I didn't do that to you, did I?" He says each syllable with pain etched in his voice. He gently touches the marks on my back; all the while a frown is placated on his face. "Does it hurt?" He asks, looking back into my eyes.

I shake my head back and forth, and cup his cheek making him look at my eyes, not at my back. "Look at me!" He does. "It doesn't hurt, and I like it." His eyes widen and darken all in a breath. "You didn't do that to me. We did that together, baby. When I saw it this morning I was shocked at first, but then I remembered how we felt together. How badly I wanted you—want you now. We were so caught up in the moment that I never even felt the pain." His eyes move back to the marks on my back as he moves behind me. "To me, those marks are beautiful," I whisper as he wraps his hand around my stomach. He lowers his lips to the marks on my back where he kisses each spot. I forget how to breathe.

Then he lowers the zipper of my skirt and glides it down my legs. I'm left standing here in my silver heels and my black sheer bra and panties set from Emily, facing the bed. "You are so sexy." His words are like a breath of hot air along my neck. *Oh God.* I press my butt into the front of him as he reaches his hand into the front of my panties to feel me. Then he does this thing that has me gripping for any restraint. When he undoes his pants and lowers them down his legs, he lowers down to the floor with them. He kisses my ankle and licks all the way up the inside of my leg as he slowly stands back up. He gently bites my ass, and softly kisses his way up my back. I moan loudly and then feel embarrassed. I shut my eyes and drop my head. He grips my chin and turns my head to look up at him. "Don't hide your eyes. The sounds you make are the sweetest fucking thing I've ever heard." I bite my lip painfully because he pulls me close to him and tugs at my hair.

You liked it rough?" His question is a husky whisper in my ear.

"Yes," I breathe.

He's pressed against me, and I can't help but whimper, my head falling back on his shoulder as he tickles his fingers up my rib cage and to my breasts. He moves his hand to the nape of my neck. He gently pushes me down to the bed, my hands catch my fall on the bed as I gasp, shocked by the movement. I have no idea what he is thinking, what he plans to do from here. His hand moves down my back and to the backs of my thighs. I look over my shoulder and find him standing back staring at me with heated eyes. His eyes move from my ass back to my eyes. "As much as I'd love to take you like this, I don't want to fuck this time. I want to take my time enjoying you, to feel every inch of you shiver when I make love to you. I want to crawl inside of you and watch you come undone." I can't speak. I'm so turned on. I'm beginning to think that sex with Josh will never be gentle and sweet, and right now as I watch his eyes penetrate mine, I don't care. I push against him, silently begging him to do it that way. He just grins and shakes his head. He's taunting me, making me wait. "I've watched you all damn day tempting me with your lip biting, your lollipop licking and just being you. Do you want me, pretty girl?"

I nod because speech isn't possible. "Say it!"

I stand up and turn around to face him. "I want you," I whisper as I unhook my bra, and he watches closely. I let it fall to the ground, and his eyes darken and drop to admire me. I climb onto the bed and scoot back. "I want you to make love to me, Josh. I want to give you everything I have and more, because you have given me my life back, and I love you."

He crawls onto the bed like a lion seeking its prey—his hands climbing up my body and into my hair as our mouths connect desperate for the other. Our hands are everywhere, and passion ignites something so beautiful between us. I moan as his mouth sucks on my breasts before moving to the other. He travels down my stomach and sits back on his heels in between my open legs. I lift as he glides my panties down my legs. He lifts one ankle kissing the inside of my leg as he removes my heel, and then he repeats the same process on the opposite foot.

He trails his hands up each of my legs and to the inside of my thighs. I'm trembling.

"God, you are so beautiful, Riley." He grins as I squirm under him. He lowers his mouth to mine. I love the way our skin feels against each other. He touches me between my legs and a soft moan escapes my lips. "Feel good?" His words caress my lips.

"Yes," I whisper.

"I want to taste you there." He looks in my eyes as if asking the question. I nod my head. He kisses his way down my stomach. He inhales and groans deep in his throat. *Oh, good God.* My body is taking over, and I grab his hair behind his neck and my hips roll on their own accord.

"You smell so good." He says these things and they are messing with my head. My head starts thrashing back and forth. I don't know what to do with my hands, and he hasn't even made contact yet. He's just breathing air over me.

His finger traces the musical heart tattoo that is for him sitting on my hipbone. He replaces his finger with his lips where he delicately kisses the spot on my hip, kissing the spot next to it and then next to it. He dips his tongue in my navel, and I begin writhing beneath him.

He presses his hand down on my hips to still my movements and licks his way down. As soon as his tongue makes contact I'm already unraveling. I can feel his smile against me. And then he proceeds to make me believe in magic. Everything with him is so intense, and this is no different. Everything he does to me is so perfect. He makes this sound deep in his chest, and it vibrates against me.

"Josh, oh God, I…hmm, I…please." I'm not even coherent. My head is thrown back and my back arches. I'm tugging on his hair and pushing his head where I need it. He mutters words about me tasting good and tells me to let go. As if I could stop whatever this is happening to my body.

He kisses his way up my stomach, up my neck and to my mouth. My hands are gliding along his skin. Our eyes are locked as I use my feet to guide his boxers off of his body. I've come to realize that I love how I taste on his tongue. We kiss slow and deep. Our skin feels hot touching the other, slick with sweat.

I cup his cheek trying to find the right words. "You feel so good, Josh. I need you inside of me."

His mouth takes mine in a hungry growl. "I love you," he whispers as he presses into me.

"I love you, too." I pull his face to mine as we kiss and begin to find a rhythm. Again, our bodies know just what to do with each other. I never knew it would feel so good. I never knew we would be so perfect together. That this, with him, would feel so right. He likes to talk to me when we make love, and he kisses me like he can't get enough of my lips. Everything about him intoxicates me. He's like a drug to me, and I'm completely high.

I feel myself getting close, and I shut my eyes. He grabs my face, "Open your eyes. I love watching you. It's the most beautiful thing I've ever seen."

I open my eyes and my breath catches at the look in his eyes. He rests his forehead against mine, moving faster and deeper into me. My legs are wrapped around his waist, locked at the ankles.

He reaches his hand underneath me and lifts me just a little. That's it. "Josh. Oh, God. Stop…no, don't stop." He smiles and watches me as

I come undone just like he wants. I grab his face and greedily kiss his lips as he groans into my mouth.

In the shower, I take my time to really notice Josh's body—how lean his muscles are, how strong his arms are, how beautifully sexy his hair is wet and clinging to his forehead. The motions of him lathering soap along my skin ignites yet another burning inside me. We kiss and we touch, and I have decided that I will never get enough of him. He washes my hair for me, and the gentleness in how he cares for me warms my heart. I feel high until he says, "I'm going to miss you so damn much." And now I'm hollow.

I squeeze my eyes shut as immediate tears sting my eyes. I know he has to go. I don't want to be the reason he gives up an opportunity that might be good for him. But who am I kidding? This is going to be hard on us.

My reply is tense. "I'm going to miss you too, Josh."

My back is to him so he can't see my tortured face. He turns me to face him, and the tears fall unbidden. I hope he doesn't notice the tears fall. I hope that the tears mesh with the water trickling down my face and body from the showerhead. His eyes study mine, and when his thumbs move under my eyes I know he knows I am upset. Nothing about me goes unnoticed to him.

"I can stay, Riley. Where ever you are is where I belong. You are my heart."

I want to tell him to stay. I want to, but I don't because I can't. "I belong with you, too, Josh, but you have to go. I can't be the reason you give up something that matters to you." I tell him truthfully.

"Riley, I wanted to give this up before you and I became an 'us.' You know that. I want to see your face every day not just hear your voice. *You* matter to me the most."

God, I know what he means. We are talking about college away for four years. Are we just in denial? How could we survive that? I'm going to have to transfer to be with him, or I am afraid I will lose him forever. I've already applied for the spring semester, but he doesn't know that.

I begin to tremble and shake as a sob falls from my chest. He holds me to him and sighs heavy. "I've already applied to UTA, Riley. If you want me to go, I will, but I'm not promising to stay away. You are my heart. You are my home, and with you is where I belong. Fuck the rest. Fuck football. Fuck anyone that doesn't understand why I need to be with you."

I kiss him, pouring my entire heart into that kiss. Kissing him like it will be the last time. Kissing him in a way that says, even if he were gone away for four years my heart would always be his. Nothing would change that...ever. I belong to, Joshua Parker. I am his. He owns me— mind, body and spirit.

He wraps me in a towel and places a kiss to my forehead. We brush our teeth, and I get dressed in my pajamas as Josh just throws on a pair of boxer briefs. I fall asleep to him humming a song. For the first time in a while, I don't have a nightmare.

CHAPTER 20

It's an emotional mess that is destroying us both. I've never felt so much for someone. I'm blissfully happy with her and in the same damn breath—I'm scared as fuck for us.

I awake to the smell of coconut and vanilla across my face. I smile because I can imagine waking up to her hair in my face every morning. I take this moment to study her features to memory—the way she breathes, the little freckle that is next to one of her eyes. She looks like an angel—my angel. I study the soft curve of her nose, the little dip in her lips, and how her hair covers her face and my pillow. I watch her sleep and imagine a future where we wake up like this each morning.

"So, how long will you be gone?" she asks in a soft voice. We're sitting at our spot by the lake the following day. Later, we'll be moving her into her new apartment with Emily, and then we have a few weeks together before everything changes.

"Two weeks and then I'll come back for a week." She's sitting between my legs against my chest. I can feel every breath of air she intakes.

She says, "I'm going to miss you, but I know we can do this," she mutters out loud, but I think she's speaking to herself, not so much to me. She turns suddenly to face me, sitting on her knees, looking down at her hands in her lap.

I guide her chin up with my fingers. "What is it?"

She sighs softly, and her eyes bounce back and forth between my own. "I'm just so sorry that I stole so many moments from us. We could have had so many years together if I just had believed enough. I feel like I've just finally started living, and now you're leaving. I...I promise to be strong, Josh. It's always been you for me."

My chest hurts—like it's strangling my heart and robbing me of air. I don't want to do this. I don't want to be away from her. I feel like I've just started living as well—living with her. She is the reason why I live. "Riley, I love you. I've always loved you. We may not have been together the way I wanted all those years, but I remember every fucking moment we've ever shared. There have been moments that I cherished that you may not even have known I grabbed. I'll come back to you. I promise." I tuck her hair behind her ear, and when I trail my finger down her neck, she shuts her eyes breathing shallowly. I love that her skin covers in goose bumps when I touch her.

I lean forward, closing the distance between us as I kiss the corner of her mouth. She inhales deeply. I cup her cheeks and then press my lips to hers, not opening my mouth. We just stay like that for a beat before she parts her lips slowly, and her tongue very so softly touches my lips. That's all it took for our kiss to become the kiss that has sealed my fate—I am hers. I will never belong to anyone but her.

"I can't believe her dad furnished the apartment," I state to Riley as I load up my truck with boxes of her things to bring to her new apartment.

"I know right. I'm glad, though. Now, I don't have to lose my bedroom here. There might be times I need to escape the apartment if Collin comes to visit Em, and you don't get to make it to me." I know she doesn't mean for that to sound offensive, but it does. I don't call her on it though. There may be times Collin can come home and I can't.

"Why don't you run inside and get Tink and her stuff, and we'll get going," I say shutting the hatch to my truck.

She pecks my lips and runs inside. I'm about to climb inside my truck when an all too familiar motorcycle parks at the side of the road by my mailbox. I turn my head and find Dean looking to Riley's house and then to me. He smirks. "Remember when I said I realized she belonged to you? I lied. No worries, Parker. I'll keep her warm while you're out of state." He hollers over to me with a taunting gleam in his eyes.

I ball my fist, and I'm walking towards the street prepared to remind him again of whom she belongs to. The door to Riley's house opens, and she comes walking out with Tink and her things. Her back is turned to lock up when I look over at her. Dean's tires burn as he zooms off down the street. She turns around and looks down the street with wide eyes. She looks back to me, those same wide eyes holding the question. An internal debate is going on in my head—to tell her what he said, to not? To stay in Texas and not let him have an inch, or go because it's what I have to do?

"Was that Dean?" She asks, as I walk up to help her grab Tink's litter box and a bag full of her stuff.

"Probably so," I say, avoiding her eyes as I turn to walk back to my truck.

What the hell did he mean? Like she would let him near her again. She wouldn't let him near her again. But he will obviously try, and that in itself is enough to make me crazy mad.

Once in the truck, I feel my irritation growing. Riley notices because she says, "You okay? Your ears are red, and that vein in your neck is pulsing."

Part of me wants to yell at her. *What were you thinking ever dating that prick? Why did you lead him on so long that now he thinks he has an in when I'm gone?* Instead, I shake my head, rub behind my neck to soothe the tension, take a deep breath and lie straight through my fucking teeth. "Yeah, I just have a headache coming on. Nothing to worry your pretty little head over." She stares into my eyes looking for something. I don't give her much time, because I lean over the console and kiss her lips and then turn back to the front, turning the ignition.

When we get back to the apartment, Riley goes to her bedroom and shows Tink to her new home. I'm in the kitchen fighting against my own instincts and myself. I pull my phone from my pocket and send a text.

Me: I DON'T KNOW WHAT GAME YOU'RE PLAYING BUT LEAVE RILEY ALONE!

It takes a few seconds for him to reply.

Dean: SHAME REALLY – WE WERE MAKING SUCH PROGRESS

Me: BULLSHIT – YOU NEVER CHANGE

Dean: YOUR PANTIES ARE BUNCHED – THINK SHE MIGHT GET LONELY?

Fuck! I hate this guy. I seriously hate him.

Me: YOU THINK THE MOMMA OF YOUR BABY WOULD LIKE YOU TRYING TO SNEAK OUT OF THE HOUSE ALREADY?

He doesn't reply this time, and I take a moment to calm myself. My phone pings just as Riley walks in the room. I simply place it into my back pocket and clear my throat. Her eyes track my hands and lift in question. She begins fidgeting with her hair like she does when she's nervous. To distract her, I make small talk.

"Does Tink like her new room?"

Riley shrugs and studies my eyes. She is so damn intuitive. "What's up, Josh? You've been on edge since we left my house."

"It's nothing. I just have a headache. I told you. C'mere." I crook my finger as I pout.

She sighs heavily, and I know she isn't buying my shit, but for now she lets it go. She wraps her hands around my waist, and I rest my head in her hair. *Please, Lord let me keep her. Please.*

Later that night, I'm sitting in my bed staring at her dark window. It's her first night in her apartment, and I'm here. I take a moment to look at my phone, at the text that has been blinking at me all night.

Dean: NO WORRIES WITH PRESLEE – SHE KNOWS HER ROLE IN THE GAME! ;)

What the hell does that mean?

Two weeks have flown by all too quickly. Time has run up. Thankfully, no repeat run in's with Dean have taken place. We leave tomorrow for Louisiana for summer drills. The girls are coming up to meet us next weekend, but I'm not thinking about that right now. I'm thinking about the nerves in my stomach for what's about to happen.

We are at the Rockin Fourth to watch Rebel and the Dark Angels perform Riley's songs. What she doesn't know is that I'm their opening act. I'm singing one cover song and one of my own in a few short minutes.

We're sitting on the picnic blanket with Collin and Em. They are now officially a couple. I lean over and kiss Riley's cheek. "I'm gonna go to the bathroom before the band starts up."

She looks down at her phone. "You better hurry. They go on in like ten minutes."

I smile. "No worries, pretty girl."

I'm standing to the side with Rebel and the group. "Are you nervous? I can't believe you are doing this." I look out to the audience and smile. I can. I've dreamed of singing on the Indie rock stage as far back as I can remember. They only let you hit the stage at eighteen. So here I am. The park has multiple stages set up, but this one has always been my favorite.

I have my guitar in place, and I'm to the side out of sight. I'm so nervous. I bet Riley is freaking out right about now because I'm not back.

The crowd cheers as the Dark Angels take the stage. Rebel gets the mic and glances at me, winking. "Hey, guys. We are the Dark Angels." More cheers. The girls have sort of made a name for themselves all the sudden. "Before we pull you into the dark with us, we have a surprise for you. Our opening act is a well-known guy that we all can't help but fall in love with, and he's none other than the boyfriend to our song writer." I see Riley's mouth fall open, and she starts scanning the crowd for me with the biggest grin on her face. She's proud of me. My heart swells. "Please, put your hands together for Joshua Parker!" The crowd goes crazy, something I never expected.

I make my way to the stage with my guitar. I grab the mic and smile. More screams follow. Damn, I really didn't expect it. I watch Riley stand and make her way through the crowd to come stand in the front. I bite my lip and grin at her. She's smiling so wide, it's contagious, and I can't help but smile back at her. Those eyes that I lose myself in are twinkling up at me. "This song is a cover, and I'm dedicating this to a special someone. Guys grab your girlfriends. Husbands kiss your wives, and tell them they're beautiful. Go on...do it." I smirk as I see them do it. I mouth to Riley "You're beautiful." And then I start strumming the guitar and sing *Anywhere but Here* by Safetysuit.

I sing my heart out and feel every emotion. I sing it for her. The next song is harder, because this is one I wrote *for her*. "This song is mine. The girl I wrote this for has no idea I ever wrote this or that she changed my life forever. This is *Her Escape*."

With her eyes locked with mine, I sing her song to the world.

INNOCENT WITH SAD EYES
FEARING THE NEXT CHAPTER
AFRAID OF LIES
LETTING GO
LETTING ME IN
THE WALLS BUILT SO HIGH
CRUMBLE TO ASH
HER ESCAPE SO BEAUTIFUL
THE STARS SHINE FOR HER

FINDING HERSELF
THE SLOW BURN
THE ACHE IN HER HEART
GROWS IN STRENGTH
SO MUCH LOVE TO GIVE
INTO EACH OTHER WE CRASH
HER ESCAPE SO BEAUTIFUL
THE STARS SHINE FOR HER

IN A DAZE SHE FINDS HER WAY
FINDING THE NEED TO TRUST AGAIN
I WILL NEVER FORGET
EYES, SKIN, BREATHS BETWEEN US
FALLING SO FAST
YOUR ESCAPE SO BEAUTIFUL
THE STARS SHINE FOR YOU

YOU ARE BEAUTIFUL
NOW, HERE I AM WITH MY HEART ON THE FLOOR
IT'S YOURS, MILES IN BETWEEN
IT STAYS HERE WITH YOU
WITH YOU TO PROTECT
CONSTANT WHISPERS OF REGRET

NEVER SAY GOODBYE
NEVER HIDE YOUR EYES

NEVER TO SAY A LIE
MY ESCAPE IS YOU

YOUR ESCAPE SO BEAUTIFUL
EVERY STAR IS ANOTHER REASON TO REMEMBER

NO MORE STONES TO THROW
A SLOW CRAWL
KNOWING NOTHING AT ALL
KNOWING EVERYTHING IS YOURS
LEARNING TO LIVE
FINDING REASONS TO FLY
FINDING LOVE TO LOSE TIME
COMING DOWN FROM THE HIGH
I CAN'T... I CAN'T MAKE YOU BELIEVE
THAT YOUR ESCAPE IS BEAUTIFUL
YOU ARE BEAUTIFUL

INTO EACH OTHER WE CRASH
LET THE DOUBT, THE FEAR REMAIN ASH
NEVER SAY GOODBYE
NEVER HIDE YOUR EYES
YOUR ESCAPE IS BEAUTIFUL
THE STARS NEVER LEAVE
A CONSTELLATION FROM YOU TO ME

I take my guitar off and climb down the stage to wrap my hands around Riley as she cries. "I love you. Never forget. We will make this work. I love you," I say as she nods and then I kiss her in front of everyone as they cheer.

After we watch Rebel and the Dark Angels sing Riley's music, we start roaming around. We are walking around the park when this guy walks up to us. "Sorry to interrupt, but I wanted to give you my card. I just happened to be in town to visit family, and I am definitely glad that I was. I'm one of the producers at Nashville's Next in Tennessee. You have a great voice. I don't have a lot time to talk now, but take my card. I'll be waiting for your call." He doesn't say anything else. I think nothing of it and put the card in my back pocket. Riley's eyes are on my face, but she doesn't say anything either.

We're sitting on our blanket getting ready to watch the fireworks, but it's still not dark enough. Riley keeps glancing behind her and shivering. "Are you okay?"

She looks at me and sighs. "It's just that I keep feeling like someone is watching me. It's weird, earlier when Em and I walked to get a snow cone, I swear someone was following us."

I look around, but I don't see anyone that stands out. They're hundreds of people here. I can tell that she is genuinely freaked out though, so I pull her close to me. I have her between my legs, and I'm holding her. We remain like that until it's time to leave.

CHAPTER 21

I hate change. Living with Emily is a change. Having Josh gone for the majority of July is a change. Falling back into the darkness is a change. I don't want anything to change. I want him here. I want things to stay the same. But it's all changing.

Collin and Josh have been gone a week. It hasn't been too terrible. In fact, I think I handled it well, but I knew that Em and I would be visiting this weekend. Josh and I are sitting in the bleachers of the stadium just admiring the view of where Josh will play sooner than later. Em and I drove up here to visit since they had to leave us for a few weeks. Collin took Em on a tour of the campus, and Josh took me here.

"Wow. It's kind of amazing, Josh. Don't ya think?" I say feeling a little awestruck at the stadium.

"Yep."

"I've never seen them play up close, just on TV, and you're going to be a part of that one day. It's just a little crazy, right?"

"Yep."

Every 'yep' is flat and detached of any real emotion and definitely not full of excitement. I turn to look at him and sigh when I see the sadness in his eyes.

He looks back to me. "This is a mistake, Riley. I don't think we are strong enough for this. I'll just get a job and go to school next year. I don't want to be here without you."

I stare at him unsure of what I should say. His dad would be so angry, and then he would blame me. I can't be the reason they aren't okay with each other. His dad is right. He's amazing, and he has a real shot of being great—this could be his future. If he gives this up he might resent me one day—maybe, not today, or tomorrow, but one day. It's a real possibility that I fuck this up somehow, or that he wakes up one day and remembers all the reasons his life turned to shit. I shake my head to rid myself of the dark thoughts that always remain in the recesses of my mind.

"Josh, we will be okay. I will be strong for you. I promise. You can't give up without trying. I can't let you give up without trying. I love you so much. I want nothing more than for you to be with me, but if you walk away from this, and then one day you realize that you regret it, it will be my fault…then all we have is a lot of resentment. I already have a list against me for all the reasons you should hate me. Please don't make a bigger list. One of those reasons will eventually stick, and then I'll lose you completely." I am rambling so fast, and I didn't even realize I was crying until he has me in his lap and is wiping my cheeks.

"I love you. There will never be a reason for us to not be together. You couldn't ever do anything to push me away, Riley. This is just going to be so hard for us." He holds my head to his shoulder and is threading his fingers into my hair.

I breathe him in and fight the urge to sob and beg him to do what he wants to do anyways. I finally get him, only to lose him so quickly.

★☆★

We're in Josh's truck driving through New Orleans. At first glance, I'm a little worried about where we're going, but once we park in the garage and take off walking in the French Quarter I absolutely fall in love. It's so busy and full of life.

"Have you been here before?" I ask Josh.

He shakes his head and leans down to my ear. "Another first for us, pretty girl."

I look up at him and smile. He interlaces our fingers as we walk down the street. For a moment, it's like our separate lives are entwined. I try to picture myself living in Louisiana with him, our lives together as we find our forever.

"Oh, my God—street performers. Let's watch," Em says tugging my hand to pull me along with her. I'm ripped away from Josh, and when I look back at him and Collin, they are both grinning at us. We're across the street from this beautiful cathedral and horse and carriages. A group of guys are putting on a show with flips and break dancing.

My eyes are taking in everything I can like a sponge. I don't think I've stopped smiling yet. I laugh when Emily gets called up to be part of the act. I would be bright red, but she's eating the whole thing up with a cheesy grin plastered on her face.

After the show, we walk to Cafe Du Monde and enjoy beignets. Oh, my god, those are delicious. We've just crossed the street to look at all of the art and to walk to the St. Louis Cathedral. I'm pointing and admiring everything I see.

I stop briefly to watch a magician perform a trick outside the Cathedral when Josh looks down at me giggling. "What?"

He turns my body to him and my breath catches as he leans down. His lips brush against mine, and he licks the corner of my mouth. He stands back up smirking. "You had some powdered sugar left behind, but I got it for you. I really love it when you eat sweet stuff."

I swat at his chest and turn to pull us into the church. "Oh, wow," I breathe taking in the view.

It's so beautiful. An image of walking down the aisle to a waiting Joshua Parker fills my mind almost instantly. We don't stay in here nearly long enough. Collin and Emily won't shut up, and people are giving us crazy looks for being noisy.

"We should go down Bourbon Street," Collin tells Em, wiggling his eyebrows.

I've already been warned that this street is crazy at night, with its many bars and strip clubs. It's daytime though, so I expect it to be tame. However, once we hit the street, I realize it's not all that tame even during the day. My mouth falls open as I see everything around me. Collin stops at this window and orders two daiquiris showing them his fake ID. He hands one to Em and one to me. I gladly take it.

I gauge Josh's reaction as we walk along the street. He looks curious, but isn't showing too much excitement. It makes me grin. We walk past a club to the right. A girl in a black bustier with a garter belt and thigh highs is standing in the doorway luring people in. "Holy fuck!" Collin mutters slapping Josh on the chest and nodding his head to the girl. Josh looks, and I mean really looks. It makes me uncomfortable, but guys will be guys, I guess. Will these be his temptations on the weekends when he's going out? He looks back to me. I may be naive, but I see the darkening in his eyes. I softly smile and look away.

Collin is going on and on about how he's going to love living in Louisiana. Of course, Em laughs it off and tells him he can look but he better remember their agreement, whatever that may be. She's stronger than I am. My mind is on overdrive picturing Josh partying it up and having too much fun. *Stop it, Riley. He hasn't even done anything. Quit thinking the worse.*

We don't linger much longer on Bourbon Street. I decide, though, that I really like daiquiris. We go eat at this cafe' and Josh and I share fried shrimp. Then we walk to the Riverwalk. I can't get over how beautiful everything is, how friendly people are. The energy here is contagious. It makes me happy, yet makes me sad. Josh is going to fall in love with it here.

Our hotel is back in Baton Rouge since that is where the university is located. As we make the drive across Lake Pontchatrain, I take in the view, and imagine what life would be like if I lived here with Josh. I snuggle up close to his side, thankful for the middle seat in his truck. He gently kisses my hair. "Did you have fun today?" he asks, glancing at me.

"Yeah, it's an entire different world, huh?" I chuckle lightly. "A little contagious, actually." I chance a look at his face. He's smiling and nodding, but I can see the same melancholy in his eyes that lives inside of mine.

After saying our goodbyes to Collin and Emily, Josh and I settle into our room. He realizes he left his phone in his truck so he goes down to get it. I have my ear buds plugged into my ears, and JES *Like a Waterfall* comes on my radio app. I'm belting out every word feeling the same way. This weekend is it. Our new lives in separate places begin as soon as Em and I go back home. I feel every word of this song as I stare out the window that overlooks the pool.

I actually really love singing, always have, but I hate that I do. My mom loves to sing or loved to. The music ceased to be beautiful in my house when my dad cheated. Not wanting to be anything like either of them, I decided to never embrace this love of mine. That hate I've let harbor space in my heart for far too long is slowly fading away.

I have my hands on the glass of the window as I sing the last note and feel the release of my own waterfall. I rip the buds out of my ears and turn to throw my phone onto the bed as I wipe the tears that are on my cheeks. I freeze when I see Josh standing against the wall with his mouth hanging agape. His feet are crossed at the ankle, and his hands are in his pockets telling me that he has been standing there a while.

"How...how long have you been standing there?" I ask stuttering.

He moves slowly towards me with that look in his eyes—that determined look. "Long enough to fall in love with you again. I love when you sing. Your voice is like an angel," he says, brushing his knuckles along my cheek. "That song was sad, though."

I shut my eyes. Josh leans his forehead into mine and there we remain for a few breaths, just sharing the same air. He cups my cheeks and places a kiss to my forehead. "I had a good time with you today." He smiles softly at me.

I throw my hands around him, and he lifts me up to where my legs are around his waist. He walks back to the bed and holds me. I just need him to comfort me right now. After a little while, he loosens his grip on me. "Wanna go for a swim?"

"No, I just want to hold you longer." The tears are burning the backs of my eyes, but I blink them away. This hurts. This ache in my chest is growing larger, and the lump in my throat is making it hard to swallow as I'm imagining all the time I'm about to spend without him.

He lowers to his side on the bed and pulls me close to him. I tuck my head under his chin and listen to his heartbeat.

He begins to breathe fast and then he clears his throat and swallows hard. "Remember that night at Brandt's party when um, you were so mad at me?" His whole body stiffens.

"Yes," I whisper. *Why is he asking this?*

He grips my chin, and turns my head to where our eyes are looking into one another's. "My heart broke a thousand times that night, Riley. Seeing the pain in your eyes. Seeing that dark place swallow you up, and then when you kissed that dick, I thought my heart would shatter into a million pieces. It physically caused me pain. But something you said in my truck later really bothered me, and I never said anything to you about it."

"I'm so sorry, Josh. I never meant to—,"

"Stop. I know, Riley. I know you didn't mean to act like that, and I never told you how much it hurt me. I'm not telling you now to make you feel bad. It's just that you said you hate yourself that night, and I'm scared. I'm scared that when I leave, you're going to go back to that dark place that makes you climb inside your head, and I don't want you to do that. I want you to remember how far we've come. I don't want to take those steps backward, baby. I want us to keep moving forward. I want you to remember that even miles apart, my heart is with you. It was always and will always be with you," he whispers the last part as his thumb pads along my bottom lip that is now quivering.

I know he's scared for me. I don't trust easily. I don't do any of this well. I know he loves me, and I know, without a doubt, that I love him, but in the back of my mind, I know we have never been apart like this, and we've never been tested this much. I fear we aren't strong enough.

He watches as a single tear falls down my cheek and then another. He watches my eyes so carefully, and I see the pain in his. We both feel this. "Promise me, Riley. Promise me that you won't get stuck in there." He taps my temple. "Promise me that you will hold onto us and everything I've ever told you about us and love. Promise me that when the pain gets too much that you will call me, and we will talk about it, that you won't numb it."

I nod my head, and he shakes his. "No, Riley. Say the words. Promise me that you will keep the walls down for me."

"I promise, Josh. I promise I'm yours today and forever." Tears are streaming down my face as he presses his lips to mine.

When we made love that night, I prayed it wouldn't be the last time. I prayed that somehow we would survive this test, that we would make it back to each other in one piece and stronger. We didn't fight this hard, and go through all this pain to lose each other. But I knew my weak heart, and I knew my warped mind might have made a promise I wasn't capable of keeping. My heart will always be his, but I can't guarantee the darkness won't creep up on me. The wicked whispers always linger, telling me I'm not enough for him—that it takes one moment of temptation for love to be forgotten. Look at my parents. I may have escaped the doubt about where my heart belonged, but can I ever truly escape the fear of heartbreak?

I'm sitting on my bed with my daddy's guitar. I stole it out of my mom's garage back home and brought it here. I'm not sure why. The reasons keep changing in my head. It's partly because seeing a guitar reminds me of Josh, and partly to remind me that my dad was just a man that made a mistake, but he loved my mom. Somewhere in my mind, the reason is rational. I haven't played in years, but as I sit here with my fingers on the strings I remember it all. It becomes a cathartic release, and once I start, I can't stop. I'm playing Flyleaf *All Around Me,* the words coming to me by memory. My eyes are shut, and I go somewhere beautiful in my mind, somewhere a little dark but still full of light.

When I finish the song, I hear a click from my doorway and snap my eyes open to find Emily standing there with her phone. "Did you take my picture?" I ask.

She shakes her head with a soft, mischievous smile. "No, I recorded you. That was beautiful. Everyone is right. You sing so pretty, Riley. Sorry to be a creeper, I just wanted to capture that moment of peace for you."

I place my dad's guitar back into his case and stand to put it against my dresser. "Thanks. I haven't played or sang in so long. I was just feeling something today, so I did."

"Are you excited about the guys coming home? It's still so weird having Collin as a boyfriend. I half expected to be another notch on his bedpost, but he says he misses me. Crazy right—even crazier that I miss him?" she rambles.

I smile. "Kinda crazy, but Collin just needed the right girl to calm him down. Maybe the same is true for you. Y'all are cute together." I smile genuinely.

"Yeah?"

"Yeah, let's go get dinner. I want sushi." I laugh when she gives me the crazy eye.

"Since when do you like sushi?"

I smile thinking back to the day Josh made me try it for the first time. "Since, Josh. Let's go."

Sushi wasn't the same without his flirtatious remarks. My mind kept flashing back to the way he smiled at me when I spoke about the sushi's size in my mouth. I kept dazing into an empty chair thinking about reading fortunes and making them dirty. I looked to the door as I imagined his truck parked out front, and him trusting me to drive it. Maybe, sushi wasn't the same without him.

The entire drive back home, I was thinking about how many things remind me of him and how I never realized it. A certain smell, a place, a song—so many reminders of him everywhere. I miss him so much, and the hard part hasn't even started. At least, I have one more week with him soon.

★☆★

"But you said you were coming home? You said you had one more week?" I cry into the phone as Josh informs me that he can't come home this weekend. He's been gone for weeks and classes start soon. Once school begins, he won't be able to come home at all.

First, it was drills and then it was getting school stuff situated. I understand. I just miss him, so much. Collin's already come back once without him.

"I know, baby. I can't come for a few more days. I had to get a job to pay for gas and other shit. I can't ask for time off already."

I sigh. *A job?* Just one more thing to keep him from me. "Okay, I understand. I just miss you."

He sighs heavily in his chest. "I miss you too, baby. Listen, I need to go. Collin just walked in, and we're going to work out before my shift. Can I call you when I get off work?"

I roll my eyes and plop down on my bed. I know he isn't blowing me off, but it feels like that. "Yeah, of course."

"All right. Talk to you later." The line goes dead. I have the urge to throw my fucking phone across the room—another weekend alone.

Emily comes into my room pouting with her phone in her hand. "I hate this," she says.

"Me, too." At least, she had her boyfriend visit once.

We lie back on my bed pouting and missing our boyfriends. She looks over at me. "I know we agreed to save money so we can visit them all the time, but I kind of want to do something. Maybe this pain will take my mind off of the other pain I feel."

I look over at her, curiosity in my eyes. "What?"

"Trust me?"

I nod and follow her. Anywhere is better than here stuck in my head.

As I'm lying back on this table with my shorts unbuttoned and my shirt up high, I'm questioning my trust for Emily. "It's going to be so sexy. You can't back out now."

"I'm not backing out, but when you said numb our pain with another kind of pain, I just assumed we would get drunk or something." I'm griping and the guy says, "You ready?"

I nod my head and follow his instructions to inhale and blow it out, and then it's done. I have my navel pierced, and Em has her nipples pierced. She is much braver than me. That was a definite 'hell no' for me. "We'll get drunk after. Wow," she says.

I'm standing in the mirror looking at the silver dangle with a guitar charm on it. I love it a lot. She's right. It is sexy. I just wish I could show it to, Josh. A tear falls from my cheeks, and she comes to stand behind me. I'm circling my navel with my finger. "I miss him, Em. I'm not any good at this. It makes me feel empty inside without him." I flatten my palm on my stomach as the hole there physically hurts. She pulls me to her chest, wincing slightly. I'm sure her boobs are in pain.

We stop at the one gas station that never cards us and buy a bottle of wine. We go back home and sit on the back porch drinking the wine and smoking a pack of cigarettes. I'm not a smoker, and my lungs will be burning tomorrow. Burning is nothing new for me, though.

Josh didn't call me, and I've found myself writing in my journal again.

IT'S EASY TO FORGET THE SMALL THINGS
WHEN LIFE HAPPENS AND ASH IS LEFT AFTER THE
BURNING
BUT I REMEMBER IT
THE SMALL THINGS
THE WAY YOUR FINGERTIPS LEFT GOOSEBUMPS IN THEIR
WAKE
THE LOOK IN YOUR EYE WHEN MY HEART WAS YOURS TO
TAKE
THE FEAR LEFT BEHIND WHEN I LOST IT
THE ACHE LEFT IN ITS PLACE AS I TRIED TO REPLACE IT
I NEED THEM
THE SMALL THINGS
RACING HEART, BUTTERFLIES DANCING
STOLEN KISSES AND LOVE BLAZING
I FORGOT THEM
THE SMALL THINGS
HOW YOU KNEW JUST WHAT I NEEDED WHEN I DIDN'T
HOW YOU PUT ME BACK TOGETHER WHEN I COULDN'T
I LOVED THEM
THE SMALL THINGS
LOST, FORGOTTEN AND MISSED
GAINED, REMEMBERED AND EMBRACED
THESE SMALL THINGS BECOME EVERYTHING

I wake in the middle of the night to my phone ringing. "Hello," I answer with a scratchy voice.

"Hey, baby. Sorry, you awake?" I wasn't, but I miss his voice so much that I'm now wide-awake.

"I am now. You didn't call me," I whine. I hate that I feel so needy.

He sighs. "I just got off of work. I'm calling you, now."

"Where are you working anyway?" He hasn't even told me. He takes a deep breath and gets silent. "Josh, you there?"

"Yeah, I'm here. Sorry. It's just...um, I don't want you to get mad."

My skin prickles and my stomach sinks. "Just tell me. You're not like a male stripper, right?"

He laughs. "God, I love you. No, it's nothing like that. It's just...I'm working at a bar."

"A bar?"

"Yeah, it's near campus, and I'll bartend. Some nights I might get to play. They have open mic night."

"M'kay. Why would I be mad?" I don't understand.

I can hear him take yet another deep breath. *Why is this bothering him so much?* "It's just, I'm bartending at night and playing on the weekends. It's the only job I can get that doesn't interfere with practices and games. It just means I'm going to be really busy."

Ah! I already knew he wouldn't be able to come home on the weekends because of his games. In fact, in my mind, I'm already prepared to not see Josh until the holidays, after this planned visit that is. It's painful to think about. "Okay, I'm not mad, Josh. I know you will be busy. So, if you are trying to prepare me for that, no need. I'm very much aware of this reality, Josh."

He curses, and we both get really quiet. "Baby, listen to me. I know this is going to be difficult for us. I can already hear it in your voice. You're starting to put that wall back up. Please, don't. You promised." My heart crumbles—it hurts. The fear makes me want to protect myself, put my guard up, but no matter what I do, no matter what I feel, I won't survive any of this if it means losing him. My tears start falling, and I try not to cry into the phone, but I can't help it.

I hear him growl, and something crashes. "Fuck!" He shouts, and I cry harder. I can hear him breathing heavy into the phone. "Please, baby. Please don't do this. I'm doing this for us."

For us? I sniffle and choke on the sob. "I...I...I'm not doing anything."

"You are. You are shutting down on me. Don't. I need you, Riley. I can't do this if I know you're over there in tears. I can't have you go back to that dark place. I fucking hate this already, and we haven't even started it. I only took this job, so I have money to save and come back to you, baby."

Oh. "I just miss you." I whisper and roll over to look at the picture of us together on my nightstand.

"I miss you, too. I miss you more than you realize. I'll be there in a few days. I promise. I'll be home for a week, and we will spend every single minute of each day smothering each other. Okay?"

I nod my head, but realize he can't see me. "Okay, I'll try harder. I promise."

"Remember the stars," he says. I reach over to my nightstand to pick up my silver box. I set it on my chest remembering his words. I flip it over, push the button and let the stars illuminate the ceiling in my room.

"I remember." I breathe the words into the phone, but I know he's already gone.

I didn't get much sleep after we ended our conversation. I just needed to make it a few more days, and then I would have him for a week, but then I wouldn't have him at all for months. I lie there snuggling Tink, and looking up at the stars on the ceiling in my bedroom remembering that's how much he loves me. I glance at her snuggled on my chest, and remind myself of all the things he has done for me. That he loves me that much. He loves me.

The next morning Em and I are sitting on the couch eating crunch berry cereal. We have a vase sitting in the middle of the coffee table, and I just stare at it thinking about something Josh said last night. He took the job to save money, to get back to me. I turn to Emily. "I think I'm going to get a job."

"Huh?" She looks over at me like I've grown another head.

"I need to stay busy, or I'm going to go insane." I put the bowl of cereal down and pick up the vase. "I'm going to get a job, and every bit of the money I make is going in this jar. This is going to be my Louisiana jar. I'm going to save enough money not just to visit, but also to go to school there with him. I have to try. He can't give up on football, so it should be me to go to him. I have nothing to lose but him, and I'm not letting that happen."

She squeals and jumps up off the couch. "I love this idea. I'll get a job with you. We can go together. I know just the place we can work. They'd hire us in a heartbeat."

"Where?" I walk to the counter and write on a paper 'Jar of Hearts' and then I grab some tape and attach the paper to the jar. I empty the change out of my wallet, put it into the jar and then put the jar on our mantle. Step one...complete.

"We can work where Rebel's band plays on the weekend."

I plop down on the couch. "The Dark Days?" Honest to God, that is the name of this bar. They have open mic on Saturdays, and the Dark Angels have become their regulars. The name is suiting for how I feel. A little ironic that Josh and I will be doing the same thing to get back to each other.

"Yeah, it's perfect," she explains as she picks up her phone.

My phone pings with a text.

Josh: LISTEN TO THESE SONGS

He attaches two mp3 clips to *Life Left to Go* and *What If* by Safetysuit

Me: OKAY? WHAT ARE THE SONGS ABOUT?

Josh: JUST LISTEN. THAT IS HOW I FEEL

Me: OKAY. ILY

Josh: ILY MORE x

We're on our way to Dark Days for an interview. Emily made a call, and the owner wants to talk to us both, today. I have my iPhone plugged into the stereo playing the songs Josh sent me. I'm swiping at the tears that fall unbidden.

"Why are you crying?" Emily squeezes my hand.

"Josh sent these songs to me. He said to listen to them, and that's how he feels." I look over at her, and her mouth forms an O. We listen to the songs the entire ride over. My heart hurts.

We walk into the Dark Days, and I try to picture myself working here. Once inside, immediately to the right, is the bar and to the left, is the stage. The floor by the stage is empty for dancing, and around the room are tables and booths for those that order food. Straight in the back are two pool tables and a hall that leads to the bathrooms. The girls that work here wear knee high boots over fish nets, either leather shorts or miniskirts, and a white skin tight midriff t-shirt with the bar's logo, which is a heart with angel wings coming out of it in black. It's low cut, and their boobs are normally spilling out of them. Josh will not be pleased to see me in that get up. I definitely can't make him feel bad about his job now can I?

The owner is nice. His name's Peter, and we've known him for a while now. He knows I write all of the Dark Angel's music, and has asked me more than once to sing, only because Rebel told him I'm a helluva good singer—not gonna happen, though.

Peter walks out of the back with one of the other girls. I don't remember her name. She's pretty—long legs, black hair cut in a bob, and these striking blue eyes. She's every guy's wet dream. "Hey," she says, smiling and raking her eyes over our bodies.

"Hey," we say in unison.

Peter looks over at her and smiles. "What do you think, Taylor? Can you work with them? You're both eighteen, right?" We nod, and she smiles as she's walking over to us. She looks us up and down, and it's a little unnerving being scrutinized so closely.

She twirls her finger for us to turn around and so we do. She hums and looks to him. "They are perfect. Her red hair is amazing, and this one's eyes...just damn. Riley and Emily correct?"

I nod, Em answers, "Yes."

Peter smiles. "When can y'all start?"

"Now!" I reply, earning a raised brow.

"How' bout tonight, we do a training night?" he asks.

"Yes, okay. Let's do it." Emily pops in.

Taylor takes us to the back room to get our uniforms. "You will have to get your own boots—sexier the better—and always fishnets. You can wear the shorts, or the skirts—mix it up. We have rules for the girls here. You can flirt, but under no situation is it okay for the customers to grope you. This is a bar, and of course you get a few drunk asses who lose their manners, just let us know, and they are out. Okay?"

We leave the bar with our new attire in hand, and we're off to find some sexy boots. Oh, man. *Maybe I should have talked to Josh about this first.* Then again, this is for him. I can do this.

Later that day, I'm sitting in the kitchen on my laptop flipping through Facebook, when a friend request pops up. One name has my insides twisted, and not in a good way—*Dean Warren.* I've only just set my page back up so I can keep in touch with friends and Josh. Why would Dean even send me a request? We haven't talked since May, and I have no intention of doing so now. He's a part of my past, somewhere he needs to remain. I decline the friendship as the doorbell rings. I walk to the door and smile wide as a man is standing there with flowers.

"Riley Shaw?"

"Yes."

"These are for you. Sign here please."

Back in the house I smell the flowers—various shades of roses. They are beautiful. I send a quick text to Josh.

Me: THANK YOU FOR MY ROSES. THEY ARE BEAUTIFUL :)

He replies right away and my heart sinks.

Josh: ??? SRY BABY GIRL - I DIDN'T SEND YOU ROSES.

Another ping.

Josh: WHO SENT THEM?

I didn't even read the card. I just assumed it would be him. I mean...they are roses after all, a flower that Josh loves—rooted in symbolism. I remove the card and read *Missing you, Dean.*

Oh, my God. No, no, no. My heart is hammering in my chest. A PM pops up on my screen from him.

Dean: LONLINESS IS A BITCH. HOPE THOSE BRIGHTEN YOUR DAY

My phone pings again.

Josh: WHO RILEY?

I'm freaking out now. How was Dean aware of where I lived, or that I'd just gotten them, and what does he mean by that? I block him and shut my laptop.

My phone rings. I guess Josh isn't waiting on my text. I answer. "Hello."

"Who the fuck sent you flowers?"

"Oh, um. It was a wrong address, after all."

Silence fills the line and then he sighs. "You're lying."

Now I sigh. "I am. Dean sent them."

"Son of a bitch!"

"I haven't talked to him. I don't know how he knew where I lived, or why he sent them. I'm throwing them in the trash now."

I hear Collin in the background talking. "Dude, slow the fuck down, before you kill us."

"We're on our way, and I'm going to kill that fucker." Josh is angry, but all I can focus on is that he is on his way.

"You're coming early?" I squeal as Emily walks out the bathroom in a towel. "They're on their way," I shout over to her.

"We miss our girls. Be there soon. I'm serious. I will have words with Dean," he growls.

"Whatever you need to do. My heart's yours, Josh. Only yours."

I see Emily grab her boots that we just bought off the couch, and everything in my body flutters. *We have to work tonight. Oh, crap.*

I'm standing in the mirror at Dark Days looking at myself. Josh will be here, soon. He's going to be so pissed at me. Emily whistles. "Holy hell, Riley. You are to die for."

I look like a slut. My black boots are leather like the miniskirt that barely covers my thighs. They have a heel, and I'm at least two inches taller in them. My navel ring is visible with the shirt being so short, and my boobs are popping out. My hair is down in a wavy mess—the red streaks I put in popping brightly. I have more makeup on than usual. My eyes look bright blue with eyeliner and mascara making them stand out.

"Josh is going to kill me, Em." I look over to her, and she looks like a fucking vixen with her dark auburn hair untamed. She wore the shorts, which look more like booty shorts than work attire. I'm looking at us and thinking all we need are whips and dog collars.

"Let's get this over with. I'm scared shitless," I say.

We make our way out to the bar, which isn't crowded yet. Taylor gives us the rundown on how things go here and assigns us our tables. My stomach free falls when I notice Dean sitting at one of my assigned tables. I'm starting to think he's following me. His eyes lock with mine, narrowing instantly. He then boldly looks up and down my body. They darken and something wicked dances behind them. I hate it. I look away. "Can we switch tables?" I ask, Taylor. Emily looks to see why I said that, and mutters a curse.

"What's up?" I explain the situation to Taylor. She looks over at the table and frowns. "Honey, he's a regular. His dad and Peter go way back, but yeah, it's okay to switch." Seriously? This shit can't go well.

We're standing at the bar getting our tablets for taking orders. "Why's he here?" Emily asks me.

I shrug. "You heard Taylor. He's a regular. This can't go well, Em. He's starting to freak me out."

After I told her about the roses, she tensed up and told me she caught him in our parking lot at the apartment the other day. He was waiting for me. They argued, and he left. I'm officially creeped out.

The night flows well enough. I don't mess up any orders, and I've succeeded in avoiding Dean's table. He hasn't left either, though. He just stares at me. And the way he's staring at me makes my skin crawl. I catch his eye on my legs while biting on his finger. His eyes slowly lift to my eyes, and I can't place what I see in his stare, it's almost like hatred laced with something sinful. It makes me uncomfortable.

Rebel and the girls are about to take the stage to sing something new I wrote. It's dark as usual, and the haunting edge that Rebel puts to it always makes me shiver. They are very Evanescence like. Speaking of, she comes over to me and says that looking at me in this uniform solidifies that I need to be a Dark Angel. I laugh and tell her she's crazy. She begs me to sing *again*, and I shoot her down *again*. I can't get up there and sing my words. That's Josh's thing, not mine—maybe one day. I can't get up there like *this* at all. Josh would die.

It's like my body is so in tuned to his, because I can sense him the second he's in the building.

Em and I are both on our fifteen-minute breaks and talking in the corner with Rebel before their act. I don't look at him just yet. "Does he see me?" I ask Rebel as Emily walks away to meet Collin I'm sure. My back is facing the tables. She grins. "Yeah, he sees you all right."

Glory Box by Portishead is blaring through the speakers right in front of me. I lean into Rebel's ear because it's too loud for her to hear me otherwise. "Does he look pissed?"

She shakes her head and whispers back to me, "Nope. His eyes are screaming sex. I'm pretty sure he'd like to bend you over one of these tables." I snap my eyes to hers. She's nodding her head enthusiastically. So, I slowly turn around.

He's standing against the wall with his eyes raking every inch of me. He's biting his lip like he does when he's picturing us having sex. His eyes are hooded when they finally meet mine. He crooks his finger for me to come to him. I walk to the beat of the music to him, smiling shyly. My legs feel weak, and I'm just focusing on not falling.

I'm half way to him when a hand wraps around my wrist halting me dead in my tracks. I turn to find Dean's brown eyes locked with mine, and years of foolishness crash into my chest. "I need to talk to you," he says in a rough voice. "Alone!"

Josh's deep voice billows over my shoulder, "Get your hands off of her." He is there, by my side in a second.

I yank my hand away from Dean, and with my other push Josh back. My eyes meet Peter's behind the bar, and he's frowning. He nods his head to Taylor saying something. She looks in our direction and glances at Dean's table. Next thing I know, she walks over to his table and leans over saying something in his ear. His eyes widen, and he stands. I watch as she walks him to the backroom. He glances at me as he walks off with her. Something rubs me wrong about this whole situation. I look back to Peter, and he nods his head without a smile. I don't see Dean again the rest of my shift.

I didn't get to talk to Josh much for a few hours, because I had to finish my shift, but I feel his eyes on me. I couldn't read his expression. He seems to be a mixture of emotions, part of him turned on, part of him pissed off. He watches other guys look at me and his jaw locks and twitches. He may be enjoying what I look like, but he clearly doesn't enjoy other men liking what they see.

We are cleaning up and about to lock up. Taylor tells us we did well. She put us on the schedule for the following weekend. That was the soonest she needed us. I couldn't help but think that was such a blessing, because I had a week of Josh to enjoy.

After Collin and Em leave, and we're about to follow behind, she stops me. "Hey, Riley? Can I talk to you for a second?"

I glance to Josh who has a brow raised. "I'll be just a minute." I tell him as I nod to her. He looks uneasy about this as his eyes bounce from her to me. I try to reassure him I'm okay by kissing his cheek. He smiles soft and steps away. Taylor pulls me just out of earshot of Josh. "Look, I took care of Dean, today. I explained to him that he can't touch you and that when you're on the clock, you're off limits. But Riley, this can't be an issue. Like I said his dad and Peter go way back, and Dean, well...he isn't going away. In fact..." she pauses and looks uncomfortable.

"In fact, what?" The hairs on the back of neck prickle.

"Peter was going to offer him a job."

My mouth falls open. "Oh."

"Look, I'll understand if you don't want to keep the job. You have a week to think about it. Peter's aware of the situation, y'all dated— whatever." She makes it seem like nothing. "Just let me know your plans. We'd like to keep you on and get you on that stage at some point...but like I said, I understand if it's uncomfortable."

"Thanks. I, um...I will."

What are the odds really? I pick the one bar Dean's dad is a regular at, and Dean is, as well? And just since when do the two of them run in the same circle? *Fuck.* The Dark Days just got darker.

Josh and I are walking out the bar and to the parking lot when he grabs me by my elbow to stop me from walking. I turn and go to say something, but the look in his eyes swallows up my words. His eyes roam my body, and he touches the dangle on my navel. "I like this a lot," he breathes. Then he crashes his lips to mine, his tongue instantly in my mouth. "I've missed you, and fuck, Riley...this outfit. You have lost your damn mind," he says between kisses and nips at my lips.

I hear a revving engine as a familiar motorcycle slows to the curb. I can't see his eyes under his helmet, but I know Dean's gaze is on us before he zooms away.

"Was that?" Josh asks, glaring in the direction of the red taillight.

I run my hands through my hair and begin shaking. Dean is starting to scare me. I'm constantly feeling eyes on me and then he just shows up places that I am at like he knew I would be there—a job at the same bar as me? Coincidence or not—it's creepy as hell.

I meet Josh's eyes, and I know he can see the fear because he pulls me to his chest, and then he takes me to my apartment.

CHAPTER 22

Rage is what I feel when I see Dean touch her. What kind of game is he playing? Sending her flowers, the comments, showing up at her job. And fuck...her job? What the hell am I supposed to do with that? How am I supposed to go back to being hours away from her knowing she looks like that?

"Good Morning," her sweet voice tells me as she stirs beside me.

"Mornin' sunshine." I kiss her forehead.

She rolls to her back and stretches like a feline. I swallow as I watch her arch her back with her hands above her head. It's damn sexy.

"What time is it?" she asks with a morning voice that is raspy and hot.

I clear my throat. "9:00 ish," I answer. It's like my hands have a mind of their own, they begin to twitch to touch her again. Evidently, my body has missed her just as much as my heart has. Last night when I brought her home, I couldn't wait to get lost in her. It clearly is not enough. I want more of her.

She sits up suddenly, throws her bare legs over the side of her bed, and is about to get up—wearing nothing but a t-shirt and panties. I wrap my hand around her stomach and pull her back causing her to squeal.

I lie on top of her, burying my head in her neck and inhaling her scent. "Where are you going?" I begin kissing a path from her collarbone to the spot behind her ear that always makes her squirm.

She giggles. "I have to pee."

I ignore her response and continue inhaling her. "Have I told you that I love the way you smell?" I whisper into her ear, and she shivers.

I'm pressed in between her legs, and I know she feels how much I've missed her. "M'hm. Uh, I like really, *really* want to kiss you right now, but I have morning breath and want to brush my teeth first." She's embarrassed and holding her hand over her mouth.

I chuckle at her and sit back on my heels looking down at her with hungry eyes. Her t-shirt has ridden up her thighs, and I can peek at her pretty coral panties. She blushes, and I can see her chest rise and lower. *Damn.* After everything we've done together, she still gets flustered. It's adorable to me.

And then her eyes widen as knocks against the wall and moans erupt. She covers her mouth as I smirk.

Oh Collin. Oh yes. There. Don't stop!

Baby! Shit. I've missed our fucks.

"Oh, my God. We can't stay here." She giggles.

"I could take you to get breakfast. Are you hungry?" Part of me wants to join the fuck club, but she didn't insinuate that.

As if on cue, her stomach growls and she laughs hiding her face ever so cutely. I place a kiss above her navel. Jesus, that piercing is hotter than hell.

"Yeah, guess so, huh?" She mumbles under her hands. I pry her hands away and tap her nose with my finger. I wiggle my brows. "What are you hungry for, pretty girl?" She smiles and something devilish twinkles in her eyes. I know her mind just went somewhere I'd like to explore. So maybe?

She just looks over my frame, admiring my chest. I love that she is attracted to me. "Hey, did you get a new tattoo?" She asks, sitting up to touch the elegant verse scripted across my rib cage.

She traces the letters, cursive words so beautiful.

Wings among angels fly with beauty

A cherished rose embraced in ash

Another love not dead but thriving

Hope for peace forever to last

"I got it right before I left to go to Louisiana. Farewell gift from Brandt," I explain.

She places her hand right on my bare chest and begins venturing—feeling. I begin to breathe shallow. "It's beautiful," she whispers so softly before kissing it.

"You're beautiful." I put my index finger under her chin guiding her face up to mine. The urge to kiss her is so strong. Her eyes flick to my lips. She wants to kiss me, too.

She crawls her way to me and straddles my lap, wrapping arms and legs around my body, she hugs me with all of her might. "I love you, Josh. I've missed you like crazy."

I squeeze her tight, holding onto her like she might slip away. "I love you, Riley...so much. I've missed you too, baby."

I kept my promise of spending a week smothering, Riley. We've left her bed for food, water and necessities—every moment spent in one another's arms. She even sang for me like old times. We've been in our own private bubble—until today that is.

Riley and I are at the lake after leaving her house in a state of shock. She's sitting on the swing with me propped against the tree. Riley's mom called and asked her to come home to talk, and then she drops a bombshell on her and Tatum. She announced that she's going to have a baby. Of course, Riley freaked out on her. Tatum was even quieter than usual. After all of her talks with Riley about birth control and protection, her mom slips up, *again*. Riley yelled at her, and told her that she better not blame that baby for her new responsibilities the way she has blamed her. Her mom cried, and then they had a heart to heart about what her mom truly feel's for Riley. In the end, they hugged. No mention was made of the baby's father.

"I'm still so shocked, Josh. I was worried about her with all her headaches and dizzy spells but this...I didn't expect this," she says touching the necklace on her neck. She looks to me, "And she doesn't go on dates. I had no idea she even had a boyfriend...and ewww...having sex? This is just so weird. I'm going to have a baby brother or sister, isn't she like too old to have a baby?"

I shake my head, "Riley, your mom's only thirty five. She had you so young. Maybe she doesn't have a boyfriend. I don't know what to say. Just that maybe you should take this moment and let it be something to bring you and your mom closer together. She might not have someone to be there for her. Maybe she just had sex." She scrunches up her nose. "I'm just saying. She's an adult without a guy in her life. Maybe she just needed to—,"

"Oh, God. Stop, stop. I can't hear this. Ugh. That's my mom."

Another thought crosses my mind, something Riley and I have never discussed, only because I knew the answer since I overheard her talk to her mom in her room that morning. "Not to change the subject, or freak you out, but we haven't exactly been careful...at all, actually. I've never even worn a condom with you."

At first, her mouth falls open, and she looks horrified, but then she smiles shyly. "No, we haven't, but I'm on the pill, and I take it religiously every night before bed. Honestly, I have never even thought about it."

"That's good because we aren't ready for that yet, but know that I see us sharing that moment one day." I tell her looking her right in the eyes. She sucks in a deep breath as I lower myself to one knee and pull out a velvet box.

"Wha...What are you doing?" she asks stuttering.

"Riley Shaw, I love you more than anything in this world...and I'm not proposing us get married, but I want you to know that I'm promising to love you forever...to cherish the heart you've trusted me with. This next year is going to be so hard on us, and I believe wholeheartedly that we will make it out of this stronger and closer." I open the box, and she gasps. She wipes a tear that falls. I pull out the silver band that I had engraved with *Let it be beautiful.* I grab her right hand and slide it on her ring finger. "With this ring I give you my promise to remain faithful to you, to try my hardest to be everything you need. I promise to love you and remind you all the time of it. What do you say? Do you promise to see forever for us, too?"

She's breathing so heavy, and tears are streaming down her face. She's looking at her hand in mine and then she looks up at me and smiles. She throws herself at me causing me to fall back onto the grass.

"Of course, I promise. I will love you, forever…as if it were ever a question, Josh." Her lips press against mine and the world ceases to exist except for her and me and this one moment.

The first month of school flies by pretty quickly. So much is happening all at once that I almost can't keep up with it. I am glad for the constant distraction, because I don't have to think about how much I am missing, Riley. It's not just missing *her*, though. I miss my sister and my dad. I scheduled fourteen hours this semester, and I know juggling class work, football practice, work and calling home are going to eventually catch up with me. My one escape is the time my hands are on my guitar. The music is my moment when I'm playing on Thursday nights, or any weekend the bar chooses to have bands play.

Practices are kicking my ass. My new coach is hardcore, and this is a whole new ballgame. Training is more intense, more vigorous, as is the time I need to dedicate to it. My every move is under a microscope since Bridges graduates this year, and there is already talk of him signing early and leaving. *Just more pressure.*

By September, I'm struggling to keep up. My grades are slipping. I'm tired—very tired. I've missed a few phone calls with Riley. In fact, our conversations started out as every day, then every other day, and now maybe three to four times a week—not enough. My GPA is turning to shit, and coach has already warned me that I need to focus more on my studies—easier said than done. Thank the Lord for video phone calls, though, because I think I would go crazy if I didn't get to see Riley's face, at least, a few times each week. I just wish I could reach my hand into the screen to touch her. It's been too long.

Now it's October, and I'm on the verge of losing my shit.

"Dude, you look like death," Collin says walking into my dorm room.

"Shit, I know. I'm fucking tired, man."

He sits on my roommate's bed. Yeah, that's another sour topic. That guy is a douche, but at least he stays gone a lot with his girlfriend. I think I hate him for that reason alone. The silence can be sometimes deafening, but walking in on them having sex too many times is no picnic either.

"You gotta get out more. C'mon, they are having a costume party at the Sig house for Halloween. You know bitches use this as an excuse to dress slutty, while guys like me reap all the benefits." Love Collin to death, but he's same ole Collin—always looking for a party and some chick to bang—part of the reason he was invited to pledge Sigma. I've asked him about it, considering he's with Emily now, but he says they made an agreement, whatever that means.

"Dude, I've got a long ass paper to write, and then I need to call Riley before I go into work."

He huffs and falls back onto the bed. "Look, man, I get it…but this is college. You're always doing this or that. We should be having fun, Josh. C'mon. I'm sure Riley and Em are going out and shit."

Are they? Something about her partying without me there to protect her makes me nervous. As if on cue, my phone pings with a picture of Riley dressed in a Dark Angel costume. I send her a quick text.

Me: DAMN PRETTY GIRL. WHOSE SOUL ARE YOU STEALING?

Riley: *BLUSH – YOURS

Me: HOW SO?

I run my hand across my face. I look over at Collin and find him grinning like an idiot just as a knock on my door happens. Collin says, "You gonna get that?" with a devilish smirk.

"Yeah. Hey, call your girl and find out where they are going. Riley just texted me in this naughty as sin costume."

"You're pussy-whipped, bruh. Just open the damn door."

I open the door with my eyes cast down. "Someone say pussy?" I hear Emily's voice. My eyes are stuck as they leisurely travel up. I'm met with black heels with silver spikes, black skintight leather pants on the legs I imagine in all kinds of ways.

"Holy shit," I mutter as my eyes make it to the guitar navel ring, further up to a black leather corset tied with red satin strings, and just shit... I can't breathe. Her tits are on display, and my hands itch to touch them. Black angel wings, long wavy curls with red streaks around the face of my dark angel. My angel is a vixen. Her blue/green eyes are even more perfect, more beautiful than I remember. Fuck! She is breathtaking. My dick agrees. That black halo on her head doesn't match the outfit on the girl I love.

"Damn," I breathe. She's standing in my dorm room, and I have no words but damn? I had no idea she was coming. I'm on the verge of coming just by staring at her.

"Oh, my God, quit eye fucking my friend. Where's my boyfriend?" Em says walking into the room in a Jessica Rabbit outfit. "Hey, baby." Emily says in this sugary sweet voice, quickly followed by a moan as he obviously claims her mouth.

"Are you happy to see me?" Riley asks, biting her lip nervously.

"Happy? Are you fucking kidding me? I'm ecstatic. I've missed you so much." And without another word, I take her mouth hungrily. She moans, and just hell, I want to bury myself so deep in her and forget everything.

She puts her hands on my chest, and grips my shirt at the same time my hands reach down to cup her ass. I don't even realize it, but I've pushed her out into the hall, and have her pressed against the wall by my door.

Whistles erupt and someone yells, "Getcha some," from across the hall.

Riley pushes me back giggling and touching her lips like she always does when we kiss. I press my forehead to hers and whisper, "I can't believe you're here."

She smiles softly and runs her hands through my hair. I lift my head to look at her, to make sure she is real.

"It was Em's idea really. I can't take the credit. She wanted to surprise Collin. She said he needs a reminder fuck, or something like that, but then she slipped up and told him we were coming. So, it became your surprise. I wasn't passing up an opportunity to see you. Besides, I have so much to talk to you about."

I trail my finger along the skin exposed on her stomach. A soft whimper escapes her throat. "I've missed you." She breathes the words almost like a moan. Oh, it's been too long.

Just before I lean into her to taste more, Collin and Em come walking out.

"Let's do this," Em says smacking me on the ass.

What the...? Riley just rolls her eyes and the four of us together again head to Collin's house for a party.

Collin's house here is party central just like it was back home—only change is a lot more guys and a lot more girls. It should be interesting with Emily here.

We walk in, and right away I spot trouble dressed in a naughty maid costume with a naughty smile plastered on her face. Carly, one of the Chi O chicks and a random hook up of Collin's, begins to head in our direction as soon as she sees him, not even missing a step when she clearly notices Emily's hand in his. Carly is cute, but Collin's eyes tonight are all over Em.

"Hey, Collin," Carly slurs as she places a hand on his arm. He looks away from Em. The asshole actually has the balls to look Carly up and down with a smirk.

Emily glances to Riley, "Like I said, *reminder fuck*, it's time to crack the whip." She smiles and pushes up her breast. She reaches up, grabs Collin by the chin, and turns his lust filled eyes back to hers. "We agreed, right?" He nods his head and then she kisses him, and it's not just any kiss. It's the kind of kiss that claims him. Carly's face falters, and then she looks to me, but I shake my head and kiss Riley's cheek, so she walks away disappointed.

Em whispers something in Riley's ear, and then she and Collin walk away together. Go figure. The dick pulls me here with his girlfriend, and within minutes is bringing her to his room. I debate on asking Riley to leave with me, but then she says, "Wanna play?"

I quirk an eyebrow, "You wanna play King's cup?"

She shrugs, "Why not?" She pulls my hand to follow to the table.

"Holy shit, if it isn't, Parker. Welcome to civilization." Sean, one of my teammates announces. We fist bump.

"Yeah, yeah, yeah." I can feel Riley's eyes on me questioningly, and I see their eyes on her. I put my hand around her shoulders and pull her closer to me. "Guys, this is Riley, my girlfriend." I kiss the top of her head. "And this is a few of the guys. That's Sean, Chad and the one with his tongue preoccupied is Tristan." I skip over all the scantily clad dressed girls around the table.

"Nice to meet you," she says, in a sweet voice with a shy smile.

I hold back a growl at Sean's eyes not leaving her cleavage. I bite my tongue when one of the girls who I probably should know, but can't remember her name says, "Awww Joshua, she's so cute."

Riley laughs, but it's not her 'I find that funny laugh.' It's the bitchcraft laugh. The one where she smiles and laughs sweetly—too sweetly, and inside she is cussing you out like a sailor. I look down at her to gauge her reaction. She's grinning and staring at the girl across the table that is staring at me. I guess I should have warned her that I have a few fans, between football and playing at the bar—some girls have crushes—definitely one sided. My heart is with the angel next to me, the one's whose fiery eyes are telling that chick to go-to-hell.

"Cute? Bitch you crazy. My girl here is fucking schmexy as sin," Emily says walking over, bold as ever and wearing a very satisfied grin. That was fast. It makes me laugh.

Tristan comes up for air and pushes aside the girl he was just kissing. His eyes darken as he takes in Emily first, and then he bites his lip when he looks over to Riley. Love him on the field. However in the game of life, he is a dick. Collin growls, and I give a warning glare across the table.

"So, are we playing?" Riley asks, completely oblivious to the fact that she and her best friend are being visually undressed.

Tristan smirks, obviously ignoring the fact that the two he's eye fucking are taken. "Ya wanna play, sweetheart?" he asks in a flirtatious tone and then winks.

Riley snorts a laugh. "Does that usually work for you?" she asks grinning.

He shakes his head as the guys at the table laugh. Sean holds his fist out for her to bump. "Ha. Josh your girl is cute as hell. I like you, angel." She lifts a brow and looks to me. I just grin, and she bumps fist with Sean.

After several rounds of cards, and the game definitely not in her favor, my girl is a little tipsy. I lean into her ear to whisper. "I need to go into work for a few hours. I didn't know you were coming, otherwise, I would have taken tonight off."

She turns her head and her lips almost brush mine. She smiles. "I'll go change. Can I come with you? I need to talk to you about something."

I nod and wonder about what? "Where were you staying tonight?" I grab her elbow before she walks away.

"Well, here with Em. Unless—,"

I shake my head and cut her off. "With me. You're staying with me." She just smiles and nods her head, grabbing Em's hand on the way to the back.

I was standing there having a conversation when I notice Riley's phone on the table in front of me. She left it sitting there, and the screen lights up with a text that has me seeing red. I pick it up and read the text. "What the fuck?" I say, showing the text to Collin. "What the fuck is this?"

Dean: MISSED SEEING U 2NIGHT. WHERE R U?

Collin reads it. His eyes widen as he averts his eyes from mine. My eyes narrow as I notice he doesn't look surprised one bit by this text. I tilt my head in question, and he rolls his neck. "You knew," I state.

"It's not the way that looks. You need to talk to her about it," he says, finally meeting my eyes.

I clear my throat. "Talk to her about what exactly?" I feel the weight of those words squeeze the air out of my lungs.

He doesn't even get to answer, because Emily and Riley walk up dressed in different clothes. Riley is standing there in the same heels with the studs, a white frayed miniskirt and a black top that hangs off her shoulder. Damn. It's been months since I've seen her. For a moment, as I take in her appearance I forget why I'm pissed—for just a moment.

My eyes harden and she tilts her head. That soft smile she had is now a frown. I hold out her phone for her. "You have a text. It lit up your screen with an interesting piece of information."

She looks confused and grabs her phone. Sliding her fingers along her screen, she curses and hands her phone to Emily, who also curses. She looks up to me, walking up close, but I'm already backing away from her. She's seeing Dean again, while I'm here missing her. "It's not what you think," she says.

"You don't know what I'm thinking," I snap back.

She sighs and reaches a hand out to touch me, but I step further away. I get outside, but she is right there calling my name. "Josh, stop. Let me explain. You have it all wrong."

I turn, and she almost runs right into me. "Go for it. Explain how he is missing seeing you tonight."

"Dammit, Josh. Listen to her. You need to hear her out," Emily pipes in with Collin nodding his head beside her.

I didn't even know they followed us out. "Explain," I gesture my hand toward Riley to go for it. "Evidently, everyone already knows something I don't."

She begins wringing her hands and chomping on her lip. She's nervous. She should be. "I'm not seeing him, Josh. I never even text him back. He's been...he...well, we—,"

"FUCK! Just say it."

"He's working at Dark Days with me. Well, not with me, but there. I was supposed to come in tonight. That's what he means. I ignore him all the time, Josh. I never text him back. I'm not seeing him at all. I promise."

"He's working with you now, while you're dressed in that barely there outfit?"

"Yes."

"Since when?" She tenses and looks to Emily.

"SINCE WHEN?"

"Since August," she whispers.

"You have got to be fucking with me right now, Riley. Are you telling me your ex-boyfriend, who is obviously not done with you, has been working with you for two months, and you never told me?" I run my hands through my hair, and then I turn to Collin, who is standing there so quiet. "And you knew this, didn't you?"

"Fuck, Josh. I knew you would be pissed. I told her to tell you," he explains.

"And why didn't you?" I ask her.

She looks at Emily, and I notice a tear fall down her cheek. She meets my eyes, and there is a lot hidden in her gaze. "Because, I didn't want to lose you. Dean won't leave me alone, and I knew if I told you everything that is happening, that you would be mad. I didn't want you to worry. I didn't want you to see things that weren't there. I didn't mean to lie to you about it. I'm handling it."

"Handling what?"

She chokes on a sob and wraps her hand around her waist like she needs it there to hold herself together. She covers her mouth with her hand. Emily is there in a second, holding her up. She doesn't continue.

"I don't have time for this shit. I need to get to work. When you figure out what the hell it is that you need to tell me, I'll be at the bar. See ya." I walk away from her.

My heart wanted to comfort her—make her feel better, but my mind didn't know what to believe. None of this made sense to me.

I can hear Collin on the phone yelling at someone, and I hear Emily telling Riley to go after me. She doesn't, and I don't stop.

The entire walk to work, I replay the past few months, and how the distance between Riley and I was changing us. I replay Dean's comments to me before I left. I knew he had every intention of making a play for her while I was gone. I didn't know what to believe when it came to her. Her reasoning behind not telling me didn't add up.

I'm at the bar with Natalie one of my co-workers. "You okay?" she asks with her hand on my chest.

"No. I'm not in the mood to talk right now, Nat. K?" I start my shift and begin keeping myself busy.

I feel her enter before I actually see her. Riley sits at the bar, but I don't acknowledge her, not even when I feel her eyes on me. Chris walks to her to get her order. She shakes her head, which surprises me. Natalie looks to her and then to me. "That her?"

I look away from Riley and to Natalie. "Huh?"

"Your girlfriend?"

"Yeah, that's her."

"Interesting," she mutters popping the cap off a beer and handing it to someone.

"Interesting?" I question leaning against the bar.

She bites her lip. Natalie's cute. A little taller than Riley, long, blonde, straight hair, with big brown eyes—they make her unique. She and I have become friends over the past few weeks, even though I know she would like to be more.

"I figured you were either gay, or happily in a relationship to constantly say no to your many offers here. I don't get told no often, and as many numbers as you get, I just assumed…but as I see you standing here, and not even looking at her, I wonder…"

She moves to stand in front of me and touches my shoulder. "Wonder what?" I ask, glancing to Riley. She looks pissed. Good. I'm tired of always being the one that feels the pain as I watch her with someone. How's it feel when it's you, I think?

Natalie turns my cheek back to her, and I smile. "I wonder if you're happy."

Her comment hits my heart in the worst way. Am I happy? I look back to Riley, and see the pain in her blue/green eyes—the eyes that I have always loved more than any in this world—the ones I picture every night when I lay alone without her. I'm not happy, but I love her. No matter how hurt my heart is, or how pissed my head is at her—I love her.

CHAPTER 23

Breaking into two again. I'm losing him, and no one else is to blame but me. I knew keeping this secret would backfire on me. I just hoped Dean would leave, would back off, but he hasn't. If anything, he is scaring me more. But to explain that to, Josh? I don't know how.

I'm sitting here watching him purposely try to hurt me. Not only is he ignoring me, but he's also blatantly flirting with girls in front of me. This version of Josh is new to me, and I don't know what to do with it.

It's been an hour without him acknowledging me once. An hour of him allowing the girl he is working with to touch him in small ways. He meets my eyes, smirks and then smiles at her. I know what he is doing, and it fucking hurts. Josh oozes sex appeal. All he has to do is wink, give a curve of his lip, or even a breath in another female's direction, and I have no doubt they would drop on their knees for him. He has that power. I've seen him use that power to his advantage before, but never so cruelly as to do it this way to hurt me.

Three giggly girls have been hanging on his every word for the past half hour, and he's been entertaining them with his gorgeous bedroom eyes and his lip pulled in between his teeth.

"Here. I think you need this." I look in front of me to see a glass with sugar around the rim. I look away from my boyfriend breaking my heart and to the other bartender whose nametag reads Chris.

"What's this?"

"Lemon drop. It's sweet. Might make the sour feeling you've got taste a little better," he says, looking between Josh and me.

"That obvious, huh?"

He laughs and leans into the bar. "Honey, if your eyes could speak words, they'd be saying a helluva lot."

I pick up the cup and lick some of the sugar. Chris looks to my lips and clears his throat. I swear I heard a growl from the other side of the bar, but I don't look over to see for sure. "So, I haven't seen you around here before. You know him?" he inquires.

"I go to school in Texas. Yeah, he's my boyfriend."

And now he looks confused, which makes me uncomfortable. "Hmmm. I didn't know he had a girlfriend. Doesn't look like he knows that either. Does it?"

I catch Josh's eye as he glares at me. I lick more of the sugar off the glass. "No, it doesn't." I take the lemon drop in one gulp, licking my lips after. Josh squares his shoulders and crosses his hands over his chest. Two can play this game. I look back to Chris smiling sweetly. "Thank you, that *was* sweet. Can I have another, please?" I tilt my head and bite my lip.

He reaches for my glass and lets his fingers graze mine as he smirks. He walks across the bar to make me another shot, Josh meeting him halfway. The two seem to start up a heated conversation just as the bitch he's been working and flirting with all night walks over to me.

"So, you're the girlfriend, huh?" Really? She knows about me, but Chris didn't.

"That I am. And you are?" I ask in my best bitchy voice.

She laughs, and I want to slap her. "I'm Natalie. Josh calls me Nat, though."

"Is that so? How cute. A nickname, huh?"

She seems taken aback by my attitude, but what the fuck? She came over here and has been knowingly flirting with my boyfriend— and then tells me shit like that.

"Funny, you obviously know who I am. Chris over there didn't seem to know who I was." Something isn't adding up.

She smiles a fake smile. "Well, Chris only works weekends, so he doesn't know Josh well."

"But you do?" I ask feeling more peeved with every word that comes out of her mouth.

"Yeah, kind of. Josh and I work together during the week, as well. Lots of hours, so we talk a lot, I guess."

I just stare at her, and then glance at Josh, who is staring at me. She pulls my attention back to her. "We're just friends, not that I wouldn't mind being more, but he's been pretty honest about being taken…until tonight, that is."

She has officially pissed me off, smiling the entire time. What the hell is that supposed to mean. Until tonight, that is? Is he saying he isn't taken? Well fuck that. She walks off, and I watch her walk near him—her pinkie grazing his hand as she does. He looks down at it and very slightly touches his own to hers. When I look up, I see him staring right at me. He knew I saw it, and he still did it. I search his eyes for an apology, for an explanation, and I get nothing but cold.

Next thing I know, Chris has another drink in front of me. I reach for the glass, but Josh is there in a second taking it from him. He leans down real close to my face, holding the glass in between his hands. "Is this what you're going to do? Drink until you feel nothing? Did you even card her, you prick?" he asks with venom. Feel nothing? Isn't he trying to make me feel all of this?

"I guess I am." I lean around him. "Thank you, Chris. You're very sweet. My ID say's I'm twenty-one. You're *good*, Chris." I look back at Josh satisfied.

"What the fuck?" He seethes through his teeth.

I snatch the glass from his hand and very slowly lick the sugar for exaggeration, and then I tip the glass to my lips. I slam the glass down onto the bar. "What the fuck is right, Josh? You want me to feel bad for working side by side with someone I ignore as best as possible, while you're here working side by side with some bitch you obviously have intentions of fucking later. Well, FUCK YOU!" I pull out a $20, kiss it and hand it over Josh's shoulder to Chris.

Josh's mouth hangs open, and I go to leave just as Emily and Collin come stumbling in. "Heeeeeeyyyy!" Em slurs hanging on my shoulders.

"Let's get a table." I say, grabbing her hand and pulling her to the back of the bar where the band is playing. I wonder for a moment if Josh is playing later. He never said. Collin stays by the bar with Josh. I look at him, and his eyes are saying a lot of things. Anger, sadness, love, and lust—I can't read him anymore.

I proceed to tell Emily all about Josh and the bitch at the bar. "Riley, he wouldn't cheat on you. You know that."

"I did know that. But now, I'm not so sure. You should have seen him, Em. He practically held her hand. It's like he was trying to hurt me, and he did," I explain.

She frowns. "You need to tell him that Dean is stalking you, Riley. You shouldn't be keeping this from him. All he knows is that you and your ex are talking again. He's probably scared, and so he is trying to hurt you."

"Dean's not stalking me, Em. He's just too close for my comfort." I explain not even sure if I believe my own words. Dean is randomly showing up where I happen to be. I catch him watching me from a distance, all too often. It is unnerving, and he's never with Preslee. In fact, I haven't seen her in months. He leaves notes on my car, at my apartment and in my locker at work. Never once, have I played into his game. I just ignore him, but it isn't working anymore.

"What-the-fuck ever, Riley. He is around too much. I mean shit, he rented an apartment in our complex, got a job at our bar, parks his bike right next to your car half the time. It's weird…and I don't buy for a fucking second that Preslee and he are together. She's never even around."

I laugh at her, but her words are too close to home. "Seriously, Em. I don't want to talk about this. You're killing my buzz."

I can't stop staring at the band playing. One guy is playing on the piano keyboard, another playing the guitar and one on the drums. I don't recognize what they are singing, must be original, but it has me entranced. I get an idea, and I have no idea where it comes from.

I came here to talk to Josh, to explain what was going on, not to lose him. I know he's angry, but he wouldn't go through with hurting me like that. I know he wouldn't. I'm not losing him.

"Hey, where are you going?" I hear Em ask, but I keep walking. I reach the band that announced they were done, and the next act would be up in fifteen minutes. I step up on the stage to talk to the guy by the keyboard. I explain my plan, and ask if they know the song. I fear they won't, but he smiles and tells me he does. He waves over the guitar player who is also the guy who's been singing. He asks what he thinks.

They both eye me appreciatively and shrug. "Why the hell not?" They talk to the drummer.

I look up to the bar as they set up, and see Collin nudging Josh to get him to look over, and when he does I can't read him, yet again. He leans forward on the bar locking eyes with mine. I'm standing next to the singer who introduced himself as Steele. He grabs the microphone off the stand.

"Well, guys and dolls, we have a lovely surprise. This young lady..." He cups his hand over the microphone and leans over to me. "What's your name, darlin?"

"Riley."

"This lovely lady, Riley, is going to be singing a cover for y'all."

He hands me the microphone, and I look to the piano player with a nod. He begins to play *Pieces* by Red.

I close my eyes to listen to the piano as it envelops me. Once the guitar starts, I begin singing. I'm lost in the words. I'm reaching into my hair and swaying slowly as I let my heart bleed out on this stage.

When the chorus starts for the second time, I open my eyes for the first time as I realize the room is as quiet as a mouse. Everyone is listening to me in awe. I lock eyes with Josh standing right in front of me as the drummer kicks in for the build. He is in shock. I can see it all over his face.

I let the rest pour out of me because I mean every word. I did try. I tried so hard to make this with him work. To be everything I thought I couldn't—to be enough. The music softens and so does my voice. I meet his eyes and find the coldness of before now gone. I need him to understand, to hear me. He is my missing puzzle piece, he always has been. Even if I'm a jumbled mess of jagged edges, he puts me back together. He fixes me, completes me. I see so many questions, so many thoughts in his gorgeous hazel eyes.

My eyes shut and the rest becomes pure emotion as I glide my hand down the microphone string. When the song ends, the crowd applauds and whistles. "Thank you," I smile.

Steele takes the mic and smiles widely. "Damn girl, you've got some lungs. That was beautiful, honey. Wasn't it?" He looks back to the crowd going wild again, but my eyes are on Josh's. I step down and walk over to him. He doesn't touch me. He just stares, his eyes bouncing from one to the other—reading me—thinking—completely resolute. Giving me nothing.

Parker! Parker! Parker!

The crowd begins to chant, and I realize now that *he is* the next act. His eyes flick to my lips for a brief second, and then he walks to the stage leaving me stunned without a word. His face is guarded. I walk to sit beside Em and Collin now. "I recorded the whole thing," Em says smiling wide. I can't smile back, though. I thought he would understand what I was trying to say, but maybe he didn't.

Josh seems flustered and not his normally composed self as he escapes into music. His hands are shaking as he grabs his guitar and barstool to sit on. He adjusts the microphone stand. His eyes meet mine as he just stares with that same composed, guarded look. I don't understand his eyes. He clears his throat.

"Well, um, not sure I want to be following that act—hauntingly beautiful," he murmurs. "I've got two songs for y'all tonight. One my own and one a cover I just came up with on a whim," he says, locking eyes with mine. I swallow hard, and the urge to look away is so strong, but I'm trapped in his gaze. He breaks the contact first. "How many of you have loved someone so much that it physically hurt you when it fell apart?"

What? No!

"How many of you have had someone crawl under your skin so deep that it fucked up your head? Loved that person so fucking much that you can't breathe when they aren't by your side? Loved them to the point that it left you broken, because they were broken, but you still kept trying to fix them?"

I look to Emily. "Why is he saying this?"

She shrugs and squeezes my hand. I try to blink the tears away, keep them from falling, but it's to no avail. He begins strumming his guitar as his eyes meet mine. "This song is Without You."

NO!

I don't recognize this song. It's soft and haunting—hauntingly beautiful, like he just said. It's new, and he titled it *without you*? My heart is thumping so hard in my chest. I just poured my heart out to him, is he about to break mine?

MILES SEPARATE US
OUR LOVE BINDS US
LETTERS HERE AND THERE
PHONE CALLS TO MAKE THIS EASIER TO BEAR
BUT YOU'RE GONE, AND I'M HERE WITHOUT YOU
LONELY, BROKEN, MY HEART LEFT BEHIND WITH YOU
NOW, I KNOW THAT I NEED YOU MORE
MORE THAN I HAVE EVER BEFORE
BUT IS IT ENOUGH?
TO KEEP US TOGETHER, LOVE?
I CAN'T THINK WITHOUT YOU
BREATHE WITHOUT YOU
IT DOESN'T CHANGE
I AM HERE WITHOUT YOU, BABY
UNDER MY SKIN, IN MY HEAD
THE END IS WHAT I DREAD
WAS IT ALL FOR NOTHING IF I LOST YOU?
WAS ANY OF IT EVER TRUE?
HAUNTED BY THE MEMORIES OF YOU IN THE RAIN
OF LOSS AND OF PAIN
THE TASTE OF YOU LINGERS ON MY LIPS
THE FEEL OF YOU BENEATH MY HIPS
THE SMILE ON MY FACE
JUST THE THRILL OF THIS RACE
BUT YOU'RE GONE, AND I'M HERE WITHOUT YOU
LONELY, BROKEN, MY HEART LEFT BEHIND WITH YOU
NOW, I KNOW THAT I NEED YOU MORE
MORE THAN I HAVE EVER BEFORE
BUT IS IT ENOUGH?
TO KEEP US TOGETHER, LOVE?
I CAN'T THINK WITHOUT YOU
BREATHE WITHOUT YOU
NOTHING CHANGES
I AM HERE WITHOUT YOU
I AM WITHOUT

BREATHING EMPTY AIR
NOTHING HERE TO CALM MY FEARS
LOVING YOU BLINDLY AND SCARED TO DEATH
THE PAST ALWAYS BINDING AND I CONFESS
THAT I MIGHT NOT BE STRONG ENOUGH
WE MAY JUST FUCK THIS UP
TILL NOTHING'S LEFT
BUT THIS REGRET
CUZ, BABY YOU'RE GONE, AND I'M HERE WITHOUT YOU
LONELY, BROKEN, MY HEART LEFT BEHIND WITH YOU
NOW, I KNOW THAT I NEED YOU MORE
MORE THAN I HAVE EVER BEFORE
BUT IS IT ENOUGH?
TO KEEP US TOGETHER, LOVE?
I CAN'T THINK WITHOUT YOU
BREATHE WITHOUT YOU
WITHOUT YOU NEXT TO ME
EVERYTHING CHANGES BECAUSE I AM HERE WITHOUT YOU
WITHOUT YOU
ALWAYS WITHOUT YOU

I blink through the tears that are streaming down my face. His eyes that have been closed the entire time land on my face, and he frowns. I can't even wipe away the tears. I can't move. I'm in too much pain. *What is he telling me? That it's not enough?*

The cheers around us make me remember that we aren't alone. He nods his head without a smile. We are bearing our souls in a room full of strangers. He looks away and begins *Broken* by Seether.

I'm crumbling into pieces. He is ripping out my heart. Doesn't he know that I am broken too without him? Doesn't he realize I can't breathe, I can't eat and I can't sleep without him? That he is everything to me.

He doesn't.

I'm losing him. I might have already lost him.

I'm scanning the room looking for an escape. This hurts too much. I can't listen anymore. He's almost done with the song, but I can't hear any more of it. I've never wanted to not hear him sing before.

I stand, and begin to weave my way through the crowd to the back as he ends the song, and officially breaks me. I can barely see through my tears. I'm almost to the edge of the crowd where a hallway will lead me to the exit when I realize he is no longer singing.

I gasp when a hand grabs me around my waist, and pulls me into a room just offset from the bar. I turn ready to fight like hell when my mouth is sealed shut by lips I know by memory. Josh pushes me against the wall in this dark room. I hear him click a lock as he licks the tears falling down my cheeks. They won't stop falling.

"I hate you," I whisper.

"No, you don't," he says, kissing a path along my jaw as he cages me against the wall.

"I want to," I admit.

"I want to hate you, too. You're such a bitch."

"You're such an asshole." That's the last thing I say before his mouth is on mine at a feverish rate. My hands are in his hair, pulling at his shirt—everywhere. I feel like a crazy person—loving, hating and wanting him so badly.

He lowers his head to my neck. "Damn, you smell so fucking good. And you singing—just fuck." He moves his hand up my skirt to my warmth. He puts his hand inside my panties as I arch into him.

"I'm sorry," I breathe. I'm moving my hands to his jeans as he tears away my panties. It makes me gasp.

"Shhh..." he lowers his jeans and lifts me against the wall. My legs wrap around his waist and within a moment, he fills me the only way he can. He growls, and against the wall, he claims me all over again.

My eyes shut as I feel him, for what I fear will be the last time. He rests his forehead against mine. "Open your eyes."

"I can't."

"Yes, you can. Look at me, baby," his soft voice pleads with me. I listen and meet his gaze as we near the edge together.

His eyes lock with mine. "I've always loved you and will always love you," he says groaning.

Speech isn't an option for me. His mouth takes mine, and I fall over the edge with him. But why does this feel like goodbye?

Tears are falling from my eyes from pleasure and pain. He's resting his head on my shoulder as he lowers my legs to the ground, and we both catch our breath. I feel wetness on my shoulder, and realize he too is crying. I run my hands along his cheek and make him look at me. I see it, his decision. My eyes widen, and the lump in my throat strangles me. "I love you, Josh," I whisper.

"I know you do…and…I love you," he says as a breath of air almost against my lips.

"But it's not enough anymore for you?" I ask, not wanting, not ready for his answer.

He stares long at me, his eyes moving along my features as though he is memorizing them. He shakes his head as the tears continue to flow. I've lost him. In one night, I've lost him.

He kisses me one last time and then he walks out, leaving me there in a mess of a person I hate to be, with broken promises. I crumble and fall against the wall, sliding down to where I'm sitting as a sob overtakes me. My hand is covering my mouth. I've lost everything I want most in the world.

"Riley?" I hear Em's voice from the door. "Are you in here?"

I croak out my reply, "Over here."

"Oh shit, honey, are you okay? Josh just stormed out of the bar."

I shake my head as I choke on my words. "He…he fucked me and…and he left me. He broke up with me. I lo…lo…lost him." I cry harder than I ever have in a long time. She grabs me up and pulls me into a hug.

"I'm so sorry. So sorry," she says holding me up.

I reach down to grab the panties he tore off of me in a frenzy, and toss them in the trash.

When we walk out the door a bunch of stares land on me.

"Oh damn, baby girl," Collin mumbles as he comes around to my other side. I must look like hell—my hair a mess from what we just did—my makeup running down my face from crying. My entire world is over.

I climb into the back seat of Collin's car and curl up into a ball as I silently cry.

"What the hell happened?" I hear Collin ask Emily.

"She said he broke up with her."

"What the fuck?"

I grab my phone and send him a text.

Me: I'M SORRY I PUSHED YOU TO CHASE YOUR DREAMS. I'M SORRY I GAVE US UP. I'M SORRY I DIDN'T FIGHT HARD ENOUGH TO KEEP YOU. I'M SORRY I WASN'T ENOUGH. I'M SORRY I LIED TO YOU. I WILL ALWAYS AND FOR EVERY BREATH I TAKE LOVE YOU, JOSHUA PARKER. ONLY YOU!

He didn't reply. I didn't expect him to.

EPILOGUE

DECEMBER

 *Dean*

"You were never pregnant were you?" I yell at Preslee on the phone after being told she was back in town without a baby that should have been due. She took off months ago, no explanation—nothing.

"Why do you care, Dean? You told me to fuck off, remember? I did as you told me as I always do, and now you want to talk about what I was and wasn't to you?"

I can hear her start her car. "What you were to me? What is that supposed to mean?" I shout into the phone.

"I was just a fuck filler for you, Dean. You didn't want a baby. Well good for you, you didn't get one. I have to go," she sniffles and hangs up.

A sickening pit in my stomach swallows me up. I know I said all of that, but I wanted the baby—someone to love me unconditionally— someone to be mine.

I call her back and she is crying. "What do you want, Dean?"

"Why are you crying?" I ask, actually feeling sympathetic.

"You wanna know what happened to your baby? I'll tell you, in person. I'll text you the address you can meet me at. I will wait half an hour only. Don't come if you don't want the truth, Dean," and she hangs up.

I wait for the text and when she sends me the address I head outside to get on my bike.

 *Josh*

I can still feel her lips on mine even now two months later as I sit in my truck back in Texas. I've read her text a thousand times and never once replied. I haven't talked to her since that night in October. I miss her desperately. Collin told me I overreacted about Dean, and that may very well be true, but the truth is, I'm not sure I want to constantly be chased by Riley's ghosts anymore.

I'm parked outside Dean's house now and watching him get on his bike. I don't know what possesses me to follow him, but I do. Emily told me he's acting irrationally lately. She said Riley quit her job at the bar the day after they returned to Texas. I almost changed my mind and called her then, but it didn't change the fact that we were hurting each other all the time. Emily said Dean flipped out on Riley, grabbed her wrist and told her he needed her there. It was strange, and it freaked Riley out quite a bit. She never told me about it, but of course she wouldn't. We weren't together anymore.

Together or not, he needed to keep his hands off of her. I follow him and he parks at an Ob-Gyn office. I watch him walk to a Volkswagen Bug—Preslee's car. He taps on her window, and she climbs out with tears streaming down her face. He says something and she throws her hands up nodding her head. She says something, and his face falters. His face contorts into pain and then anger as he shouts at her. She puts her head down and begins to sob. He stares at her for a long time until he wraps his arms around her, and they comfort each other. It's obvious that something happened to the baby. She says something else, then climbs back into her car and pulls away. He stands there for a while lost deep in thought.

He taps away at his phone and gets back on his bike. I follow him all the way to Riley's apartment. *What the fuck?* I sit in my car gripping the steering wheel so tight my knuckles turn white. Their apartment faces the parking lot, and thankfully, I can remain parked unnoticed and watch as my blood boils.

He rings her doorbell and Emily answers. Her face is angry, but then he says something, and her mouth forms an O. Collin opens the door further, and I watch as Dean rubs his hand over his face and paces back and forth. Collin walks all the way out of the door, and he and Dean start walking back to the parking lot together.

Two things happen at once. Riley's car pulls into the parking spot next to Collin's car. She gets out of her car and heads in the same direction they are leaving. Then my heart stops beating in my chest.

She sees them and freezes. I look at her face and see fear in her eyes. It throws me off guard. As soon as Dean sees her, he stops moving and says something as he rubs behind his neck. Her face appears confused and then she frowns. She looks to Collin like she is unsure of what to do. He rubs at his eyes like he is crying, and then she hugs him. She hugs him, and everything in me becomes ice cold.

I'm frozen, my heart racing, adrenaline pumping in my veins, and confusion in my mind. I climb out of the truck and walk over to her where her arms are still wrapped around his neck. Her eyes clock mine, and she jumps back away from Dean. He has the nerve to grin. I have my hand fisted at my side ready to punch the shit out of him when Collin pushes me back. Riley's mouth opens and shuts. "Cat get your tongue?" I yell at her. She shakes her head back and forth and looks between Dean and me—her eyes wide in fear or guilt. "Shocked to see me, huh?"

"Dude, it's not what it looks like. He's not here to create trouble. He just found out Preslee miscarried their baby a few months ago and never told him. He had no one to talk to. He came to see *me*. He texted, and I told him I was here. Riley wasn't home. She was supposed to be back in Grandbury. I figured it was okay."

"Well it isn't," I yelled.

"He wasn't here for her, dude. Just chill, okay?" Collin says. Of course, I can't say I know about Preslee, because I would have to explain that I followed him. Truthfully, I'm surprised by this information, as I believed she was faking the entire time. I feel like such a dick because a part of me believes this is karma. I would never wish that on anyone, and the feeling throws me off balance.

I look over to Dean, who appears more satisfied than distraught. I hate him. "I'm sorry for your loss." My eyes move to Riley who is still standing in shock. I haven't seen or spoken to her in months, and I find her here comforting him. "Can I talk to you?"

She nods her head and moves away from them. I grab her hand and pull her towards my truck. She gasps when I push her against the door and kiss her roughly. She's tense at first, but eventually relaxes as our tongues find their rhythm. God, that soft moan she makes drives me insane. I've missed the way she tastes. Then she shoves me back. "Stop it. You can't do that."

"Do what?"

"That," she points between her I. "Kiss me like your claiming me."

That one statement pisses me off so much. "Do I need to claim you?"

She narrows her eyes and glares at me, equally pissed now. "You broke up with me, remember? Why are you even here?"

I sigh and look away. *I'm here for you, because you're mine.* I can't speak.

She doesn't say anything. She stares at me—waiting for an answer that doesn't come—so, she turns to walk away. I halt her by her elbow, and she stops, but she doesn't turn around. I move to stand in front of her and tuck her hair behind her ear, trying to ignore the hurt I see in her eyes. She shuts them, and her face looks like I'm causing her pain. It hurts to see it. "I'm sorry. I'm out of my mind, lately. It's just when I saw you hug him I...I just hate it."

Her eyes flutter open, and she frowns. "I was just being nice, Josh. He just told me his baby died, and I didn't know what to do or say, so I hugged him. It didn't mean anything," she explains.

"Do you have to be so nice to him, though? Maybe that's why he's always coming around you." I regret it the minute the words leave my lips. I didn't mean for it to come out so harshly, or sound like I blame her.

Her mouth falls open and her eyes glass over like she is soon to break out in tears. "Josh...I—," she looks away and takes a few deep breaths. She turns back to me with unrecognizable eyes—cold and hardened. "Please, leave. It's obvious you don't want to be here with me anymore, and I don't want you here to judge me."

What?

"I want to be here, Riley."

"I guess that isn't enough, huh?" She tosses my words back at me from months before.

I stare at her for a beat without a response. What am I supposed to say? To explain why I did what I did, when I can't even explain it to myself. "I never stopped loving you," I whisper.

She makes a strangled noise, but doesn't comment. We stare at each other with all of these unsaid things in between us. When I feel like nothing is left, I turn to walk away as I hear her almost whimper. I want to beg her to forgive me, to take me back, but I don't.

Instead, I climb inside my truck and punch the steering wheel over and over again. "FUCK, FUCK, FUCK!" I'm so pissed at myself. I'm so out of my mind and crazy. I can't do anything right. I'm barely holding onto my scholarship, because I can't pass any of my classes, because I'm always thinking about her and here. I've fucked up on and off the field, disappointing everyone—her and my teammates. I miss my family. I miss her. I miss everything, and nothing makes sense in my head. I crash my head to the steering wheel, shaking as the gates open in my heart, and the tears actually fall from my eyes. I haven't cried since my mom died, and that night after I left Riley the way I did, and here I am crying like a pussy in my truck because the girl I love yelled at me. Except it's not just that she yelled at me—it's that I'm hurting her, and I'm hurting. I hate this. I hate this so fucking much. I just want to tell her I take it back—that I love her, and I can't breathe without her.

After several deep breaths, I lift my head and find her standing a few feet away watching me with tears streaming down her cheeks. I wipe my eyes, turn the ignition and drive away from my heart. Once again, it stays behind with her. Eventually, my life will end without it beating in my chest.

JANUARY

I'm back at my house in my old room for the holidays. It's been a week and knowing Josh is back in town, I've been staying back at my apartment, but I had to come home for Christmas, which was ridiculously hard. I didn't tell my mom we broke up, and obviously he hadn't told his family. So, we pretended for the sake of it. It hurt a hell of a lot because he kissed me, and everything in my heart wanted it to be real. It wasn't. Not anymore.

I am in my room looking around at everything that reminds me of him. I look at the window that holds so many memories, seeing him in his room. I stand up and head to the living room. Ready to tell my mom I'm going to Collin's New Year's party. I only declined out of fear that Josh would be there, but he's not, and now I want to be anywhere but here. I freeze when I hear her voice outside on the porch with someone.

"I know what you mean. Sometimes I can still smell his cologne in my room. It was making me so crazy the other night that I pulled out one of his shirts that I kept and never washed," she says to the person.

The door is cracked open, and I'm standing on the other side of it, out of sight, but I can see them perfectly. And then I hear his voice— Mr. Parker.

"I know what you mean. At least, you don't have a son. This is going to sound terrible, but every time I look at Joey, my heart breaks just a little more. She looks and acts so much like Jessica. The older she gets, the more I see Jess in her eyes. Certain little traits in her tone when she gets mad at me or Josh. She even nags me the same, you know?"

Oh, God. They are reminiscing about their spouses. I see my mom pass a look to him, and it's a strange look—one full of sadness, of remorse, of understanding. Then she says, "I'm so sorry, James. I regret that night with Evan every single day. Not a day goes by where I don't wake up and lie there just wondering what is real—just hoping it was all some blasted nightmare I've slept way too long, through—but then I roll over and the cold spot that used to be his is empty, and I know. I know that I destroyed his heart that night with my lie, and he took your heart away. And now, you and I both are stuck here alone in misery with kids that don't trust, and kids that hurt and miss them. If I could do it all differently, if I could have just learned to forgive him of his past and let it stay there, then maybe we could've been happy."

Wow. I knew she felt guilt but just, wow. I watch Josh's dad wipe a tear that has fallen from my mom's cheek, and they stare at each other for a long time. My heart is beating so fast in my chest, I was sure it has to be audible.

"Claudia, we talked about this before, and it's the same thing Josh tells Riley all the time. You can't keep blaming yourself for the decision he made that day. All this guilt is going to swallow you up. All of our lives changed that day. It's how we move on that will make us who we are. I know your marriage wasn't perfect. Jessica and I were happy, but don't think we were perfect. We had our ups and downs just like everyone else."

"Dammit, James, my daughter walked in on him having sex. She was just a little girl, and had no idea what was going on. She thought they were playing dress up. I've never felt so betrayed in all of my life. How could he do something like that and love me, love her? She was in the next room, in *our* house, James."

It's so strange how memories are when you grow older, because I remember that night, but it's almost fuzzy, like it's an almost memory, or a kind of forgotten one. Even her face is blurry to me. I can't remember what her face looks like exactly, but I remember that I thought my babysitter was beautiful. I think I even loved her, and she loved me. I haven't thought about her in a very long time.

Josh's dad sighs and touches my mom's cheek gently. She turns into his touch. *Why does she do that?* "I know, Claudia. She's a strong girl, and you are a strong woman. Josh loves her, and he would never hurt her like that."

Loved me, and he has hurt me.

He swallows hard, "and I—," his voice trails off.

He what? No, no, no.

"You what, James?" she asks studying his eyes.

I think I'm going to be sick. Bile is rising in my throat. I think they are about to kiss. Oh, my God. Oh, my God. This can't be happening.

"I don't regret it," he says simply as he tucks a piece of her hair behind her ear.

Doesn't regret what? What does he not regret? Fuck...I need to be a mind reader right now.

"I don't either," she whispers leaning into him.

NO!

"What are you doing?" I jump back so high hearing Josh's voice behind me. I catch Mr. Parker's eyes lock with mine as I stumble back away from the door. He curses and they both stand walking into the doorway to see us. My eyes are wide, and my hands are shaking. They were going to kiss each other. I know it. Oh, God.

The baby.

Josh is looking back and forth between them and I, and he is completely confused and unaware of the puzzle I think I just put together in my head. Mom never goes on dates. She doesn't have a boyfriend. She has a good friend who lives next door, who understands her.

Fucking hell.

"What's going on?" Josh asks, still in the dark. "Why do y'all look like the cat that just ate the canary?" He looks to me. "And why do you look like you're about to pass out?"

"How did you get in here?" I ask, knowing he just climbed in through my bedroom window, but why? He looks guilty and doesn't answer me.

My mom's worried eyes meet mine, and Mr. Parker's gaze drops to the floor.

"Riley, were you listening?" My mom asks.

"Listening to what?" Josh asks.

His dad walks past me and pulls Josh into our kitchen.

My mom sighs and walks to sit on the couch. "I made a mistake, Riley. I'm good at those."

"What mistake, Mom?" My stomach sinks. "Does this mistake have anything to do with your baby?"

Her eyes were cast down, but now they are on mine. She nods her head. *Oh, God. Oh, my God. This can't be happening!*

"I was listening. I heard what y'all said to each other. I saw the way you looked at him." I point to the kitchen and feel the knife stab me in the back.

"We didn't mean for this to happen, Riley."

"What to happen? I need you to say it, mom. My head is forming all kinds of conclusions here, and it sounds to me like you are saying that you and Josh's dad are going to have a baby together. Tell me how that happens without some thought!"

She wipes a few lost tears, and I can't even bring myself to tear up. I'm pissed.

"Are you sure you want to hear this?" Her voice is barely audible.

I was until she said that—like that—even still I nod.

She takes a deep breath. "We've always been friends. After work one night, I was at Pete's having a drink. I was remembering everything that happened that awful night as I just stared at the table where your dad and I sat when I lied to him and left him there. The memories haunt me every day. The hate I feel for myself, sometimes, just gets too much to bear. All the pain it caused you girls. I just didn't want to feel the ache anymore, and when he came to the bar and smiled at me—I thought just one night would make it all stop hurting so much. He said some nice things, and for a moment, I let go because he understood pain like mine. We didn't mean for any of this to happen." She touches her stomach and mine sinks. Mine grows into this wide pit of anger and reaches up to grab my heart and crush it.

Her eyes lock with mine, she reaches for my hand, but I pull it away. "He understood pain?" I ask the question like a breath of air.

She nods and swipes at a tear that has fallen. "It was a mistake, Riley. A moment of weakness. It won't change anything for you and Josh. I promise. I won't let it."

Oh, God. Everything is already changed between us.

She's always with him. I never saw it—like it could never be a possibility. I'm already backing toward the door. "Riley, please? Try to understand."

I halt and turn to her seeing Josh standing in the doorway to the hall with wide eyes. My sister is right behind him with the same shocked expression.

"Understand what, Mom? That you had sex with Josh's dad and changed everything? Can you just for once not ruin my life with your fucked up decisions?"

She gasps at the same time as Tatum. Josh punches the wall on a curse. His dad puts his hand on his shoulder, but he shrugs it off.

"Riley, I'm still your mother. You can't talk to me like that." *She gets all motherly now? Well, it's too late.*

I square my shoulders and grab my keys to my car. "I don't have a mother," I state harshly and then I leave.

My mom is on the porch hollering at me through tears to come back in the house. I'm ignoring her. Josh is running after me, but I don't stop, though. My entire world is caving in on me, and I can't breathe. I am completely alone. I climb inside my car and leave. I have no idea where I'm going. Just that I can't stay there. I can't believe she did that to me—to us.

There is no us, remember?

This is some twisted shit. What would that baby be to us? If they became a couple, raise the baby together, would that make Josh and I step siblings? *Just great.* I will forever be attached to him. I will never escape this pain—ever.

Tears are streaming down my face, and I can barely see. It's flurrying, and the roads are icy, but I can see enough to know that's Josh's truck following behind me, honking his horn at me to get me to stop. His name is flashing on the phone that is ringing in the center console. I scream as I see the place I've somehow driven to. I climb out of the car at the cemetery and take off running to my dad's grave. I'm yelling and screaming at him. "Why did you do this to me? Why did you leave her? Ahhhhh. I hate you! I hate you both so much!" Tears are burning my eyes. I feel sick.

I fall to my knees in the wet grass and bang my fist onto his grave. I feel Josh kneel down beside me, and he pulls me into his lap. I'm crying so hard and hitting at his chest. He grabs my wrist and ceases their movement. "Shhhh. Calm down. It's okay. Shhhh..." I slow my breathing and try hard to compose myself. He smells so good. He loosens his grip on my wrist, and his hands glide up to my cheeks, where he rubs his thumbs under my eyes to catch my tears. We're both on our knees staring into one another's eyes as our future becomes more uncertain with each breath we take. It's always their fault. We're both breathing so fast with wild, crazed eyes. "Baby?"

"Don't call me that, please, it hurts," I beg.

His eyes study mine as he sighs, and they are full of the same pain I have. It's below freezing outside, and I'm dressed in my jeans, a t-shirt and my flip-flops. I'm shivering and sobbing, my tears sticking to my cheeks painfully. He picks me up and carries me to his truck in his arms. He puts the heater on and wraps his leather jacket around me as he holds me to his chest with my head on his shoulder as my body trembles. I miss the way his heartbeat feels beneath my cheek. We sit there for the longest time in silent reprieve, but eventually he loosens his hold on me.

I climb off of his lap and curl up in the passenger seat with my knees pulled up. My heart is crumbling. The air with him is suffocating me. We sit in the truck in the quiet watching the flurries fall. I don't know what he's thinking, but I know that what I'm thinking is breaking my heart in two. For as long as I can remember, the odds have been against Josh and me. There have been so many damn roadblocks, whether self-made or cruel twists of fate. It's all starting to make sense, how we fell apart. I feel like someone is stabbing me in the chest, turning the knife and letting me bleed out.

I turn to look at Josh, and notice the deep frown line on his forehead. He mirrors my move of leaning into the seat, and looks over at me.

"Thank you for coming to find me, Josh," I whisper.

He brushes his knuckles along my cheek, and I shut my eyes consumed by that one touch.

"I will always find you," he says with all sincerity.

I believe him. He will always find me when I'm lost because he is my best friend, or was. But what happens when we are both lost? Who finds *us*? I guess that's why we are here—broken and without each other.

 *Riley*

I don't know how one survives without their heart, survives when they are splintered into pieces. I'm crushed and hate the evil bitch that is fate or life. I just hate. That is what I feel...hate.

I've spent the past hour listening to Em and Collin having sex— twice. I'm sick with envy, with rage. I'm in the kitchen debating on drinking some more when they both come in the room looking well taken care of. Fuck them! I hate them. Another visit home for her, another knife in my heart as Josh stays behind.

"Riley, you have to come out with us tonight. You can't stay here moping around anymore." Em declares. Who made her ruler of my decisions?

"You mope around here?" Collin asks, concerned.

"Yes, she never goes to parties, never leaves this apartment much. All she does is sit around here drinking until she pukes. Does it make you feel better? Is Josh home moping around like that? Fuck him, Riley." I hate her right now. I don't want to know if he is or isn't.

Collin's eyes meet mine, and I see the pity. He knows if he is or isn't, and everything I see in his eyes makes me think Josh isn't moping at all. "Fine, I'll go but I'm drinking. So, don't expect me to be your fucking DD. Got it?" I sneer and head to my room to change.

"What the fuck, Ri? I'm worried about you. You don't need to be such a bitch about it," she says following me.

"Fuck you and the way you worry about me, Em. I love you, but just don't worry about me so much. I'm good." I stare at her, waiting for her to leave my space.

She just stares at me, dumbfounded at my outburst. "We're leaving in half an hour. K?"

"K."

"Where are we?" Collin asks as we walk into a house littered with people.

Emily shrugs, "I found some paper about it on campus. Figured it's a party, what the hell."

We walk through the pit of people scattered throughout the yard and make our way inside. Once inside, the stench of smoke is overwhelming, the air thick. There is a long hallway open to a large living space, which sits a couch and some chairs, but mostly writhing sweaty bodies dancing to The XX.

I haven't made much of an effort to make many new friends on campus, although, I do recognize many faces that I see.

"Want me to go get y'all drinks?" Collin asks.

"Beer, please." I say, plastering my fake smile onto my face.

"Em?"

"Surprise me, baby." She places a lingering kiss to his mouth. It makes me sick. I roll my eyes and look away. As if my heart wasn't already cold and pissed off, I catch sight of Dean in the corner—his eyes locking with mine, instantly.

He's always around—watching me.

A girl is grinding all over him; he just lets her—as he watches me.

I look away.

Fucking perfect. The one I love is never around and throws me aside, while the one I hate and loathe is always lurking in the shadows.

"Here you go." Collin hands me my beer and Em something in a cup. Of course, they immediately begin to snuggle up against each other. I take a long pull of my beer and realize this isn't going to numb what hurts enough.

Bad by Wale filters through the speakers—this is Em's favorite song. "Hey, Riley. Will you hold this? We're going to dance." She hands me her cup, not even waiting for my response. *Bitch.*

I watch them dance seductively and decide to fuck it. I drain whatever is in her cup—Jack and coke—good option. I head to kitchen where a guy is taking keys and serving drinks.

"What's your poison, princess?"

"Jack and Coke—mostly Jack, please." I tilt my head sweetly and smile.

He eyes me instantly, looking me over with appreciation. It makes me want to vomit. He hands me the cup, and I swallow down the burn in several gulps, placing my red cup back down for a refill. His eyebrow quirks up and he holds out the bowl of keys. "Keys?"

"I'm not driving."

He nods his head and makes me another. "Thanks," I smile sweetly.

"Any time, sweetheart," he smirks.

I bet.

Several drinks later, thanks to a few strangers, I'm well on my way to feeling numb, just how I like it. I hate that I do this to myself. That I can't handle pain—that I drown it in liquor. It's not healthy. It's just tonight...I don't care about it. I don't care, anymore. I'm tired of life giving me what I want and then ripping it away from me. I'm tired of thinking about Josh all the time, and yet even numb I'm thinking about him.

Valentines had come and gone as I had held Tink in my arms. That night a few days ago, I remembered everything I lost. *Stop thinking about him, Riley.* My legs feel like jelly. My head is swimming.

Crave You by Flight Facilities is playing, and I climb on top of the coffee table as I begin to dance. My hips are moving from side to side, and my hands are running up and down my body and thrashing in the air.

I haven't seen Collin or Em since they went upstairs. I'm sure to fuck again in one of the spare bathrooms. I'm so hot. I'm sweating. Next thing I know my shirt is off, and people are cheering for me. I use my shirt to wipe the sweat beads off of my chest and stomach.

But now I'm sleepy—so sleepy. I stumble off the table as guys catch me and attempt to help me and grope me at the same time.

One guy tries to steer me one direction with him, but Collin appears with his hand firmly around my waist pulling me away.

"Oh, my God. Are you drunk?" Em asks, looking pretty tipsy herself.

I laugh, and lean my head back on Collin's chest because it's so heavy. I hold up my thumb and index finger like pinchers and say, "Just a li'l bit."

"Fuck, Riley. You can't keep doing this. Put your fucking clothes on. Dammit." She scolds me like a parent would a child. I know I can't keep doing this, but for tonight it's too late to realize that and change my mind.

Collin is watching me intently as I try to put my shirt back on. He's concerned about me. He should be. I'm damaged. "He wouldn't want you doing this to yourself, Riley," he says in my ear since it's so loud.

Now, I'm pissed. "Who the hell asked you? He doesn't even care about me." And now I want to cry. No, no, no. I snatch the drink right out of Em's hands and down it.

"Shit, Riley. Stop this." She snatches the cup back. "I have to pee, but we need to get her out of here. Keep an eye on her, okay? She doesn't make the best of decisions when she is like this as you can tell." And then she leaves up the stairs to the bathroom.

I stare at Collin, contemplating my escape as he pulls me into the hall. I don't want to go home with them. I don't want to hear them anymore. I don't want to picture Josh's hands on me, wishing he were with me like that. I can't.

"Hey, Collin. I'm sorry. You're right. I um, I need to sober up. Would you mind getting me a water?" I ask, smiling sweetly—somehow managing to get the words out.

He studies my eyes for a moment but nods his head. "Stay here," he demands, but as soon as he steps away, I make my escape.

I need fresh air. As soon as I get outside and round the corner of the house, my stomach empties some of the contents of the liquor. Apparently, Jack and I aren't agreeing either. When I stand back up—although, barely standing on my own, I stumble a few steps before I fall.

I feel his eyes on me—they are always on me.

"Riley?" Dean's deep voice fills my ears.

"Huh?" I ask looking up from the ground.

"What are you doing down there?" he asks.

I laugh. "It's these damn shoes. They won't work on my feet. Fuckers," I say, pulling my heels off and throwing them to the side.

He watches me with an unreadable expression. It sort of creeps me out. "What are you doing out here...alone like this? It's not *safe*." He kneels down and grabs my curl. Something about the way he said 'safe' makes a cold chill sweep across me, and I hate that he twirls my curl like he has a right to.

"Collin and Em wanna make me go home, but I don't wanna go with them." I sound whiny and ridiculous. *Why am I even talking to him?*

He's smiles, takes my heels in his hands and offers me his hand. I don't take it. He sighs heavily. "I can drive you to your mom's if ya want?" he asks.

I stare at him, knowing the right answer in my head is NO. This is Dean. Creepy, stalkerish, Dean. I lay my head on the grass and feel the drowsiness pulling me under. I can't keep my eyes open.

I feel him pick me up, and I know I should scream, I should fight for him to put me down, but I'm too tired. My brain won't make my body do what it should.

He places me in the front seat of a car and buckles me in.

My eyes are so heavy, and my head becomes clouded. My veins feel tingly, and everything is blurry.

I feel lips press against mine. "Josh?" I mutter.

"Yeah, baby. It's me." Something bright flashes against my eyes and I turn my head towards it seeing a familiar face on the outside of the car.

"Preslee?" I swear that's her taking my picture with—I turn my eyes and find Dean smirking with evil dancing in his eyes. OH, MY GOD!

To be continued...

Synopsis for Emerge into Forever (The Shifting Series, Book 3)

Available now

She escaped the doubt, and he embraced the moment. Shifting apart then shifting together. Could they finally emerge into forever?

One secret broke his trust, which led to both of their heartbreak. They both learned that sometimes love just isn't enough. Until now.

Nothing with them had ever been simple and coming home to right his wrong would be no different. Josh was prepared to say or do anything to fix his mistake and mend what he had broken between them. He wasn't expecting to find out his worst nightmare had come true. As usual, though, not everything is as it seemed.

Riley had been slowly spiraling into a dark hold of loneliness and despair without Josh. Rebuilding walls he had once broken down, pushing away everyone around her. One self-destructive mistake left her unguarded and vulnerable causing her past to slam into her present with painful force. Destroyed by Josh's assumptions then given hope by his reassurance, she climbs out of the dark and back into his arms. He's her light and she's his music.

Enough is enough and communication is key. No longer hiding behind walls and past screw-ups, they fight like hell for what they want. One another. Always wanting more.

Apart they are a mess, but together they are music.

Not recommended for anyone under the age of 17 due to underage drinking, sexual content and adult language.